THE WINTER OF MAGIC

ONDINE BOOK 3

EBONY MCKENNA

ebook ISBN 978-1-922486-36-3

Please note, as this book is set in Brugel, it uses Brugelish English spelling. Some of it even makes sense.

This book has footnotes. They will provide you with a further explanation of terminology, cultural notes or sometimes simply a cry for help.

I'd like to thank the Scottish ferrets who acted as sensitivity readers for the Ondine Series. I learned so much from this incredible but often overlooked community. Any mistakes in fact or interpretation are my own. They made me say that. It's not fair, they want money now, and Brugelwürst.

CHAPTER I

December is a fun month, wherever you are in the world. If you're in the southern hemisphere, you have long summer days at the beach ahead of you. If you're in the northern hemisphere, winter snow dusts everything with soft magic. All over the globe there are festivals galore and New Year celebrations. December is also way more interesting than March, which everyone agrees can be a bit of a dud. If December happens to be the month of your name day, it's also cause for a fair bit of excitement. Ondine de Groot, the star of this story – and the two that came before it – has her name day in December. [1]

Two days after her name day, Ondine's eldest sister Marguerite will marry her fiancé, Thomas Berger under the ceremonial elm tree in the botanical gardens. But before the wedding

---

1. In Brugel, name days are not birthdays. They are far more important than that. It's the day you celebrate the saint you are named after, rather than the accidental day on which you were born. If you're not directly named after a saint, you'll be given one as a middle name. One of Ondine's middle names is Benedicte, named after the patron saint of spelunking. Benedicte is also the patron saint against witchcraft, which is pretty convenient considering the situations Ondine has been in.

– and Ondine's name day – the de Groot family has customers to serve at their family pub, *The Duke and Ferret*, in downtown Venzelemma. [2]

On this particular Saturday in December, the day was short and wet, the night dark and cold. It rained and sleeted something miserable, but the weather didn't stop people from going out in the evening. Saturday nights were always busy in the pub, but in December they were frantic. This is because in Brugel you simply must "catch up" with all your friends before the end of the year, or you'll have hideously bad luck in the New Year. This entrenched tradition has necessitated the creation of "second dinner", a meal service that slips between the first evening meal and supper.

Even the new East Asian restaurant across the road, *On The Fang*, was booked out – for both dinners – every night. Ondine suspected they had somehow created a third dinner, but she was so busy she had no chance to check the truth of it for herself. [3]

Meal times – all of them – were so busy Ondine felt run off her feet. Or more precisely, run off her *hands*, which were permanently submerged in hot soapy water as she cleaned dishes day and night. [4]

Henrik the chef and Cybelle, Ondine's middle sister, worked together like an old married couple at the stoves, knowing exactly what the other needed at just the right time. Henrik had a pudding bowl of a tummy, which was a generally accepted work hazard in the cheffing world. He did have hair, and Ondine tried to remember what colour it was. It was hard to know,

---

2. Venzelemma is the capital city of Brugel, a country in Eastern Europe that still hasn't made a dent in the Eurovision Song Contest.

3. In Brugel, eating is the new black.

4. They do have a dishwasher, which is brilliant for crockery, but everything else has to be done by hand. Beer goes flat if detergent residue is left on the glass. Flat beer may be all the rage in neighbouring Slaegal, but in Brugel it just won't do.

because he always wore a tall white chef's hat firmly on his head. Da, Ondine's father, p, Ondine's oured drinks in the public bar. He still had shocking white hair and the dark hairy caterpillar of a monobrow, which made Ondine and her sisters simply itch to pluck it.

Da had a television on the wall to keep himself and the patrons entertained. The monitor was a 16:9 rectangle, but nobody knew how to set it properly so everyone on screen looked fat and blurry. Tonight the channel was set to the news, with a miraculous story of a plane crash at an airport in neighbouring Craviç, in which everybody walked out the wreck completely unharmed. (Some were suggesting magic had to be involved.)

And Hamish? The handsome lad with eyes full of mischief and a mop of dark hair that fell tantalisingly over his forehead had the easiest job of all. Ma had him waiting tables. With his Scottish accent, cheeky smile and boundless energy, Hamish had a knack for charming the guests. His sparkly green eyes only added to the package. In return, the tips had never been more generous. And these days he hardly ever turned into a ferret, which made Ondine all kinds of happy.

A defeated-looking Marguerite, her long wavy hair hanging lankly over her shoulders, walked into the kitchen with a tray of dirty beer mugs from the bar. Automatically Ondine pulled up her gloves and re-filled the sink with detergent and scalding hot water.

Ma intercepted Margi. "Darling, you're wrecked. Take a break or you'll have bags under your eyes for the wedding." Ma took the tray of dirty glasses and added them to Ondine's workload.

"Can I have a break too?" Ondine asked.

Ma shot her a sly grin. "When a fish dances on the table." [5]

Marguerite's soft chin wobbled as she touched her fingers to her cheeks. As the eldest daughter, Marguerite had worked for her parents from the moment she could carry a bowl of soup without spilling it. Tonight she looked far older than her twenty-one years. Long nights and hard work had a way of doing that to a person. Ondine felt exhausted too, but nobody urged her to put her feet up on the off-chance she'd look tired for her name day.

"Get some rest." Ma kissed Margi on the forehead. "I'll help Thomas and Josef at the bar. It's winding down now anyway."

At which point Thomas came in with another tray of dirty glasses. "Have you seen the news? The Dentate is changing the laws of succession." [6]

No, Ondine hadn't seen the news because they didn't have a telly in the kitchen. Ondine has been too busy to have the luxury of catching up on Brugelish politics. Nobody had brought a newspaper into the house ever since that food writer Dee Gustation gave them that excoriating review way back in summer.

"Really?" Ma said with extra-high raised brows. "Who's it to go to after Duchess Anathea then?"

"The daughters I guess," Thomas said with a shrug

Ma said, "That will put Vincent's nose out of joint."

At the mention of the young lord's name, Ondine rolled her eyes. [7]

---

5. Something that is incredibly unlikely to happen. A fish can dance on the table, but few of them want to.

6. At the risk of becoming bogged down in footnotes before the story can gain momentum, there have been huge ructions in Brugel lately. Duke Pavla is too sick to rule, his wife Kerala is responsible for that sickness and is being kept under high security lock and key. As a result, the Duke's sister the Infanta Anathea is only too happy to take control.

7. Lord Vincent is almost as gorgeous as Hamish on the outside, but under the skin he's rotten right through.

Ma shot her a look. "They can change the laws all they like, won't make any difference to us. Because we won't have anything more to do with that lot, will we Ondi?"

"No, course not," she said.

Talk of Brugel's royal family reminded Ondine that she was still grounded for sneaking off with Hamish so she could work for Duke Pavla at his Autumn Palace. This had been expressly against her parents' wishes. The punishment Ma and Da meted out on her return was both swift and hideous. No friends over. No parties. No extra-curricular school excursions and she couldn't visit anyone either. Just working at home and studying at school and that was it.

All things considered, she accepted the punishment and got on with it. Because being grounded wasn't that different from normal life in a busy pub. Plus, Hamish was here in the pub all the time, so why would she want to be anywhere else?

The dishes kept piling up, so Ondine kept on with her routine. In her peripheral vision, she watched Ma walk back towards the dining room and then suddenly gasp in shock.

Her first thought was, *Uh-oh, what's Hamish done?* [8] The next moment she chastised herself. She should have more faith in him – just because Ma got a shock didn't mean Hamish was the cause of it.

Silence enveloped the kitchen as everyone stopped what they were doing and looked at Ma. The family matriarch was rooted to the spot, staring at someone in the dining room.

A stranger's voice cut through the air. Female and demanding, she summoned the will of a field marshal and brought everything to a stop. "If I may have your attention please. Nobody is to leave."

"What?" Ondine shlucked off her gloves and raced to her

---

8. Let's face it, Hamish is a trouble magnet.

mother's side to see what was going on. Her jaw dropped. There in the dining room stood five official-looking people in dark blue suits, (three women and two men), each holding aloft shiny official-looking badges for everyone to see.

Two suited men moved into the taproom, effectively blocking the remaining exits. They were serious; nobody was leaving.

Their leader, the woman who'd brought the evening to a screaming silence, had a voice that could shatter glass. "We are from the Department of Immigration and Employment. Pursuant to legislation passed this week in the Dentate, we are here to check everyone's identity documents, to make sure nobody is working illegally."

Cold dread filled Ondine as her gaze homed in on Hamish, who at that moment turned towards the kitchen with arms full of empty plates. Ordinarily you might say 'dirty plates' but the hungry customers had used their complimentary soft bread to scoop up the last of the sauce. It must be the cold weather making people extra hungry, because lately the diners were sending their plates back, licked clean.[9]

Hamish winked at Ondine as he walked toward her. He was still in the dining room, she still in the kitchen, but he closed the distance between them. Happy harp music played in her head as she looked upon her wonderful, gorgeous, charming – and a teensy bit naughty – boyfriend. Uh-oh. The invisible harps clanged as reality intruded. The moment Hamish opened his mouth, the immigration inspectors would know he wasn't from around here. The lead inspector spotted Hamish moving closer to the kitchen.

---

9. In neighbouring Slaegal, bread rolls on the table are not complimentary. Nor are they all that edible. They are, however, very effective for stabilising a wonky table leg.

"You there, do you have your work card?"

Fear for her beloved kept Ondine glued to the spot. Mentally she sent her thoughts to him, as if by sheer will she could keep him safe. *Just keep walking. Don't say a word.* Not that she had any psychic powers to speak of, but the will was there.

Behind her, she heard someone pick up the phone, dial out and then murmur down the receiver. It was Henrik the chef, saying things like, "warning", "immigration" and "get out". The compressed voice at the other end said, "too late".

"What's all this about then?" Ma walked into the dining room to create interference. Hope soared. Ma had magical powers of timing and could usually interfere just at the right moment. Alas, her hopes sagged as the leading inspector paid Ma no mind, charged forward and clapped her hand on Hamish's shoulder.

Hamish's eyes turned round like golf balls. Ondine's mouth dried up with fear.

"Show me your work card," the woman said.

Every single guest looked at Hamish and held their breath. You could have heard a knife and fork drop – which is exactly what happened. The plates wobbled in Hamish's hands and cutlery slid onto the floor with a clatter. Movement caught Ondine's peripheral vision and she looked to the pub's front windows. There, across the street, were people running out of *Fang's*. Some of them looked like diners. Two of them were wearing aprons, which meant members of staff were fleeing too.

"Tell me your name and where you're from. You look Slaegalese to me," the inspector said.

Silently, Ondine begged, *I know you don't like authority, but Hamish please keep quiet and –*

"I'm Scottish ye toerag."

– Jupiter's moons! Why did you open your mouth?

The inspector said, "Close enough. You're coming with us."

"No!" Ondine charged into the dining room without a thought as to what she should do or say when she got there. No way would she and Hamish be parted again, not after everything they'd gone through. Hamish dropped the rest of his plates in a series of sharp clangs and crashes. In the next half-second, he fell away into nothing, leaving only a pile of second-hand clothes on the floor. The inspector's palm clutched at nothing but air, her eyes astonishment-wide. As one, every guest in the restaurant gasped and looked at where Hamish used to be.

Ondine took advantage of the confusion and screamed at the inspector. "What did you do to him?" She bent down to scoop up the fabric, hoping against hope he would be in there somewhere. Also hoping she didn't stab him with the broken crockery lying about.

A ruckus broke out as everyone talked at once.

"– gone."

"– was just there."

"– what's in this plütz?" [10]

"– will they let us out?"

" – told you we should have come for first dinner."

Ma stepped forward and said, "Please, Ondine, you're making a scene. Tidy this mess up and get back to work." To everyone else she sounded like a peeved mother. But to Ondine, Ma provided life-saving interference.

"Yes Ma," she said, carefully carrying away the bundle. The clothes felt warm and smelled of hot dinners and Hamish. Something scratched at her wrist. It might be a chunk of broken plate but she didn't dare look. She kept walking, every moment wondering if one of the inspectors would grab her and drag her

____

10. A ravishingly demented drink made from sozzled peaches. The consumer feels no ill effects for the first few minutes, then they stand up to find their knees don't work.

back to the dining room. Heart thumping, she tore through the kitchen and jogged up the stairs to the room she now shared with Cybelle – they'd set up Ondine's room for Thomas's parents so they had somewhere to rest after the wedding reception.

She kicked the door shut behind her and dared to breathe again. Heart crashing against her ribs, she put the bundle of clothes on her bed. There in the middle of it all, a lump began moving. Then the lump poked out from the neck of a shirt to reveal the face of a whiskery, black ferret.

The ferret looked up and grinned. "Didye miss me?"

CHAPTER 2

The shock was *not* that Ondine's beloved Hamish had turned into a ferret – she'd had two whole books to get used to that – but that he'd transformed so quickly. He'd been in agony when he transitioned at the Duke's palace a couple of months ago, so the super-fast version tonight must have been super-painful.

"Are you hurt?"

Shambles – for that is how he was known in his ferret-form – winced and said, "Naw. Weil. A wee bit."

"Oh my poor darling." Ondine scooped him into her arms and gave a gentle hug, followed by a kiss on the top of his furry head. An ache took hold at seeing him like this. Just when she'd become used to him being human – complacent even, if she were honest with herself – he'd changed. He'd had to. Otherwise the inspectors may well have hauled him away in handcuffs. And seeing him hauled away simply wouldn't do.

Ondine knew she could put up with anything so long as she and Hamish were together. Yet she may as well be cursed too if they couldn't *properly* be together. And here they were, alone in her bedroom and everything.

"Oh would ye look at that," he said. "Get tae the window hen, there's something afoot."

"The inspectors have raided *Fang's* as well. I heard Henrik on the phone trying to warn them," Ondine said.

Shambles pressed his soft nose to the window and made a foggy pattern with his breath. From their vantage point, what with being upstairs rather than ground level, they could see the restaurant's outdoor decorations shining brightly in the dark night. Ondine loved their neon dragons with loaded kebab skewers for fangs. Shiny things like that really lifted the neighbourhood. The lights flickered on and off in a chase pattern, then suddenly they didn't come back on again. A trio of dark-suited inspectors escorted the last of *Fang's* staff into the back of a white van, which was parked on the street.

"There but for the grace of Old Col, go I," Shambles said. [1]

Ondine rubbed at her head. "Are you telling me you don't have a work card?"

"I didnae think I needed one, what with being a ferret for so long. And then, weil, I was with you."

Yes he was. He hadn't been human in decades, thanks to Old Col cursing him a good one at her debutante ball. [2]

He hadn't rediscovered his handsomely human form until he'd met Ondine all those months ago. Even then he couldn't always be relied upon to stay human. But when he was, Hamish and Ondine had spent so much time busily falling in love; they

---

1. Mustn't forget Old Col. AKA, Miss Colette Romano, Ondine's great-aunt and all round fabulously batty witch. And lousy chaperone. See *ONDINE: The Autumn Palace*.

2. See *ONDINE: The Summer of Shambles*. Look, we could get bogged down in backstory if we're not careful. You *have* read the first two books, haven't you? Oh for goodness sake. Go read them. I'll wait . . . OK, you're back? You're fast! Are you sure you didn't skim?

hadn't spent any time contemplating the mundane practicalities of everyday life. Why did those realities have to intrude now?

"We'll have to get you a work permit," she said.

"Or I could stay like this for a while until things cool over?"

"No you can't." Ondine wanted Hamish to be human all the time, because her relationship with Shambles the ferret was nothing compared to her relationship with Hamish the lad.

"Och . . . we'll think of something." Shambles said, shifting his weight from side to side. "Oh dear. I just thought of something."

Ondine looked at him, too scared to speak.

"I just realised . . . I'm a lot older than I look."

"What?"

"Weil, on account of the fact I was like *this* fer so many decades, the real me didn't age. Remember yer auntie put that staying spell on me. If I had've aged, I'd be nearer Auntie Col's age."

Originally Ondine had been very glad of the staying spell and considered it a blessing. Now his advanced-age-yet-youthful-demeanour created only fresh problems because he didn't look as old as his birth certificate would say he was. That's if he could find his birth certificate.

And she'd so hoped after the awful time they'd spent at the autumn palace their problems might be over.

"So ye see lass, even if I had me work card, with me right date of birth and all, nobody would believe it was true."

"Oh dear." A washing machine churned inside Ondine's tummy.

Ma arrived at the doorway and bustled in. "Oh dear is right. You OK love?"

"Oh yeas, all ticketyboo." Shambles crawled into his trousers and began transforming into his lovely Hamish self.

Ondine rolled her eyes. She was fairly sure her mother was

talking to her, not Hamish. All the same, pride surged in her heart at his bravery. He must have felt the worst pain in his life during that lightning-fast transformation, yet he hadn't complained one jot. Now he was back as his good self without a whimper. What a man!

Ma nodded. "Can't have you zapping down to ferret size every time the inspectors come –"

"Aye."

"– They had a lot of questions about how you vanished. I told them you were a hologram. Can't say they bought it, but as they couldn't find you, I took advantage of their confusion and said they must have imagined the whole thing."

Ondine's forehead creased. "And they believed you?"

"Not for a minute. But then they were called over to *Fang's* so they let us off with a warning. Hamish, we need you back on your feet. Promise me if they turn up again, you'll disappear, do you hear me? We can't afford to lose you."

"Aw, yer all heart Missers G."

"No I'm not. We can't *afford* to lose you because you bring in the most tips." [3]

Trust Ma to think of the business first. Ondine gave Hamish a hug. She then helped him into his shirt, but only because her mother was right there and it was the good and proper thing to do.

"Ondine, un-Velcro yourself from Hamish. He can't be seen in public again tonight, so I need you to finish up in front-of-house."

---

3. Because this is a family pub, all tips are shared. If people enjoy their meal, they're not simply tipping Hamish for being gorgeous and attentive, they're tipping Henrik and Cybelle for the sumptuous food and Ondine for the sparkling clean plates they're eating from. And for Da for keeping such a well-stocked bar. And Ma for keeping it all running smoothly.

"Ma, we're in huge trouble. Hamish doesn't have a work card."

"I'm aware of that. You'll have to pick up the slack until we can get him one," Ma said.

Oh dear, her mother had completely missed the point. Ondine curved her hand in a 'come here' motion. "Have a look out the window."

The three of them watched the last staff member of *Fang's* stagger into the van. The inspector had his hand on the top of the woman's head so she didn't injure herself on the door frame on the way in. [4] The van zoomed off, leaving nothing but a dark, closed restaurant.

"That's not good," Ma said.

"Exactly. And they'll do the same to Hamish if he doesn't have a work card," Ondine said.

"Stop catastrophising everything, love. Hamish will simply have to fill out some forms at the nearest British embassy."

Hamish turned to Ondine and then Ma. "I'm afraid it won't do any good, Missers G. Me birth certificate would say I'm old enough to be retired. Unless my name is Dorian Grey, they'll not believe me." [5]

"Oh dear," Ma said. Time stretched as she pursed her lips, deep in thought. "Then we may have to appeal to the Duke."

"You mean the Duchess," Ondine corrected.

Ma shook her head. "Sorry. Force of habit."

---

4. Isn't it nice when they do this? "Mind your head, that's it, watch how you go, gentle."

It's all part of the Courtesy in Custody program, which began in neighbouring Craviç and has spread throughout the world.

5. "Dorian Grey" is a camera filter setting used to make ageing movie stars look like ingénues, to convince the public that anti-wrinkle creams work. Or a devilishly good novella by Oscar Wilde, about a dashing youth whose portrait ages instead of the man.

It had taken a bit of getting used to, having a duchess as head of state instead of a duke.

Duchess Anathea was only the third ruling duchess in Brugel's history, so the entire country had a fair bit of adjusting to make. She wasn't even the proper duchess as such, she was merely standing in because Duke Pavla was too sick to rule and Lord Vincent too young to take over.

Something scratched Ondine's memory. The Duke knew Hamish could transform into a ferret, but did the Duchess? The last person Ondine wanted to deal with was the batty Duchess Anathea. They'd become sort-of-friends towards the end of their stay with Duke Pavla, but all the same Ondine wanted to steer well clear of the lot of them. Every member of the royal family made Ondine uneasy in the same way having a heaving mass of spiders on one's shoulder made a person uneasy.

Ondine, Ma and Hamish looked at each other, and as they kept looking, they kept saying nothing, which meant none of them came up with any alternative ideas.

Up and down went Hamish's Adam's apple as he swallowed hard. "Go to the top, eh lass?"

Ondine said, "Back to Bellreeve? I feel sick just thinking about it." [6] [16]

Hamish grimaced. "Mebbe we send her a letter explaining the situation?"

"Good!" Ma said, "That's sorted. Now, Hamish, you stay in the kitchen, out of sight. Ondi, you're with me. We have to clear up second dinner and reset the tables for breakfast."

And to think, before tonight, Ondine's worries had been all about her name day and what excitement lay ahead for her. This

---

6. Bellreeve is where the Autumn Palechia is located. It's also the setting for a fair amount of trauma in the previous book. No wonder Ondine felt sick at the thought of going back there. They won't be – going back to the palechia that is – just in case you were thought this third novel would push the reset button.

pushed all those lovely, excited, buzzy feelings aside and replaced them with niggly, naggly worries. Hardly a fair trade. Although she was only going downstairs to work, Ondine wrapped her arms around Hamish as if fare welling him for an eternity. "Please be careful," she said.

"Aye," he kissed the top of her head, "nothing will keep us apart lass. I'll make sure of it."

When they reached the kitchen, Ondine rolled up her sleeves to get back to the washing, only to find a towel, mid-air, drying a plate, also mid air.

"Wh –" She started to say. The towel dropped the plate, which smashed on the ground, the towel fluttered over the broken pieces.

"You're overtired," Ma said as she walked in. "Look at all these gleaming plates. I was crossing my fingers they'd be done quickly. Thank you Ondi, you've done a wonderful job."

Puzzled, Ondine looked at what her mother was gabbling about. That's when she noticed the neat stacks of clean, dry plates and bowls on the drying bench, next to the sparkling glassware and tubs full of glistening cutlery. So much work done in such a short time had to be the result of magic, but Ondine couldn't fathom where the magic had come from.

CHAPTER 3

Two mornings later, Ondine woke to the lads and ladies on the radio discussing the magical qualities of the day. This appealed to Ondine no end, because it was her name day, so it was indeed already special.

Snuggling further under the covers, she listened to them blather.

"Green lights all the way to work," the host said, before adding, *"That never happens."*

The other said, *"My toast fell off the plate and it landed butter side up, which I think breaks all the laws of physics!"*

"We've banished Monday-itis. Today is officially Magic Day here in Venzelemma."

"Small amounts of magic. Give us a call and share your moment of magic with us."

That suited Ondine just fine as she listened to the shared stories of good fortune. Being a Monday, she should be getting ready for school. What a shame the magic they were talking about on the radio couldn't chase Monday and the cold weather away.

Judging by the heavy grey skies and the tree branches

scraping against the window, a properly cold arctic north wind was dancing through the streets. [1]

A rumble set off in her tummy and a ping of excitement went off in her head. What sort of name day breakfast might Ma and Da have in store for her? After all, it was still two days before the wedding, so she could get a little Ondine attention before everything turned Margi-wards. Thrills zapped through her and she lifted the end of the duvet off her bed to have a sneaky look underneath. Perhaps her parents had snuck a pressie under there during the night? Disappointment weighed her down. The only thing under her bed was a warren of dust bunnies.

No matter, there would be presents downstairs, she was sure of it.

The moving lump in the bed beside her showed Cybelle still asleep, so Ondine dressed quietly. This took some doing, because there wasn't much room and she kept fumbling and losing her balance, what with it being so cold her fingers could barely move. At this time of year she needed thermal underwear, t-shirt, polo neck and cardigan. She also wore leggings under her denim jeans and two pairs of socks. Then she remembered she had to shower and relieve herself, so it all had to come off again.

Being a school day, she put her summer uniform dress over the top of it all. You may be wondering why she didn't wear her winter uniform. That's because they were twice handed down from her sisters and therefore threadbare and revolting. So the summer uniform stayed. Not that you saw much of it because

---

1. At this time of year, Brugel's tiny strip of territory along the Black Sea would be deserted, the beach chairs and umbrellas covered in snow. The Venzelemma Tourist Bureau And Committee For The Prettyment of Brugel leaves the chairs on the beach all year round, but they are chained together to prevent thefts. They also have 'anti-towel-technology' fabric, which makes towels slide right off them, so tourists can't reserve a chair and then wander off for the rest of the day. However, the fabric is so slippery tourists have also been known to slide right off them, especially if they put a towel down first.

when she went outside she wore an ankle-length life-preserver coat and fur-lined hat with *Orschlappen*. [2]

Thoroughly trussed up, Ondine walked bulky-legged down the stairs to find her mother stacking folding chairs into their private room behind the kitchen. It used to be a family room, with a table long enough to fit everyone around it. Now it had one small round table where only three could sit, at a squeeze. This was particularly unfair considering how much her family had grown to include three new beaux.

The rest of the space was taken up with boxes of kitchen supplies including doilies and extra thick plastic food wrap. In fact, loads and loads and loads of boxes of extra thick plastic food wrap. Not forgetting the teetering towers of boxes of things for Margi's wedding. Boxes of *bonbonniere*, ribbons, linen chair covers, linen tablecloths and napkins, silk flowers and dried rice and carrot seeds for throwing on the bride and groom. [3]

Sneakily, Ondine shifted the boxes and peeked around them, wondering which one was her present. It was the perfect place to hide a box of something, in amongst all these other boxes. Huh? None of them looked remotely like a name day present for Ondine.

Her mother walked in with her arms full.

Ondine said, "More boxes, Ma?" Maybe one of them had her present in it?

"Yes, dear. Give us a hand, will you love?"

"Um . . ." She wondered if her mother was pretending to forget the importance of the day, or if she had forgotten it for real. "Where's Margi, by the way?"

---

2. Orschlappen is the Brugelish term for earflaps. The huge coats and warm hats made Ondine feel like she was wearing a duvet, but at least she didn't look as silly as those people who wear blankets with sleeves.

3. In the old days, they used to throw acorns at the bride and groom, but they hurt!

"Getting her nails done, she'll be back soon." Ma wiped her brow as she gave an inventory of where the rest of the family was. "Thomas is picking up his suit, Da is having a haircut and Chef is at the markets. I assume Belle is still asleep. And you, my dear, are helping me before you head off to school. Come on, there's more in the van."

"I didn't think anything was open this early?"

"It's December, dear," her mother said, as if that explained everything. [4]

The north wind took bites out of Ondine's neck as she walked outside. The glums gripped harder than the cold weather as she wondered whether her parents really had forgotten what day it was. True to Ma's words, the delivery van had many more folding chairs that needed to come inside the pub.

"Can't we stack them in the garden instead?" Ondine hefted a chair in each arm and walked back inside.

"No, Ondi, they'll get wet."

"Can I at least have some breakfast first before doing more? Hang on a minute, Where's Hamish? He's good at carrying things."

"Right here." Hamish walked into the room, which was becoming more crowded by the minute.

Ondine's heart soared and sweet harp music played inside her head.

Hamish beamed. "Happy name day, Ondi love." He held out a decorative bag.

"Aw, thank you!" Ondine threw her arms around his neck, whacking her knuckles against cardboard boxes in the process. "You remembered!" Thank goodness someone had! Ondine gave him a rather too saucy kiss, which made her feel warm all over.

---

4. Because of the huge spike in weddings, every service provider opens their doors super-early to cope with the onslaught of customers.

Behind them, Ma cleared her throat.

Ondine unclasped herself from Hamish and checked out the bag's contents. She pulled out the first present and unwrapped the tissue paper.

"That's from all of us," Ma said.

Ondine looked to Hamish for verification. Surprise filled his face. Ondine rolled her eyes at her mother's attempt to be inclusive and ripped the tissue paper away. It was a book, *All For Love: The Life and Times of Elmaree, the First Grand Duchess of Brugel*.

"Oh wow, thank you so much."

"Ye like it?"

"Yes. Can't wait to read it."

Hamish beamed again. "There's something else in the bag too."

Ma cleared her throat again. "That's from all of us as well."

Ondine took hold of the small square box and showed it to her mother. "Nice try." Then she turned back to Hamish, unable to stop grinning. Light beamed from inside as she lifted the lid and saw the sweetheart ring within.

"Oh Hamish." She held the silver ring up to the light – what little light could get in considering the boxes covering half of the window – and gazed upon the tiny writing on the inside.

"*'Mo ghaol ort'*. What does that mean?"

Hamish's warm breath tickled her sensitive skin as he leaned in close and whispered, "It means, 'My love with you'."

Happy tears blurred Ondine's vision. "It's beautiful! How could you ever afford it?"

He grinned. "The tips have been very good."

"Yes, we have been rather busy," Ma interrupted the moment. "Give us a hand with wedding things. There's a van outside."

"Of course I'll help," Hamish said, giving Ondine a sweet

kiss that warmed her all the way to her toes. "Get yerself some breakfast, I'll help yer Ma with the boxes."

"Thank you." Ondine gave him a quick hug and snuck in one more kiss, then headed to the kitchen.

The light was much better in here as she slipped the ring onto her third finger, left hand. It spun loosely, so she slipped it onto the index finger, where it felt snug. [5] A thrill shot through her, because it felt just right.

FOR THE FIRST time since Ondine could remember, they did not have a breakfast crowd to feed that morning. The hotel was closed now, just to get them through the next couple of days so they could prepare for – perhaps even enjoy – the wedding. Which would probably go on for a fair while as half the wedding guests were staying on at their hotel afterwards. Ondine stood in the kitchen in the unfamiliar silence, a silence broken by her loud tummy rumble. A hearty warm breakfast for herself and Hamish would be just the thing.

Knowing her family, they'd all want some, so she made double-double measures and set about creating a pan full of scrambled eggs. With bacon chunks and chives.

"Oh it's you. I thought it might be Chef," Marguerite said as she trotted into the kitchen, following the smells. She held her fingers out, trying hard not to touch anything so she didn't mess up her manicure. "That looks fantastic. I'm starving." With care not to scratch her nails, she picked up the tongs and piled food high on a plate, then added extra cheese, black olives, roquette

---

5. In many western countries, people wear their wedding bands on the fourth finger of the left hand, but in much of Eastern Europe it's on the right. In Brugel, it doesn't matter, as long as it fits one of the fingers and doesn't slip off.

leaves, sundried tomatoes and potato crisps over the top of her plate, before heaping another spoon full of eggs. [6]

"Jupiter's moons, are you all right?" Ondine asked.

"Yes!"

"You're going to eat all that?" There would be plenty for everyone, but not if Margi kept shovelling at her current rate.

Marguerite looked at her like she had two heads. "I wouldn't put it on my plate if I wasn't."

Hamish sauntered in and delivered a beaming smile. "Yer a wonderful lass, making all that. And on yer name day too."

"Oh! Happy name day Ondi." Marguerite gulped down a wobbly fork full of eggs. "I've got your present on order but it hasn't come in yet."

This time it was Hamish's turn to roll his eyes, making Ondine giggle. At least Hamish hadn't forgotten her special day. Butterflies took hold in her tummy as she looked at the ring on her finger. How was she going to concentrate at school when every time she looked at her hand – and she'd be looking at it a fair bit – she thought of Hamish?

A twinge of hope – or maybe it was desperation – lodged in her heart.

Maybe her family was teasing her and she'd get her presents at the end of the day.

Or had they completely forgotten about her in the lead up to Margi's wedding?

---

6. Breakfast should be an uncomplicated affair, or as they say in Brugel, "It's not roquette salad."

CHAPTER 4

Aheavy schoolbag slung over her shoulders, Ondine bounced through the back door with a cheery, "Hello family!" and headed straight upstairs to make a dent in her homework. It wasn't that she loved homework, but heading upstairs to study would give her family time to organise the surprise.

There *would* be a surprise, wouldn't there?

Somebody was bound to come to her room and say there was a job for her in the kitchen. And she'd head down there and they'd surprise her when she walked in. At which point she would act surprised and touched that they'd gone to so much trouble.

Hamish came up with a plate of biscuits and lidded-mug of hot chocolate. "I'm not interrupting ye, just making sure yer all right."

How she loved to see him in his human form, not least because when he was himself, he could carry treats like these to her room. "Thank you," she said with a knowing smile. She was positive he was simply making sure she wasn't aware of what they were up to downstairs.

"I'm nearly done. I'll be down for dinner later."

"When yer finished, can I get ye tae look over something for me? I'm writing tae Duchess Anathea for a pardon. Or whatever it is I need tae ask her for tae get the goon squad off my back."

Worries niggled. This sounded real. Not some made up problem to get her to stay in her room. Ondine felt sure their country's newest Duchess would remember how Hamish had played an integral part in her rapid change in fortunes. Memories of the Harvest Ball at the Autumn Palace played in her mind. The Duke had been sick, poisoned by his own wife. Hamish had spoken up when it would have been far easier to stay quiet. And they'd discovered the former Duchess's secret bank account. Surely Anathea would reward his good deeds with some kind of special consideration?

"Absolutely," she said. "You know I'll do whatever I can to help." The admiration in his smile made Ondine feel lovely and warm inside. Until fresh doubt deflated her. "I just realised. I don't think Duchess Anathea ever knew you could be a ferret. We'll have a lot of explaining to do."

"Aye. That's par for the course for us." He kissed her sweetly on the lips and gave her the smile she loved so much.

"Hamish?" Fear shot through her system. She grabbed his hand as if it might be for the last time. "Promise me if the inspectors come back you'll get straight out of the dining room, right away?"

"Of course, hen." His trademark confident smile stayed in place, which only made her worry more.

"This is serious. If anything happened to you . . . well it doesn't bear thinking about."

"Och, dry yer eyes lass." He leaned forward and kissed her forehead. It was a little patronising and not at all the sort of kiss she expected from him. "Nothing's going to happen to us."

"Promise?"

"I promise. I'll stick to ye like a limpet to a ship's belly."

"Not such a great image there."

"Sorry sweetheart." He kissed her properly, making her tummy flip at the loveliness of it. When he broke away, his face showed fresh mischief. "Never was much of a one for words."

He placed the letter to the Duchess into Ondine's hands, kissed her again and left her to it.

The room felt colder without him. The sooner she finished her homework, the sooner she could traipse downstairs and be with him again. Working at whiplash speed, Ondine powered through her media studies chapter, plotted an essay for Brugelish literature and made ten pages of notes for legal studies. By the time she finished, she felt her brain might leak out her ear, but at least her homework was done for the night. Time for Hamish's letter to Anathea. She took a deep breath to cleanse her brain.

My Lord Duchess Anathea, *(Nice start.)* [1]

My name is Hamish McPhee and I am a resident of Venzelemma. Until recently I worked at the Bellreeve Palechia for the former Duke, and was present at the evening of the Harvest Ball. You may recall I came forward at a particularly stressful time for all concerned, and helped discover the former Duchess Kerala's transgressions. *(Skirting around the issue a bit. I'm sure I can make this more to the point).*

Recent law changes have resulted in demands being made to produce work papers. As I have none of this I am writing to you to ask for an exemption to this rule. You see, I have none identification at all and don't want to be deported also. *(It's getting messy. And the grammar's all over the place. Mercury's wings I'm sounding like my mother.)*

Chewing the end of her pen, Ondine jotted down the main

---

1. These are Ondine's thoughts, in bracketed italics. Just in case you weren't sure.

points of Hamish's situation on a notepad; finding the right way to say , "you owe us a favour because we were there for you when it mattered". Much like plotting an essay – except she had to be very, very careful in the wording of the letter. If she failed, it wouldn't mean low marks, it would mean Hamish's deportation.

No way had they survived the trauma at the palechia to be split up again later.

Not.

Going.

To.

Happen.

Happy with the re-writes, she found a stamp and an envelope, addressed it to the Duchess and had it ready for Hamish to read over, sign, and pop in the post.

HER PARENTS HAD CLOSED the restaurant on Monday evening – for both first and second dinner. Cybelle and Henrik prepared a grand meal for the family to have in the dining room. Well, the extended family which now included Thomas's parents and Thomas, along with Ma, Da, Margi, Cybelle, Henrik, Hamish and Ondine.

It felt strangely quiet, being such a large room but having so many empty tables and chairs nearby. Ma piled more logs and coal into the open fire to keep them warm. By this time, Ondine was in full funk as it became patently obvious her parents had overlooked her name day. She was ready to blow her lid.

"I propose a toast," Da said. "To Margi and Thomas."

Steam could have poured out Ondine's ears.

"Margi and Thomas," everyone said. Everyone except Margi and Thomas, because you don't toast yourself.

Not feeling hungry – high dudgeon will do that to you – Ondine cleared her throat to let rip. "Thank you for my lovely *name day* dinner, Henrik." She pushed her chair back and dropped her napkin on her plate.

Henrik looked horrified. "Oh! I'm sorry! I didn't know. Belle, why didn't you say something?"

Cybelle came over all defensive. "I've been flat out like a banker in a hammock with bridesmaid duties. I haven't had a chance to think! Ma, why didn't you organise something?"

"What are you all looking at me for?" Ma said. "I've been doing more than the lot of you combined! Anyway . . . Ondine, you're still grounded . . . so it's hardly punishment if we throw a party for you while we're trying to teach you a lesson. And I'm terribly sorry that Mr and Mrs Berger should witness such poor behaviour."

Should Ondine do the dignified thing and pretend everything was fine? No way! "Hamish, thank you so much for remembering how important today is for me. The rest of you can all . . . you can all go to Slaegal!" Then she burst into tears and ran out.

"Ondi wait!" Hamish gave chase.

Tears poured down her face. It took four drags of her sleeve to dry her cheeks. Even then it only lasted a moment before more tears splashed down. Mercury's wings, her nose started running too.

Hamish caught up with her at the first floor landing. "Hen, stop." He rubbed her shoulders, then guided her into his chest and wrapped his arms around her, holding on tight.

"You've every right tae cry. They should have done more for yer name day."

Footsteps sounded on the stairs. "Come on Ondi, stop making a scene." Ma said, "We can have your name day in a few weeks when all this is over."

"You're just saying that because you're feeling guilty that you didn't do anything for me. You didn't even make a cake!"

Ma pulled up short. "Did you have a bad day at school and now you're taking it out on us?"

Petrol? Meet the lit match: "School has nothing to do with this! And you know what? *I've* got nothing to do with this! It's all Margi, Margi, Margi. I'm not even a bridesmaid!"

"Of course it's all about Margi, she's getting *married*! You can have a name day every year but you only have one marriage in your life." [2]

"They should have set a different date!"

"Now you're being stubborn. There's only one more Wednesday after this one until Christmas. You know they have to get married before the New Year or it's bad luck." [3]

Somewhere in her subconscious, Ondine knew about the end of year marriage rush. But still . . .

"She could have set it for November."

"Without you? We didn't know when you would be coming back from the palechia. Or even if you'd *be* back. Which is why you're grounded in the first place! Having a wedding without all the family present? Your Da was beside himself with worry though he did his best not to show it. At one point I pressed Margi to go ahead without you but she wouldn't hear of it. To see the way you're carrying on now . . . well it's breaking her heart."

---

2. Unless you are Linda Lou Wolfe from Indiana, USA, who has married 23 times, making Elizabeth Taylor look like an amateur.

3. In Brugel, it's traditional for weddings to be held on a Wednesday. Linguists claim Wednesday derives from the Norse god *Woden*, but Bruglers are positive it's derived from the Olde Brugelish word for *Wedding*. Being a superstitious country, it's considered good luck to marry within the same calendar year as your engagement. Nobody has a clue why, but nobody is brave enough to buck convention. Hence the sudden rush of marriages in December and very few of them in January.

Really? Off kilter emotions gave her a wobble. She wiped her face and took a step back from Hamish. "But, she barely even notices I'm back."

"She's a *bride*, Ondi, her head's spinning faster than a hamster wheel. Now look, I am sorry for how this has turned out. I will make it up to you, I promise." Ma held her arms out for a hug of reconciliation.

"All things considered, your ma's had a lot tae take in," Hamish said, giving Ondine a gentle nudge in her mother's direction. Well, he would say that. He needed to stay in her parents' good books because he relied on their grace and favour.

Ondine threw herself into Ma's hug. "I'm sorry."

"There, there." Ma wrapped her warm arms around her. "I'm sorry too. I think we're all a bit strung out with so much going on. Things will settle down soon I promise."

With a huge sniff, Ondine pulled away to see tears in Ma's eyes.

"Ye should be savin' yer tears fer the weddin'," Hamish said. "I'm bringing industrial-size hankies."

LATER THAT NIGHT, as Ondine chased sleep, a soft tapping sounded at the door. Thinking it might be Hamish, she jumped up and opened it. "Oh." How disappointing to see her father standing there.

"Don't look so pleased to see me," he said.

"Sorry Da."

"It's all right." Da glanced up and down the hallway to make sure nobody was looking. In his hands he held a cupcake on a bread plate. "Chef's been making double dozens. He won't notice one missing."

"Oh yum!"

"Shhhh!"

Ondine whispered, "Sorry!" then snaffled a bite. The cake was soft and perfectly moist. The frosting buttery-smooth, tasting of chocolate and something else she couldn't quite put her finger on.

"He swished a little plütz in the mix," Da said. Next, he pulled a small box out of his pocket. "Don't tell your mother, because you're still grounded and you're not supposed to be having parties or presents."

She put the cupcake on the plate and reached for the package. What a thoughtful father she had. "Thank you. I knew you couldn't have forgotten."

"This is just between us. The punishment was your mother's idea and . . . I went along with it because we have to put up a united front."

Tears sprang free as she opened the box and found a silver necklace with an oval locket. The kind you can open up and put photographs in. No prizes for guessing whose photo she would put in there. "Thank you, Da," she managed as her throat closed over with emotion.

"Now get some sleep. You're still grounded."

Looping the chain around her neck, Ondine leaned into Da for a hug. With his free hand (the other held the plate) he stroked her hair and said, "My little girl, you're growing up too fast."

"You'll be saying that when I'm twenty, won't you?" she said, giving him a kiss on the cheek.

"I still say it to Margi," Da said, and then he winked and snuck out the room.

The pendant warmed against her skin as she snuggled down into bed. All things considered, she felt happier than anyone grounded for life had a right to. Well, not grounded for life, but probably until the Christmas and New Year rush was over. Her mother had never actually put an end date to it all. She'd simply said, "You're grounded until a fish dances on the table," and there was no knowing when that would be.

The door squeaked open. Could it be Hamish this time?

The footsteps sounded shorter and heavier than Hamish's. When she looked up, she found her mother creeping in. Quick as a flash, she hid the cake plate under her pillow, just as her mother sat on the end of the bed. Thank goodness it was dark and she couldn't see the crumbs on her face.

"Ondi darling, can we talk?"

"Yeah, Ma," she said as she wiped her mouth.

"I am sorry about today," Ma began. "It was your father's idea and I didn't want to undermine him. I didn't forget your name day, but we had to follow through."

Despite her mother's serious tone, Ondine felt a giggle threaten to break free. She stuffed the bed sheet into her mouth to hold back the laughter. All she could do was nod and steady her breathing so she didn't give herself away.

"I brought you this," Ma held out a cupcake on a plate.

Tears spritzed from her eyes as she fought off laughter. "I'm so sorry," Ondine managed to say through the sheets stuffed in her mouth.

Ma misread the emotion and moved in for a hug. She stroked Ondine's back in lazy circles, making soothing noises. All the while Ondine's body shook in silent laughter, which her mother read as tears and only hugged her tighter.

The only way to break free from this giggle trap was to think of horrible thoughts. Things that put her in a bad mood.

Stop laughing. Think of something horrible. The way her parents had swiftly hugged her then proceeded to punish her within minutes of arriving home from the palace with Hamish.

That had been miserable.

Hamish stuck as a ferret. That always made her tummy swirl with worry.

Hamish being taken away from her. Where had that thought come from? She didn't know, but the more she thought of it, the clearer the image became. Faceless people in uniforms grabbing him and tearing him from her arms.

It felt *awful*. It felt so terribly *real*, as if she were finally developing some kind of magical skill. It also did the trick, because she stopped laughing and felt utterly despondent.

"Don't tell Da, this is just between us." Ma gave her the cupcake. "And you're still grounded."

Ondine nodded, all traces of happiness gone as that hideous image of people tearing Hamish away from her replayed in her head.

I'm not going to let that happen, she promised herself. *Never, ever, ever.*

CHAPTER 5

The morning of the wedding dawned crisp and cold. Each breath Ondine exhaled created plumes of steam. She put on two dressing gowns and her thickest socks and stepped over to the window. Opening the drapes, the fog was so thick she couldn't even see *On The Fang* across the street.

"Don't worry, it's a good sign," Cybelle said on her return from the bathroom. "Fog in the morning means it will be sunny later."

Cries of anguish carried up the staircase.

"That will be Margi, getting it out of her system," Cybelle said as she reached for the hair dryer.

Judging from the noises, Marguerite sounded borderline hysterical. Curiosity – and a need for breakfast – took Ondine downstairs toward the source.

"It doesn't fit!" Marguerite wailed. "You took the seams in too far!"

Definitely hysterical. Ondine had never seen this side of her eldest sister. The stress of the wedding must have got to her.

"Calm down, love. Take it off, I'll fix it right now," Ma said with a calm tone. Considering the circumstances, the early hour and the importance of the day, Ma sounded heroically calm. *Suspiciously* calm.

Ondine found Margi standing on a box, wearing a pale slip. On the floor next to her lay a mountain of rich blue satin and fake white fur. Ma was burrowed underneath all that fabric. Her muffled voice came through the layers. "Morning Ondi, make us some breakfast would you love? Bit busy with a needle and thread right now."

"This is a disaster!" Margi stifled a sob. "The dress doesn't fit!"

Considering how much food Margi had been putting away lately, Ondine wasn't surprised. The filter kicked in and she decided now wasn't the time to mention that fact. [1]

"Now, now, mustn't worry. It will be all right," Ma said.

Margi burst into fresh sobs. Ondine had heard brides could become stressed, but she'd never seen her sister like this.

"There, all fixed, try this now," Ma said as she crawled out from underneath the rustling fabric and slipped the dress over Margi's head.

Wow, that was quick.

"Wow, that was quick," Margi said out loud.

"Yes, it was rather," Ma said. "It's amazing what you can get done when you set your mind to it. Let's see, oh yes, you look stunning. Josef, come and look at your radiant daughter."

Margi looked beyond amazing. She must be using some kind of magic because Ondine had never seen her sister look so gorgeous.

"In a minute!" Josef called back from somewhere near the kitchen. "I need to set the hot rocks."

---

1. The filter we all have in our brains, that stops us – just in time – from saying the wrong thing. Unfortunately, it's not always possible to find the 'on' switch in time.

Ondine beamed with pride as she made her way to the kitchen and set about making breakfast. The hot rocks were Hamish's idea. He'd told her about the tradition of placing smooth stones of granite in the oven to warm them. When wrapped in a sturdy blanket, they would keep the bridal party warm as they stood at the foot of the elm tree on a cold winter's day. [2]

"Nothing for me!" Margi yelled out. "I'm too nervous to eat and knowing my luck I'd spill something on my dress."

Ondine could hear Ma's voice carry all the way to the kitchen. "We'll wrap a towel around you. You must have something. How about a boiled egg?" Then she yelled out a bit louder, enabling her to carry on two conversations in two rooms. "Ondi, put a few boiled eggs on for us, love!"

A 'few' became sixteen, because Ondine had a feeling it was going to be one of those days where everyone would need to keep their strength up. Shame she didn't take her own advice – Hamish walked in wearing his wedding usher suit and she turned wibbly at the knees. He'd become freshly handsome all over again. The cheeky rascal had been holding something in reserve all this time! The suit fitted him perfectly, creating a tapered waist and broad shoulders and . . . somehow making him taller.

"What do ye think, lass?"

Did any words come out? Ondine didn't have a clue; she just stood there next to the bubbling pot of eggs, grinning away. Steam billowed over her line of sight, making it seem as if Hamish were walking through mist.

"I take it ye approve, lass?"

"Very approve." What a man, and he was all hers! "That

---

2. When the granite stones turn cold, they can be used for a curling match, which is a popular form of post-wedding entertainment.

reminds me, have you posted the letter to Duchess Anathea yet?"

"Oh yeas, did it yesterday."

Good. Now she could begin the mental count-down for how long it would take for the Duchess to reply to their appeal for clemency regarding the paperwork for Hamish's identity. She didn't want to think about what would happen if Hamish were deported over such a trifling bit of bureaucracy. Ondine's thoughts drifted all over the place, from thinking herself the luckiest girl in the world because Hamish was here, to wondering where the sound of harps had come from.

Seriously, *harps*?

"We need to relax," Ma said, walking through the kitchen with a portable stereo. A symphony of strings strummed through the pub as Ma turned up the volume. "That should do it. Ondi, thanks for the eggs but you'd better get dressed. We need to stay on schedule."

"Oh!" The steaming pot beside her bubbled with enthusiasm. She grabbed a spoon and pulled the eggs from the water. More steam poured through her vision. A moment later, everyone descended on the kitchen and grabbed one.

Cybelle, wearing an enormous tea towel bib to protect her bridesmaid's dress, ate her egg – shell and all!

"Urgh!" Ondine said, "What are you doing?"

"The shell's the best part," she said, giving Ondine one of those 'you're bonkers' looks she did so well.

"She knows it's not an apple, right?" Ondine looked to Henrik, hoping he'd talk sense into Cybelle. The chef only shrugged and followed Cybelle's example, biting into the egg without removing the shell.

Hamish stood there and made a circling 'cuckoo' motion with his finger to his temple.

Ma walked in, "Ondi, get dressed, the hairdresser will be here in ten minutes."

"Right." Ondine picked up her egg, still warm to the touch. Curiosity got the better of her and she took a bite through the shell. Jupiter's moons but it was revolting! All sharp angles and chalky. "Ptah!" She spat the shell into the closest sink and had to rinse her mouth three times to remove the grit from between her teeth. In the doorway stood Cybelle and Henrik, doubled over with laughter.

They'd set her up! For a fraction of a second she felt stupid and angry, then Henrik made a grimace and scraped shell out from between his teeth.

For his part, Hamish looked from Cybelle and Henrik to Ondine, in open-mouthed shock. Cybelle and Henrik high-fived each other and ran off, laughing at their successful prank. The laughter spread to Marguerite – "You made her eat the *shell*?" – who stopped crying hysterically for a moment to join in the fun.

Sure, they'd cheered up the bride, but it was at Ondine's expense, which only added one more item to the growing list of things that irritated Ondine about her family.

AS THE MORNING ROLLED ON, everyone calmed down and got on with their roles for the day. Ondine changed into her usher outfit; a long blue satin skirt – she could wear two pairs of leggings underneath and nobody would see – white ankle boots, white cashmere cardigan and white faux-fur bolero jacket with a thick collar she could turn up if the wind turned on them. Judging from the immovable fog out the window, it didn't look like they'd get the slightest breeze.

The hairdresser arrived in a floor-length pleather jacket and made a bee-line for Ondine. [3] She primped and teased and pulled Ondine's dark wavy hair into intricate curls and twists, slotting blue satin flowers here and there. She wrapped a tablecloth around Ondine's jacket and started on the makeup, dusting her face with powder, then moved at lightning speed to do her eyes, and (ouch!) pluck a few stray brow hairs away.

Ondine checked herself in the mirror. Wow! The blended eye shadow really brought out the colour in her dark eyes, the mascara looked sweet without going over the top. The first hints of an ache tugged at her forehead from her hair being tied up too tightly. But the tightening effect on her face was incredible. When she smiled, the corners of her eyes barely made a crease. She looked so much older, almost regal. She couldn't wait to show herself off to Hamish.

The reaction she wanted came soon enough, as she took to the stairs and found him standing at the bottom. His eyes locked with hers and her tummy flipped over. A look of adoration crossed his face as he put his hand over his heart. If she didn't hang on to the banister, she'd miss a step and land with a splat. Hamish said nothing, imperceptibly shaking his head, mouth falling open before slowly transforming into a broad smile.

"Well?" She stood on the last step so they could be at eye level. "What do you think?" She liked this newfound feeling of power over him. He looked speechless, which sent flurries of wonder through her body.

"I . . ." Hamish started, but couldn't finish.

Henrik walked past. "Ondi, you don't look half bad when you make the effort!"

If she could, she would have rolled her eyes, but her forehead was stretched too tightly to move a muscle. Instead she looked to Hamish to see what he'd say.

---

3. Pleather looks just like real leather, but is much kinder on cows.

With a scratchy voice he said, "I hope you have more lipstick."

"Pardon?"

" 'Cos I'll be kissing it *awff* all day." He closed the distance between them and kissed her with such tenderness she nearly came undone. Warmth spread through her and lovely fuzzies tickled her skin. It may have been Margi's big day, but Ondine felt like the beaming bride. For the first time since she'd found out she wouldn't be a bridesmaid – Thomas's sister and Cybelle had those roles – Ondine felt grateful for her reduced status. It meant spending the day working with Hamish. Sneaking in more kisses when everyone's attention was focused on the bride and groom. Truly, what more could a girl want?

"I hope that's not an example of your work ethic?"

Reluctantly, Ondine pulled away from Hamish to find Thomas smiling at them. He looked dashing in his groom suit, complete with a blue satin flower in his lapel. Not as handsome as Hamish, though.

"Is my bride ready?" Thomas asked. "The photographer wants her."

"Just upstairs getting her hair done with Cybelle. She'll be down in a minute," Ondine said.

"Good. If we can all gather in the front bar, he's setting up some lights to take group shots."

Suddenly, crashing metal rang through the air. Car horns blared. Tyres skidded on the cold road outside. *Crash! Crash! Screech-Bang!*

"What the?" Ondine grabbed Hamish's hand and ran to the window to see a seven-car pile-up at the intersection.

"The world's gone whirlypits," Hamish said. "Would ye look at the lights, they're all on green."

"Oh dear. Should we go out and help?" Ondine asked as she

surveyed the damage in the street. Crumpled cars, steam escaping from radiators, broken glass all over the road.

"Aye, let's call for an ambulance first."

"Already on it," Henrik called out from the kitchen. "You two grab aprons and head on out."

Aprons? Good idea; it would protect their wedding clothes.

As Ondine and Hamish stepped outside, they found loads of people standing around shouting at each other. They had various cuts and bruises on their faces, from biffing them against the steering wheel or the inside of the car doors. [4]

"We've called for an ambulance," she said to nobody in particular.

"And I've called for my lawyer," one of the drivers said, his face red from anger rather than injury.

"And I told you the light was green! You were the one going through a red light!" That came from an hysterical teenager on the other side.

"I have never driven through a red light in my life!" another woman said.

"We might stay back here a bit, lass." Hamish took her arm to keep Ondine on the footpath. "They're fair affronted."

Nobody looked too badly hurt, so Ondine tried not to feel too relieved when Ma called out they were needed inside.

Inside, Ma said, "Best we don't tell Margi about the crash, she'll stress about getting to the elm tree on time."

The radio blared out a traffic report. There were pile-ups all over Venzelemma! Desperate to hear more, Ondine turned up the volume. Worries twisted inside her as she thought about the strange coincidence of so many weird things going on.

Henrik switched the radio off just as Margi walked through.

"What?" Margi asked.

---

4. Few Brugelish cars have airbags.

"Nothing!" they all said at once.

Nothing was going to ruin Margi's big day.

CHAPTER 6

The photographs at the pub took up the next hour and a half.

The bride and groom exchanging gifts. Click.

The respective parents (Ondine thought Thomas's mother's hair looked a bit too *foomphy* but that's what mothers tended to do). *Click*.

The bridal party. *Click*.

Just the bridesmaids pretending to straighten Margi's skirts. *Click*.

Now the groomsmen handing Thomas his tie (he took it off so he could pretend to put it on again). *Click*.

Ondine and Hamish stayed back, nibbling their cold boiled eggs – without the shell this time – and sitting together patiently. Every now and then they were needed for the 'everyone' photo, but most of the time they could take it easy and enjoy one another's company. Ondine nestled against Hamish, reading the book he'd given her for her name day about Grand Duchess Elmaree.

Elmaree

Born under a tree.
Sits on the throne
Where a boy should be.

She was up to the third chapter and it was getting really good. "Did you know she was born at the bottom of an elm tree straight after Grand Duke Savo and Flora Venzelemma said their wedding vows? Oh wow, I've just realised who our city was named after. That's so sweet!"

Hamish gave her a smile and hugged her again. "An elm, huh? Is that why Bruglers get married at the tree?"

"Must be. I wonder if it's the same elm?"

They snacked on triangle sandwiches that didn't drip (roast beef or cheese with no condiments) then the horse-drawn carriages arrived to take them to the botanical gardens. Henrik had been monitoring the news and thankfully the traffic snarls had cleared.

Ondine travelled with Hamish, Henrik and Cybelle in the first carriage, which was excellent because Henrik carried a vast picnic basket full of nibbly food and flasks of hot chocolate. They put the hot rocks at their feet and had extra blankets over their knees.

As MUCH AS Ondine enjoyed sneaking kisses with Hamish in the gardens, they did have a job to do, so she peeled herself away from him and welcomed guests as they arrived.

"Hamish look, Mrs. Howser plus one is on the list."

"So she is."

"How did she score an invite?" Ondine asked. It wouldn't be Auntie Col inviting her; they had been friends many decades ago, but lately they were barely on speaking terms.

A thoughtful look filled Hamish's face. "It's only fair she should come. If ye invite someone to an engagement party, ye should invite them to the wedding as weil."

True, Mrs. Howser had been at Margi and Thomas's engagement party back in summer, but only because her parents had made a contra deal with the witchy Psychic Summercamp principal to make up for their outstanding fees.

Seeing the old witch's name on the list made Ondine uneasy, and she had a hard time explaining exactly why. "I didn't think she was that interested in my sister," she said. "She didn't stay long at the party."

"Aye, she disappeared pretty fast that night. Mebbe she won't turn up today?"

"Ah Hamish, you don't understand. Weddings are old-lady-magnets. She'll be here. I wonder who she'll bring as her plus one?"

They greeted more guests and took them to their seats. Soon enough, Mrs. Howser did appear, with an imperious look on her grey, wrinkled face. She was dressed in formal travelling witch attire: A heavy brown cloak, sturdy boots and multi-pocketed skirt. On her head she wore not the clichéd pointed black hat but a far more sensible deep brown fur-lined hat with earflaps.

And her plus one was –

"Melody! How are you?" Ondine beamed as she embraced her friend, who wore clothing that matched Mrs Howser.

But oh dear, there was so much less of Melody than Ondine remembered from their days together at Psychic Summercamp. Mrs. Howser must not be feeding her. Guilt pricked her conscience at their lack of contact in nearly six months. They last time they'd seen each other was just after Duke Pavla visited the pub and offered Hamish and Old Col a job.

"I'm good," Melody said, her cheeks pink and bright in the

winter chill. Then she added in a whisper, "my stars, Ondi, Hamish is even more gorgeous now."

"Oh . . . you!" Heated embarrassment rushed up her neck as she stepped out of the embrace. "It's good to see you. Come on, I'll show you to your seats."

"So . . ." Melody leaned in closer to Ondine's ears. "What's going on with you two? Are you planning a walk to the elm yourselves?"

Behind them, she heard Hamish chatting to Mrs. Howser. Ondine figured if she could hear Hamish, he must be able to hear them. She chose her words with care. "I'm the happiest girl in the world, Melody, but this is Margi's special day and that's all I can think about. Look, here's your seat."

When Ondine turned around, she got the strangest look from Mrs. Howser. Almost as if she were trying to smile and trying not to smile all at the same time. Ondine's belly did a strange twisty thing. Thankfully, none of this interior concern could express itself on her face, because of all the pins in her hair pulling her skin so tightly.

Just as Cybelle predicted, the fog dissolved to reveal a sunny day. Not exactly balmy, but the wind held off. Clouds of steam rose as their guests sipped hot drinks to stay warm.

The gardens looked beautiful, with garlands of blue satin flowers on the chairs. The wedding elm took centre stage, its huge bare branches fanning out above them. It was such a shame it couldn't have been a summer wedding, when the tree would be covered in lush green leaves. Or even autumn, when the changing leaves would fall gently around them like confetti.

Ahhh, but if it had been an autumn wedding, Hamish and I would have missed it.

Great-Aunt Col turned up with a beaming smile and formal witchy attire, similar to Mrs Howser's, complete with the heavy travelling cloak and boots. Altogether a sensible option for a snowy outdoor wedding. "Ondine my love, you're glowing," she said, giving her a kiss on each cheek. "Hamish you're far too handsome for your own good." She kissed him on each cheek as well.

This had to be a good sign, because Ondine couldn't help remembering that it was her great-aunt who, in a fit of pique, had turned Hamish the handsome lad into a ferret in the first place.

"This way Auntie Col." Ondine led her towards her seat in the front row.

"Aw nae," Hamish said as he turned away.

"Wha –" The words died on Ondine's lips as she saw three people in suits step out of a van. They looked exactly like the ones who had raided their restaurant the other night, and had then rounded up all the staff at *Fangs*.

Just as the thought, *They can't seriously raid a wedding for illegal immigrants, can they?* passed from one side of Ondine's brain to the other, the man who had become so impossibly handsome from the mere act of suiting up, dropped to the ground.

"*Boak*." [1] With a grimace of pain he vanished into a pile of clothes on the snow.

The snow on the ground wasn't nearly as cold as the ice roaring through Ondine's veins as she looked on her hapless boyfriend who'd had to ferret-ise himself to avoid deportation.

With a soft nudge of her foot, she scooted him and his clothes under the nearest row of seats and tried to act as if nothing was going on. Inside, she wanted to cry. Would life with Hamish ever be normal?

Oh, why had he only *posted* the letter? They should have delivered it to Duchess Anathea personally, then they could have

---

1. Boak = "Oh dear, something I have eaten does not agree with me."

had an answer straight away. Mentally Ondine counted the days until she could expect a response. Two days for it to be delivered, possibly another few days before she looked at it. Then a few more days and . . . oh it was so frustrating.

The string quartet started playing. The celebrant, a woman wearing a high-collared, navy blue woollen cloak to ward off the cold, walked to the base of the elm. She had a calm but happy expression, as if she were excited for the couple about to marry, but perfectly in control of her emotions and nerves.

The three men in suits walked towards their party. Fear pumped Ondine's pulse as they came closer. They weren't going to stop the ceremony, were they? Mercury's Wings, they *were*!

With a quick dash, Ondine intercepted them. "Can I help you?" Her panting breath made great gusts of steam as she spoke.

"We need to check the credentials of the bride and groom."

"Oh them!" Relief crashed over Ondine. "They're up the back, this way."

"What's going on?" Ma said as she and Great-Aunt Col came over.

The suited man held out his identification badge. "We need to check that the bride and groom are Brugelish nationals."

The quartet slowed down, so Ma turned and made some hand gestures at them to keep playing. Then she turned back to face the interlopers. "Why are you targeting us?" Ma put her hands on her hips.

He said, "Far too many marriages at this time of year: people desperate to become citizens and duck the paper, that sort of thing." [2]

---

2. Ducking the paper is the local expression for avoiding filling out forms or completing other brain-drainingly horrid paperwork. It's usually achieved by signing the blank paper at the bottom of the page, then handing it back to the official with a crisp ẞr100 bill at the top.

"Come with me then," Ma said to the officials, then she looked at Ondine and said, "back to your post, you have a job to do."

"Yes Ma," Ondine said, doing her best to look chastened in front of the suit-squad, while dancing with relief on the inside. Thomas and Margi would be fine.

Back at her post, more worries added to the party of woe in Ondine's heart. Hamish was nowhere to be seen. His clothes lay in a pile on the snow where she'd kicked them, so she picked them up, shook them out to keep them dry, then shoved them under her faux-fur jacket. Wherever Hamish would be as Shambles, he'd at least have a real fur jacket.

She looked about for that familiar dark streak of fur. How hard could it be to find him in the snow?

"Over here, hen."

Following his voice, she saw Shambles the ferret, poking his furry face out from under the snow-laden branch of a weeping Slaegalpine. [3]

Quick as she could, but also not too quick in case people saw her running and wondered what the fuss might be about, Ondine made her way over.

"Throw me thae clothes will ye, I'm freezen mah tights off."

Using her body as a shield, Ondine faced the wedding crowd and made sure nobody was paying her any attention. No, they were all watching the immigration inspectors and seeing them off.

Phew, that was too close for comfort. And also, the need for

---

3. Despite the name, Slaegalpines are not native to Slaegal, the country that neighbours Brugel. They are however, in plentiful supply in that country, and feature heavily in Norange, that country's capital. Legend has it that the first families brought the pines with them, when they arrived from somewhere much further east.

Hamish to become a ferret at the slightest provocation was starting to do her head in.

She slipped Hamish's thermal underclothes through the branches. Behind her, she heard him wincing. "Och, these pine needles are sharp."

"Are you all right?" Ondine jammed his trousers and shirt through the branches again and tried not to spill too much snow on her sleeve, otherwise she'd end up with soaking wet arms.

"Didye bring me shoes and socks?"

"Sorry, forgot. They're right under a chair. I'll grab them."

Every nerve screamed to run back and get his shoes, but again that would draw people's attention so she had to walk and act normally, retrieve his shoes and socks as if it was all part of her usher duties, and get back to the tree before Hamish's feet snapped off in the cold.

The immigration team were over at the gazebo, where the next wedding party waited their turn for the wedding elm.

"They've moved on to the next group now," Ondine said as she slipped the shoes (with the socks rolled into them) through the branches. "Talk about ruin your big day."

In a fresh shower of snow, Hamish pushed the branches aside and made his way out. "Ouch, got a splinter," he said.

"Let me look at it."

"No hen, let's get back to the weddin'."

Back in position and with the inspectors busy with some other unfortunate bride and groom, Hamish slipped his arm around Ondine for some shared warmth as their ceremony began.

The celebrant stood front and centre, a smile fixed in place. Her voice created steam as she spoke. "Welcome everyone on this magical day to the marriage of Marguerite and Thomas."

As is the Brugel custom, the parents walked in from the left and the right, meeting in the middle. The symbolic joining of families. They exchanged small gifts and kissed each other on the cheeks, then separated and took their seats.

Then it was time for the groomsmen and bridesmaids to do the same, exchanging gifts and kisses. The celebrant smiled again and looked out to the crowd. There was a touch of pantomime involved as she raised her hand to her forehead as if gazing into the sun. "Do we have the bride and groom?"

"We are here," Thomas and Margi said together, half laughing.

Everyone stood to attention and turned to see them.

"Then come forth!" the celebrant said, beckoning them with an exaggerated hand gesture.

The quartet played a stirring wedding march. Thomas and Margi walked together, arm in arm to stand before the celebrant.

Hamish stood beside Ondine and placed a comforting palm in the middle of her back. Warmth spread through her.

As Margi and Thomas reached the base of the elm, a flock of birds twittered in the air above them and landed on the branches. Then, to Ondine's amazement, the tree's bare and skeletal branches burst into bud. The crowd gasped in surprise and awe as branch after branch, going higher and higher, became covered in pink and white buds. Those buds then unfurled into flower.

Everybody applauded, scaring the birds off temporarily, but as they stopped clapping the birds returned to the branches and chirped happily.

"That's a nice touch so it is." Hamish kissed Ondine on the top of her head.

"It's amazing!" Ondine wiped away a tear. "How nice of Old Col to do that."

"Ye think it was her?"

"She's the nicest witch here," she said.

The crowd broke into more applause as doves descended

onto the branches and began to coo. Ondine rested her head against Hamish's shoulder and felt completely at peace with the world.

Old Col turned and looked at Ondine and Hamish, a puzzled expression on her face. It didn't look like the kind of face that had just made some crowd-pleasing magic. Then her eyes grew large and her mouth dropped open, as if she'd worked something out. Before Ondine could work out what it was Old Col had worked out, her great-aunt quickly shut her mouth and turned back to face the elm.

Hamish said, "Aye, nice to see Auntie Col using magic for good instead of spite."

The tree in full bloom completely changed the snowy scenery. Soon, some of the small pink and white petals dropped from the tree and fluttered down onto the crowd below like confetti.

The ceremony got underway. There were some loving words, they swapped rings, exchanged vows and held hands. Ondine and Hamish were so far down the back they didn't hear much, but they saw Thomas wipe his eye and Margi smile at him so sweetly it set everyone off in floods of happy tears. As one, the women clutched at handkerchiefs and dabbed their eyes. The men cleared their throats and coughed. The celebrant declared them joined forever. Margi and Thomas kissed and the string quartet started up. As ushers, Ondine and Hamish would need to move everyone on fairly soon. Being December, and being the wedding elm gardens, there were more brides and grooms with families and friends waiting nearby for their turn. So long as the immigration inspectors let them through.

Being so busy with her duties, Ondine barely registered Old Col approaching them.

"Making the tree burst into leaf is a charming touch," Col said.

Strings figuratively snapped in Ondine's head and she became even more confused than usual. "You didn't make the elm bloom?"

Old Col shook her head. "No."

Ondine felt sure Col's magic had made the tree bud. Was it Mrs. Howser? It seemed too nice a gesture to be from her. Perhaps Margi had extra talents she hadn't told anyone about? "If you didn't do it, Col, who did?"

Her great-aunt folded her arms across her chest and gave Ondine a searching look. "I would have thought that was obvious. You did!"

CHAPTER 7

"**M**e?" Ondine drew in a staggered breath from the shock of it all. "But I don't have magic!"

They still had to move everybody on – issuing thank-you cards with a map on the reverse side directing them to the family pub, *The Duke and Ferret*, for the reception dinner. A van pulled up and a small team of workers appeared, collecting all the folding chairs and gathering up the decorations. They were so efficient they virtually swiped the chairs while people were still sitting on them.

"It has to be you, Ondi, who else could it be?" Old Col sounded annoyed.

"But I didn't do it."

"Aye, go easy," Hamish chimed in to defend her.

"Of course," Old Col took a breath. "I'm sorry if I sound cross. I'm so cold I'm trying to stop my teeth from chattering. But Ondi, I'm serious. Whether you realise it or not, this is your doing. Yours and Hamish's."

In mute shock, Ondine and Hamish looked at each other.

Col kept on. "Why is this a surprise? Surely you've noticed all the strange things going on? It started when we arrived in

Bellreeve a few months ago. I thought it was the palace, but then the weirdness followed us back to Venzelemma. More to the point, it followed *you* back to Venzelemma."

"I'm nawt magic," Hamish protested.

"You can change into a ferret at will," Col said.

"Aye, but that was yer doing, nae mine."

Cogs turned in Ondine's head and a few twigs began to snap. A strange feeling grew in her tummy at the thought she might be capable of magic. It would be nice to be able to do some things, but what if she got cross and turned someone into a toad in a moment of anger and couldn't turn them back?

Then again, if she had magic, might that make life easier? A sprout of confusion and hope unfurled. Maybe magic could help Hamish get a work card? Questions swirled like snow flurries. If Col was right and she did have magic, why didn't she know it? Why didn't she *feel* it? Aside from feeling wonderful whenever she and Hamish were together, which was a kind of magic all of its own.

But on the serious side, if she did have magic, how was she supposed to use it to her advantage if she didn't even know when she was using it?

The last guest departed. The hired help did a lightning-fast job of clearing away any signs of Margi and Thomas's ceremony, so that the next group could set up.

Col took Ondine by the arm. "We'll talk about it on the way back. Our ride awaits."

Henrik held the carriage door open for Cybelle and helped her in, then he stepped in after her and they sat together, holding hands. Hamish followed and held his hand out for Ondine. She was so busy smiling at his gallantry she didn't register Old Col jumping in ahead of her.

Col winked at Hamish and said, "What lovely manners you have."

If her forehead weren't pulled back so tightly, Ondine would have frowned at her great-aunt's pushiness. Col sat herself in the middle of the bench seat, so Ondi and Hamish had to sit either side of her.

The hot rocks they had earlier placed in the carriage to keep them warm had gone cold but the flask still held hot chocolate, so that was a plus. Cybelle carefully poured steaming half-full cups to avoid sloshing it over their pristine clothes.

Ondine turned her collar up against the cold as the driver clicked his tongue and the horse clip-clopped down the cobblestone street.

Being a Wednesday, Ondine could see people bringing their drying clothes in from their window lines, in time for laundry curfew. [1]

Old Col made an exaggerated 'aaaaah' sound as she sipped her drink. "So, Henrik and Cybelle, have you noticed anything strange or out of the ordinary since Ondine and Hamish returned from their adventures with the Duke?"

"We're booked out every night," Cybelle said. "Not that there's anything wrong with that, but we've never been so busy. Christmas is going to be a nightmare."

"And they're eating more," Henrik said.

Ondine had noticed that too. "Everyone eats more in winter. Don't they?"

With a raised eyebrow Cybelle said, "Licking the plates clean?"

Baffled looks passed between everyone. Uneasiness spread through Ondine.

---

1. Across Brugel, the Wednesday laundry curfew is strictly adhered to, so that those getting married (on a Wednesday, of course) will not have the blight of people's smalls lowering the tone of their day.

Col pursed her lips in thought, then said, "Let's talk about the bison on the sofa shall we?" [2]

All eyes fell on Ondine. "What have I done?"

"The elm, my dear. You made that happen," Col said. "Believe me, I'd take the credit for it if I'd thought of it, but all praise to you. It was a lovely touch."

Rolling her eyes – ouch, darned pins pulling her skin so tightly – Ondine tried to control her frustration. "But it wasn't me! Maybe some of Margi's friends are witches – or maybe someone from Thomas's family?"

Col shook her head. "I was sitting close to the Bergers; the magic didn't radiate from them. It came from behind me. The moment the ceremony concluded and everyone moved forward to congratulate the bride and groom, I started walking towards the origin of the magic. I was looking for a witch. Instead, I found you. I might also add Birgit Howser looked around as well, wondering who'd done it."

Hearing Mrs Howser's name made things move uneasily in Ondine's stomach. She also wished Col wasn't sitting between her and Hamish, because she could really use more of his support right now. "I was only looking at the elm and thinking about how much nicer it would be if they'd had a summer or an autumn wedding, but that's because I was cold. Everyone's cold! I'm sure everyone was thinking the same thing.

"In fact, if it *was* me doing the magic, why didn't I feel anything? And while we're at it, why can't I make this small carriage warm up a few degrees?"

At which point Col stood up and squished herself beside Cybelle. The movement left Ondine sitting alone with cold air

---

2. Something huge and puzzling that everyone knows is right there but nobody wants to talk about.

Pachyderms are not native to Brugel, so the expression, 'The elephant in the room' never caught on.

swirling around. Hamish scooted over and wrapped his arm over her shoulder. She closed her eyes into the embrace and felt instantly warmer.

"Nice one!" Henrik said.

Ondine's eyes flashed open to see Henrik, Cybelle and Old Col buried under an enormous fleecy blanket. Henrik tucked it neatly around them and he and Cybelle cuddled closer. First eggshells, now blankets. Henrik and Cybelle were excellent pranksters. "Stop winding me up!" Ondine said. Honestly, it was as if Henrik and Cybelle had nothing better to do than tease her! "I can't believe you'd get Col involved in one of your jokes."

"Ondi love, I dinnae think it was them," Hamish said, swallowing so hard his Adam's apple bobbed up and down.

"Oh not you too?" Ondine couldn't bear the thought of Hamish being on Cybelle's side.

"Nay lassie. I think they're being serious this time."

"But I didn't wish for a blanket," she said. Hamish's warm body was no match against the cold fear nibbling inside her.

"I sure did," Cybelle said.

A look of remorse crossed Henrik's face. "I'm sorry for the joke this morning with the eggs. Because now you don't want to believe us."

Cybelle snickered behind her hand and turned to Henrik. "It was good though."

"The best." They bumped their fists together.

Why didn't Ondine and Hamish have a blanket as well then? What's the point of having magic if you can't make your own life more comfortable? A heavy feeling of dread grew in the area of Ondine's liver, then moved at a leisurely pace to her lower intestine. Ondine wished to heavens the feeling would go away, but it showed no intention of leaving any time soon. If anything, the hideous feeling invited its nasty friends over. A veritable party of sickness rocked and rolled inside her.

At least she had Hamish looking after her. He cuddled her into his body, sharing his warmth. "If I really do have magic, then why am I so cold?"

It was Cybelle's turn to roll her eyes. "You need to use it properly. Didn't you pick up anything useful at Summercamp? Apart from Hamish, that is."

A miserable, "why now?" startled Ondine with its whininess.

"Aye, I was wondering that meself. Why now, Col? Ye didnae raise this at Bellreeve and we were there fer weeks."

A look of resignation came over Col's greying face. "Because of the weird magic. Because of every light turning green and causing the worst traffic snarls we've ever seen. Because of what happened today at the elm. Because of what it signifies. I thought – mistakenly as it turns out – that things were strange at the palace because Bellreeve is an incredibly strange place and so many weird things have happened there over the years. But lately, every time something unexplained happens, you're there, Ondi."

Ondine swallowed her nausea. "You were there too! You were at the palace. The minute you crossed the threshold into the palace grounds, there was a tornado. It rained fish! And then today, you were standing by the elm tree with everyone else. Surely it's your magic, not mine?"

Col's words sounded so patronising. "My dear, when I use magic, I absolutely feel it. Today at the elm, I felt nothing."

"Well . . ." Ondine mentally scratched for answers. "You're old! Maybe you forgot what it feels like?"

Indignation radiated from Great-Aunt Col as she sat up straighter. "I will forgive you your outburst because of the stress of the situation."

"*Whoa Geta!*" So absorbed in their bizarre conversation, Ondine hadn't noticed they'd reached the pub and the horse's clip clopping came to a stop. A shingle proclaiming *The Duke &*

Ferret hung proudly from the building's corner. They'd renamed the pub partly in honour of the Duke of Brugel.

"If I have magic, why couldn't I save The Duke?" Ondine turned to look at Old Col, the woman who seemed to know everything but never gave Ondine a proper answer to anything.

"But you *did*, dear girl. We were witness to what took place at the palace. You and Hamish saved the Duke from his crazy wife Kerala. A woman who is now safely removed from society and her children, by the way."

Normally Ondine loved it when Hamish held her hand, but as he helped her out of the carriage, insecurity wriggled into her brain. "Is Duke Pavla getting better?" On one hand, yes, they'd saved him from eating more toxic pastries, but by the time she and Hamish had worked it all out, Pavla had become so sick he didn't seem capable of recovering.

"He is . . . stable." Col had that look about her, as if she knew more than she was letting on. "We may have to get used to having Duchess Anathea at the helm for a while. At least until Lord Vincent comes of age."

The mention of Duke Pavla's son made things burn in Ondine's chest. Her mind raced back to all the mean things he'd done to her, and her family, over the last two seasons.

Honestly, today was supposed to be a day of celebration and love. Couldn't her great-aunt save all this for another time?

"Oooh, listen to them talk politics," Cybelle said.

"It's no laughing matter," Col snapped.

Henrik wrapped the blanket around Cybelle's shoulders. "Let's go inside. I'm looking forward to enjoying a meal I haven't had to cook myself."

The moment they were out of earshot Col looked to Ondine, pain evident on her face. "When I said stable, I meant to say he's not getting any better. Nor is there much chance of it.

But I didn't want to be the bearer of bad news, not on such a happy day as your sister's wedding."

"Oh," Ondine said, failing to think of something wise and sympathetic to say.

"Ye cannae blame yerself Ondi, ye did the best ye could."

Col guided them in. "Come on child, let's enjoy the party."

That at least was something to look forward to. Ondine's parents, in a rare display of splashing out, had hired caterers for the day so that everyone would be able to relax.

Everyone except Ondine, who couldn't switch her brain off.

Old Col declared, "I want the two of you to stay together. For at least an hour."

"Aw that's a terrible hardship." Hamish gave Ondine a smile and a wink.

Usually when he did that she felt safe and warm and loved. But now she felt wibbly inside.

Meanwhile, the rest of her family and Thomas's were over by the windows having more photographs taken. Actually, Margi and Thomas were having more photographs. Cybelle and Henrik were chatting with Thomas's sister and their parents, who were sitting at a nearby table helping themselves to cups of tea and finger sandwiches. [3]

The tables were set out in a horseshoe shape, with several tables joined together along the top of the room for the bridal party and family. People hovered about the tables, looking for their decorative name cards to find where they should be sitting.

Col continued with her instructions to Ondine. "Remain close at hand. In fact, hold hands if you're able." Then she went off on a bit of a tangent. "Is it dark in here or am I having trouble adjusting to the light?"

---

3. In Brugel, a finger sandwich is a dainty morsel that you can hold in your fingers. This is not always the case in Slaegal.

There were candles on the tables, to provide a romantic mood, but they didn't provide much in the way of light.

"Now that you mention it, it is a little dark," Ma said.

Ignoring their concerns about lighting, Hamish clasped Ondine's hands in his and pressed them to his chest. His heart beat a steady rhythm under her palms. His easy smile and charm broke through the shroud of worry. Sunshine filled her soul.

"Beautiful light," the photographer said as he took more shots of Margi and Thomas.

Ondine, Hamish and Old Col turned to see a shaft of golden sunlight pierce the windows, creating a stunning, ethereal back-light to the bride and groom.

It looked magical.

Col crowed in triumph, "Now do you believe me?"

Ondine wanted to believe the sunshine was coincidence. But the multiple signs of weirdness were getting hard to ignore.

"Aye but it's lovely wee magic." Hamish kissed Ondine's forehead, the tip of her nose, and then her lips. Her palms, still pressed to Hamish's chest, could feel his pulse quickening.

"More than a little magic," Col said. "Take a look."

They stopped kissing and gazed around the room. "I cannae believe it." Hamish had trouble closing his jaw.

Roses and ivy grew all over the walls and ceiling beams. Vases overflowing with blooms appeared near the doorway. A look of wonder spread over Margi's face as she watched each new arrangement burst forth out of thin air.

"Thank you Auntie Col!" she said in a high-pitched squeal of bridal euphoria.

As one, everyone turned to Col, their eyes wide with stunned appreciation.

"Oh, don't thank me Margi – thank your little sister."

Margi charged forward and embraced Ondine, kissing her repeatedly on the cheeks. "It's just like I dreamed it! Ma said we didn't have the budget because we spent it on catering. Thank you so much!" Fresh kisses of gratitude rained down on each cheek, depositing lip-gloss over her skin. Then Margi let her go and charged back to Thomas to smother him in kisses.

Ondine stood there, feeling as if she were about to topple over.

"Have you worked it out yet?" Col asked her with a look somewhere between 'smug' and 'conspiratorial' on the spectrum.

Ondine asked, "Are we . . . making *other people's* wishes come true?"

"You bet you are!" Margi said, taking a napkin and wiping Ondine's face, but then she kissed her again and smudged her afresh. "Better get back to my husband. Squee! Husband!"

Margi ran back to Thomas's waiting arms. The photographer seized the opportunity and took rapid-fire shots to capture the action.

"Aye lass, making other people's wishes come true is a beautiful gift." Hamish gave her a hug and moved to kiss her cheek. "And just so ye know, ye've made my all wishes come true too."

Warm things blossomed in Ondine as she and Hamish snuck in one more kiss, not caring if anyone was looking.

The caterers arrived with fresh trays of food and made their way through to the kitchen.

"No looking!" Cybelle's voice carried across the room as she held Henrik back from following them.

"Professional curiosity," he said.

"Come on, we're not working today," Cybelle said. "Ondi, can you fill his boots with lead so he can't sneak off?"

"I'm not a performing seal," Ondine said.

"I just want a peek." Henrik inched closer to the kitchen.

Cybelle hauled him back. "You are having the day off and you are going to like it."

Ma put down her teacup and walked over to Ondine, a broad smile on her face. "I knew it would only be a matter of time before your gifts manifested. I'm so proud of you, darling." Another set of kisses rained over her face. Surely there was no room left on her cheeks for any more lipstick?

"Ma stop, please. It's hurting my head. Aunt Col, you said before that you can feel when you're doing magic. Well . . . if you're saying all this other stuff –" she waved her hand around the room filled with more bouquets than a florist shop, "– is because of me . . . then why can't *I* feel it?"

Ma's palms were up in one of those 'calm down' gestures. "We'll work that out later. It's Margi's big day –"

"And mine!" Thomas yelled out.

Ma raised her voice, "– And Thomas's. Thank you, my newly-minted son-in-law!" Then she turned to her aunt. "Please, Auntie Col, I know you've always had a soft spot for Ondine. But let's have this day for Margi and Thomas."

Which was fine by Ondine, because she didn't want to be the centre of attention if it meant people expected her to do magic she had no real control over. It didn't sit right and she wasn't sure why. The thought of having magic had always appealed – it's why she'd gone to Psychic Summercamp in the first place. Unfortunately, her experiences there had shown her she didn't have an atom of magic in her. But now she had the gift to make other people's wishes come true. That had to be a good thing, right?

On a purely selfish level, she'd rather make her *own* wishes come true. Then, as Hamish wrapped a gentle arm around her shoulders and made her feel protected and loved, she realised she already had everything she'd wished for.

So maybe it was magic?

At which point Melody walked in and made a bee-line for

the food, while Mrs. Howser walked in and made a bee-line for Ondine.

The woman pulled away her fur-lined hat, revealing masses of grey curls, skin like a wrinkled bed sheet and a glare that could cut an apple at thirty paces.

"My dear student, forgive the pun, but you're blossoming." Mrs. Howser said with a beaming smile. A smile that didn't sit right on her face somehow. As if it had been such a long time since she'd had a genuine smile, her muscles were out of practice. "And Hamish, how good to see you again," she said, the smile losing its way but refusing to ask for directions as she looked him up and down.

"Aye."

"Come now, let's not be so formal with each other" She flashed a set of pearly whites and kissed Hamish on one cheek, then the other. "My, but you're more handsome than I remember."

Did she have to squeeze his cheek?

Old Col cleared her throat with far too much gusto. "Something you wanted, Birgit?"

The last time Ondine had seen these two together, they were none too friendly. Were they about to trade insults? At a wedding?

"I think," Mrs. Howser linked her arm into Ondine's and steered her away from Old Col, "you could do with some proper instruction. You have incredible talent my dear – talent that can't be wasted here. You simply must come to CovenCon."

" – Ah –"

"No prevaricating. You are coming, and that's it. A talent like yours, my dear – oh the things you could do . . . As you well remember, Melody was on the verge of failing astral projection, but with my excellent tutelage, look at her now – she's flourishing. Oh Melody dear? A moment please?"

Any moment now Ondine's knees would turn to dough and she'd fall down from the shock. There was something very wrong about Mrs Howser being so interested in her, especially coming so soon after Old Col's bombshell about making other people's wishes come true.

At the buffet table, Melody stopped piling finger sandwiches on her plate and turned to them. Her cheeks were stuffed with food like a chipmunk preparing for winter.

Flourishing? The girl was reed thin.

Old Col took Ondine by the other elbow to steer her away. "All is well in hand here, Birgit. Ondine is under my tutelage." The words may have been sweet as syrup, but Old Col's lips were pressed into a determined line.

"Oh you sweet old thing," Mrs. Howser said, showing those shiny teeth of hers. "Of course you want to help, but Ondine here needs the very *best* instruction, and . . . no offence, but with all the goodwill in the world, she's hardly likely to get it here, is she?" [4]

"You always had a way with words." Old Col's attitude dripped with sarcasm.

Worries wormed their way through Ondine as the atmosphere turned so frosty their words were snapping as they came out.

"Don't let personal jealousies intrude, my dear," Mrs. Howser said. "You've had years to guide Ondine. It's time to let a professional take over from here."

"And you had decades with Hamish, and achieved exactly what?" Old Col shot back.

They still held Ondine by one elbow each and their grips increased as they tried ever so hard to remain polite.

---

4. "No offence". The two words uttered before the speaker always says something truly offensive.

"Come now, Colette, we're not still fighting over Hamish are we? That pot's boiled dry." [5]

They weren't fighting over Hamish, they were fighting over Ondine. She'd have bruises tomorrow to show for it.

Mrs. Howser's nails dug in as she spoke. The words were silk and kindness, the tone crafted from steel. "I think we can both agree Ondine here has tremendous potential. You would not deny her a place at CovenCon merely from spite, would you? Surely even you are not that cruel?"

"Of course I wouldn't deny her that."

Hamish interrupted with a tray of canapés. "Oh quick, ye need tae hold this, I'm gointae sneeze." His face contorted into the most bizarre shape.

Mrs. Howser let go of Ondine and grabbed the tray. He made the loudest, fakest sneeze Ondine had ever witnessed, but she loved him all the more for breaking the witchy standoff.

As wedding receptions go, Margi and Thomas's was a good one. The food and plütz flowed and everyone kept their speeches mercifully short. Da's was even funny, making Ondine wonder if she might be exerting even more magic than she imagined. When the string quartet played, they cheered as Margi and Thomas performed a Bruglish three-step. [6] Guests paired up and joined them on the floor. Hamish reached for Ondine's hand and asked, "May I have this dance?"

"Forsooth, My Lord." Ondine giggled as she made a curtsey to him.

---

5. Anything that has exceeding its statute of limitations. Whether a civil court case for negligence, or a decades-old feud between two women who fought for the affections of the same handsome lad.
6. Similar to a waltz, but less poncing and more snuggling.

"Eh?"

"Sorry, can't help it. It's the book you gave me; they're so formal and say, 'forsooth!' all the time and 'My Lord' and 'My Lady'. It's so cute."

"Ye know," he twirled her into his body as they moved among the guests, "I just remembered. I'm a lord."

Laughter bubbled in her heart, but Ondine played along and pretended she didn't know. "Oh *really*?"

"Aye, back in Scotland we say *laird*, but it's the same thing."

Batting her eyelashes for maximum effect, she asked, "And do you have a castle, my laird?"

He chuckled. "It's probably an old pile of stones by now. I havenae been back tae check."

"Then we must go one day."

"Aye. But ye wouldnae want tae go this time of year. Ye think it's cold here!"

A waiter walked past with a tray of sparkling wine. [7] Ondine reached for it just as her Ma turned to see her.

"Ondi!"

"Just a sip?"

"You're still grounded."

"Still?"

"Yes. Until a fish –"

" – dances on a table, I know." Mercury's wings but her mother loved that saying.

Hamish took a sip of his drink. When Ma's back was turned, he offered his glass to Ondine. The bubbles felt like mousse on her tongue but the taste reminded her of that awful night at the Autumn Palace when Duke Pavla nearly died.

---

7. Only sparkling wine from the Champagne region of France can be called Champagne. In Brugel, locals call it 'bubbles' or 'sparkling'. The really cheap stuff is called 'tart fuel'.

"You're too young." Ma swiped the glass away from her.

Ah well, she had Hamish instead. He made her feel light-headed at the best of times.

CHAPTER 8

The shortest day of the year arrived with hideous news blaring out the radio as Ondine woke up.

"Tributes are flowing in from across Europe at the news that Duke Pavla has passed.
He died in his sleep, attended by close family, however his estranged wife Kerala was not present.
Brugel will observe full mourning until Christmas Eve."

Guilt set up base camp in Ondine's stomach. She wanted to throw up. The words, "I should have done more. I could have done more," played in her head as she dragged on her clothes and headed down to the kitchen.

"It's nae yer fault, hen," Hamish said, giving her a comforting hug as they stood in the kitchen, waiting for the kettle to boil. "We tried tae warn him aboot Kerala and he wouldnae listen."

"I can't switch my brain off. I didn't do enough, and now Vincent's going to take over, isn't he? We should have made Pavla listen." Hindsight dumped a trailer load of "would haves" and "should haves" at her feet. With a side dumping of "if onlys".

"Hindsight is always right, hen. But ye cannae let it eat ye up. He didnae want tae listen because in his heart, he knew the truth would kill him."

"But . . . Old Col says we've got magic, so why couldn't we save him?"

Hamish rubbed her back in a comforting way. Then he too sighed and his accent came out even thicker with emotion and regret. "Mebbe he didnae want tae go on. There's not much ye can do fer someone who's lawst thae will tae live."

"You suck at being a counsellor," Ondine said with a pathetic sniff.

"Do ye want me tae stop cuddling ye?"

"No, keep doing that. You're really good at that."

"Well that's a plus. And another plus, we have tae close for the day because we're all in mourning. So ye don't havetae goe tae school."

A huge sigh escaped. "School's closed for winter, sweetheart. But thanks for trying to cheer me up."

"Aye, and at least we goat the wedding over with, so that's a plus."

Yes, at least they'd had that magical day. Thomas and Margi were on their honeymoon by the Black Sea and nothing had happened to spoil that.

ONDINE HAD NEVER SEEN SO many people wearing black, which stood out starkly against a fresh overnight dumping of snow. [1]

---

1. She hasn't been to Melbourne, Australia, where the entire citizenry wears

Everyone wore armbands with the hexagonal flag of Brugel sewn on. Duchess Anathea called for three days of mourning, which meant all non-essential services had to close as a mark of respect. Ma claimed she was deeply upset by Duke Pavla's death, but Ondine knew her mother's bad mood stemmed from their having to close until Christmas Eve. It was normally their busiest time of year. When they re-opened, not even a fourth dinner would be able to fit everyone in again before the New Year.

On the bright side, Ondine was on winter break from school, which meant more delightful time with Hamish. This in turn made her feel guilty about enjoying herself during the official mourning period for Duke Pavla, and the whole blaming-herself-for-his-death started over again. This did nothing for her state of mental health, although every time Hamish saw her looking sad – which was a great deal of the time – he gave her a warm embrace, lovely rubs on the back and beautiful kisses. Which in turn spiralled her into a fresh wave of guilt for enjoying his kisses when she should be miserable.

Because his kisses were so magical.

Both commercial networks televised Duke Pavla's funeral, which allowed people to watch from home in the warmth of their living rooms. [2]

On the fourth day, which happened to be Christmas Eve, the mourning period was over and the customers returned to *The Duke and Ferret*. Ondine was back in armpit-deep soapy water washing the dishes from lunch.

Before her hands had a chance to dry, she then raced around

---

fashionable mourning clothes all the time, even though Rock'n'Roll died years ago.

2. Brugel has two commercial networks that broadcast nationally, and the non-profit BNB, the Brugel National Broadcaster funded by the sale of Brugel-Made televisions. BNB is commercial free and broadcasts every second Sunday, and on special occasions.

the dining room with the vacuum cleaner before the "second lunch" service began. It was up to Ondine to carry the extra load, as Margi and Thomas were still on their honeymoon by the Black Sea.

"Can I help ye lass?" Hamish came up behind her.

Startled by his voice, she spun around, the vacuum nozzle slurping the end of Hamish's scarf. Before she could grab it, the machine sucked the fabric all the way in.

"Whoa!" Quick as a flash she tapped the machine off with her foot. "You shouldn't sneak up on me like that!"

"I wasnae, but ye couldnae hear me so I had tae get closer."

They then spent the next five minutes unravelling the scarf from the machine's dust bag, then had to turn the machine back on and suck the dust off the scarf, so Hamish could wear it again.

"Can you re-set the tables?" Ondine asked as she pulled the chairs out with one hand and pushed the vacuum cleaner nozzle with the other.

"Course I can." He grabbed a lace tablecloth and flicked it open, then laid it over the top of a table. Then he put the salt and pepper grinders in the central position, but just as he said "ta-da" he knocked the pepper over, spilling black and grey corns all over the tabletop.

"I'll get it." Ondine aimed the nozzle at the runaway corns, which clattered and scattered through the tube and into the bag.

"Need any help?" Old Col came sauntering in.

Flicking the machine off with her foot, Ondine looked at her great-auntie and said, "Yes, as a matter of fact. Could you magic this place clean and set the tables for me?"

Old Col gave Ondine a wink. "What's in it for me?"

Hamish answered with, "Free second lunch and as much plütz as the Old Man has left in the bar."

"Done!" The witch waved her arms in the air and flicked her

wrists and may have even snapped her fingers. At least, Ondine hoped the noise was from snapping her fingers, rather than breaking a bone or something.

In a blink, the room was ready to receive new customers.

"Thank you Auntie Col."

"Good, now we can talk." With a flourish, she withdrew a card from a deep pocket, with the Royal House of Brugel stamped on it. "I have a royal summons from Duchess Anathea, and it's for all three of us. She wants to meet at the mid-winter fairground in Savo Plaza." [3] Old Col said. "It's early evening, around four o'clock, so you'll be back in time to work for second dinner."

Ondine nibbled the inside of her cheek, then looked to her great-aunt. "What does she want with us?"

"We'll find out soon enough," Old Col said.

IT SNOWED something fierce as they walked to the train station on their way to Savo Plaza. If it wasn't snowing, or sleeting, or so cold their breath froze on their lips, they could have walked the distance. But winter in Venzelemma is not a sensible time to be walking anywhere outdoors.

Catching the train meant they were warm and dry for brief periods of time, as long as they didn't sit down on the wooden seats, which were dripping with mud and melted snow from everyone's snowcoats.

A blast of arctic air gripped Ondine's neck as they reached the station at Savo Plaza.

Her muscles cramped with the effort to keep warm and she felt like she was wearing her shoulders as earrings.

---

3. It's not called Savo Square, because it's shaped like a hexagon.

Once in the plaza, it wasn't nearly as cold, because the tall buildings formed three quarters of a circle, protecting those inside from the worst of the winter gales.

The sheer number of people packed into the plaza also defrosted the environment.

"There she is," Old Col said apropos of nothing. Her hand flew up to wave at Duchess Anathea who was standing on a gold coloured carpet, in front of a crowd at the Ferris wheel.

Nearby, a woman with a vacuum cleaner strapped on her back worked quickly to keep the carpet dry and free of snow.

A pang of jealousy hit Ondine as she wished she had someone to walk in front of her and suck up snow and slush all day.

The duchess was still in mourning for her brother, while also being dressed comfortably for the cold. A lush black coat with fur-lined collar and cuffs and matching fur trim at the hem, which came to just below her knees.

The length emphasised her fabulous mahogany-coloured boots with intricate buttons dotted up the side.

On her head she wore a fur-lined box-style hat, which sat so neatly upon her head it didn't damage her perfectly coiffed hair.

Her gloves matched her boots, but would have been made with much softer leather.

Has she had more 'work' done? Ondine wondered, as she took in the Duchess's unlined face.

Bud lighting shone from the bare trees. Decorative bunting in the Brugel colours of red, white and blue flapped in the breeze.

Paper lanterns hung in the shop windows. After all, it was Christmas Eve and people should be celebrating.

Especially after the drudgery of the past few days. [4]

---

4. In Brugel, Christmas proper doesn't begin until Christmas Eve, December

Tight security kept Anathea safely protected from the crowds. This could be tricky. They couldn't very well walk up to the Duchess of Brugel and . . . OK, apparently they could.

"Colette Romano, my very good friend," Duchess Anathea said loud enough for everyone to hear. They embraced and kissed each other on the left cheek, then the right, then back to the left again. If Ondine's eyes widened any more she'd turn into a goldfish. Since when had Anathea and Old Col been such firm friends?

"Go *aloang* with it," Hamish murmured in her ear.

She'd go along with whatever Hamish said, that was a no-brainer. Before she even questioned what they were doing next, various officials herded them into a cabin on the brightly lit Ferris wheel. It had lights in a chasing sequence, radiating from the core, in Christmassy golds and reds and greens. Double bonus, they didn't have to queue up in the cold to get a ticket.

Anathea remained outside for a moment, as she wielded a pantomime-huge pair of scissors and cut a ribbon. "Let Christmas begin!"

The crowd roared and threw cheese balls into the air.[5]

The next thing Ondine knew, Duchess Anathea plonked herself into the cabin with them. Biscuit the dog charged in and leapt upon his master's lap. The dog still didn't have his teeth back to full size. Poor thing. [6]

---

24. It's also illegal for anyone to put up Christmas decorations before December 1. This is one of the drawcards for people migrating to Brugel. Absolute guarantee, you will never read a tweet from a Brugeler complaining of Christmas merch in stores in September.

5. It's not a waste of food throwing cheese balls, because the myriad stray dogs hanging around will eat them up. In many parts of the world people employ a "five second rule" for eating dropped food – if the food has been on the ground for less than five seconds, it's still safe to eat. No such rule exists in Brugel because the dogs get it first.

6. Old Col had removed them, with a spell (which may or may not have

"Now then," Anathea said to Ondine, Old Col and Hamish, "there will be smiles for the cameras."

Cameras clicked and flashes flashed. No point asking, 'What's going on?' because Anathea was too busy being fabulous for the media. A stray thought flicked through her head. Where was Vincent? Surely he'd want to be in front of a camera at this point?

The door finally closed and the heating came on beneath their feet. How clever to have heating inside the cabins! It warmed them up and fogged the windows, which only served to confuse Ondine. Surely the point of the ride was for the amazing view?

"Now the door has been closed," Anathea said, "we shall not be overheard."

"My Lord Duchess, you are truly marvellous to see us," Old Col said, "and on such an important day as Christmas Eve."

Anathea waved her hand to dismiss her. "No time for that. What is planned?"

"Whoops!" The cabin lurched, sending an alarmed Biscuit scuttling onto the floor and Ondine into Hamish's arms. She snuck in another kiss while she was this close. When she turned around, everyone was blanketed.

"Where did they –?"

"Thanks Ondi," Old Col tucked herself in.

The Duchess cast a quizzing glance Ondine's way. Ondine was about to ask, "Where did they come from?" meaning the blankets. But then she remembered the carriage ride home from

---

included anaesthetic!) during a fraught time under the table at the Autumn Palace. And while it is terribly cruel to remove all a dog's teeth in one swoop – with or without magic, with or without anaesthetic – those same teeth were about to chomp Shambles in half, and Old Col simply wasn't going to let that happen. The teeth had begun to grow back since that incident, but the dog wasn't back to full bitey-ness at this point.

the wedding. She and Hamish must have made the blankets appear, simply from having a quick smooch or being close to each other, at the same time that somebody else had made a wish.

The Ferris wheel started again. Biscuit poked his head out from under the blanket.

They weren't too high yet, but Ondine wiped her sleeve over the foggy window to gaze out at the pretty lights surrounding Savo Plaza, which had turned the scene into a snowy fairyland.

Anathea adjusted the blanket across her knees. "Tell me what is planned?"

"Planned, Your Grace?" Ondine asked back.

"Yes, planned. There are already rumblings about bringing forward Vincent's coronation. It must be stopped."

"But um . . . I'm not sure we're the right people you should be asking about that." Ondine tried very hard to keep her tone polite, but all the same she felt she was being terribly rude in refusing Anathea. Not that she really knew what she was refusing at this point.

"You are exactly the right people to be talking to," Anathea said. "You make people's wishes come true."

How did she know this? Ondine's eyes shot to her great-auntie, who looked guilty.

Col cleared her throat and gave everyone a huge grin, as if she'd worked out something very clever. "It's all falling into place. Just as I knew it would." Then she coughed, as if to hide her real thoughts. Because Ondine suspected Col was making this up as she went along. "As we know, children, it's Anathea's deepest wish to be the fairest and best leader Brugel has ever had. This will bring certainty and stability to the country. Your magic, when you become amorous, makes other people's wishes come true. May I suggest you –"

"Huahhhtzu!" Ondine sneezed into her elbow. "Ugh, sorry."

She held her arm across her face to keep the germs in. "Does anyone have a tissue?"

Hamish shrugged and showed his empty hands. "Sorry, Ondi, I didnae think tae bring any."

"Don't look at me," Anathea said as all eyes fell on her. "I'm only given this purse to match the shoes. I have no idea what they've put in here." She opened her clutch purse to find it stuffed with butcher's paper. "Would you look at that. It's so new there wasn't time for the stuffing to be taken out."

Old Col rummaged around in her bag and produced a crumpled handkerchief.

"Danks," Ondine grabbed it in time for another volcanic sneeze. Then three more for good measure. By the time the sneezing stopped and they'd all said, 'Bless you,' Ondine felt her brains turn to goulash. "I'm sorry Your Grace, I must have picked up a bug on the train ride here."

"The train? Why were you not brought here by a taxi?"

"Couldn't get one for love, money or magic," Old Col said. "The traffic pile-ups we've been having must be contributing to the shortage."

Which made Ondine cringe in shame. The traffic situation had been getting worse, according to reports on the radio every morning. Like the multi-car collision the morning of Margi's wedding. Had that been a result of this newfound magic answering everyone's wishes at once? Every driver always wished for green lights at intersections, but if they were approaching from different directions and their wish was granted, they'd all crash into each other.

Cold air tickled Ondine's nose and she sneezed again.

"I take this to mean there will be no kissing?" Anathea asked.

"Weil," Hamish shifted in his seat as he moved away from her germs.

"Would you look at that?" Old Col wiped the fog from the

window so they could see. Immediately next to Savo Plaza, in all directions, the city was pitch black. Like a doughnut of darkness spreading into the immediate neighbourhood. The only lights they could see were from car headlights as they tried getting through intersections without crashing into each other.

"Glad I'm not old enough to drive," Ondine said.

"The continuing power supply problems are being wished by Vincent, I'm sure of it," Anathea said. "Don't you think it's suspicious he's not here? Wouldn't he just love to be associated with something wonderful like Christmas Eve? Unless he's hoping things go badly wrong and people associate that calamity with me."

That got Ondine's attention. And Hamish's. Even Biscuit looked up to his master in surprise. They all looked at her and waited until she finished her dramatic pause.

"There are rumblings and rumours that Vincent should inherit early," Anathea said. "No doubt he is spreading them. There are those who say a woman at the helm is bad luck. There are those that might hasten Vincent's ascension."

"Yer saying the city is full of troublemakers," Hamish said.

"You catch on quickly," Anathea said. "What we're up against can clearly be seen. The darkness must be Vincent's work, but he's not doing it on his own. He must be getting help, and he must also be stopped. Brugel needs certainty and security. I can provide that. But the people don't yet trust me or love me. It must be remedied."

The thought, *we're in serious trouble*, plagued Ondine.

Old Col looked royally miffed. "Much like this ride, we're going round and round in circles and getting nowhere."

Anathea sat up to her full haughty height. "The answer to our problems can be easily grasped. I must be the most popular leader Brugel has ever had."

Even with magic on their side – and Ondine still wasn't all

that comfortable with her magic – the Duchess was asking for the impossible!

"Is that all?" Old Col said.

"You're saying you're not up to it?" Anathea shot back. "I know you need something from me. I'm merely suggesting we help each other in our times of need."

"Er," Hamish spoke up. "Ye mean my work papers, on account of not being Brugel born."

"That has not been forgotten," Anathea said as their cabin slowed. "You'll be wanting this." She retrieved a folded paper from her pocket. It had the hexagonal Brugelish flag watermarked through it. "This will be signed and handed over once my succession is secured."

Their cabin came to a stop at the bottom of the Ferris wheel. Icy worries dug into Ondine. This felt a little too close to blackmail for comfort. But what choice did they have?

"Happy to help." Hamish made the decision for them and gave Ondine the sweetest kiss. It caught her off balance. Her nose was still blocked from her earlier bout of sneezing. Ordinarily she'd luxuriate in his kiss but breathing carried a higher priority. She pulled back and panted for breath.

"Wonderful!" Anathea said, clapping her hands. Then she stepped out of their cabin to face a phalanx of flashing cameras. "A wonderful time was had by all. Merry Christmas everybody!"

"Awff we go then," Hamish said, taking Ondine by the hand as the media pack followed Anathea's every step. "Let's get some cheese balls."

"Do you think the kiss made her wish work?" Ondine asked.

"I doubt one kiss will do it all, lass, but mebbe it's a start?"

A stray thought crept in. If their magic didn't work, maybe Old Col wasn't as good at guiding magic as she'd let on? In which case – the second stray thought said – perhaps she might need Mrs. Howser's help after all?

IF YOU'VE NEVER EATEN fried cheese balls, you haven't lived. Hot and crunchy and a bit saltier than is good for you on the outside, gooey and warm in the middle – they're perfect for cold months. [7] Ondine and Hamish shared some as they sat on a bench in the midst of the Christmas market, racking their brains for ways to make Anathea popular.

Cinnamon and gingerbread mixed with diesel generator smells as they set about having a big think. Everyone around them carried on being festive. Adults sipped mulled wine and the children drank hot chocolate. Piped music and puppet shows kept the party flowing. Everybody was enjoying the sights, sounds and smells of the winter fair, carefree and happy. In stark contrast to Ondine, who felt matters of state pressing down on her shoulders.

"How will we know if the magic will work?" She asked as she chomped down on a cheese ball. "And another thing. If she wants to be popular, why can't she pay some PR company to do it? They'd at least know what they were doing."

"Aye. I'm thinkin' along the same lines as you, hen. But she must think we can do it if she's asked us."

"Yes but what if while she's wishing to be loved, everyone else wishes for something horrid to happen to her. And they don't even know they're wishing because they're just thinking it." It truly hurt her brain to think of the ramifications of their canoodling. "I mean, how far does the magic extend? Just the people around us or the whole city?"

"Aye. I heard on the radio this morning there were blackouts

---

7. Fried cheese balls are banned at football matches in Brugel, as cold ones are used as weapons.

as far away as Craviç. Mebbe we should be careful about how kissy we get?"

Would they have to ration their kisses? Oh it hurt to think about that. Much better to keep her brain busy with practical matters. "She's holding a work card over your head."

"She'd call it leverage," Old Col said, bringing them a fresh basket of piping hot cheese balls. "You help her, she helps you."

"By the way," Ondine poured on the sarcasm, "thanks for telling the Duchess all about the magic. Way to blab it to everyone before I've even had a chance to get used to it."

"Because it works," Old Col said, "and it will work for Anathea."

"Yeah but, you should have told me you were going to tell her."

"There wasn't time, dear."

Muttering disdain to herself, Ondine fell upon a fresh cheeseball and bit into it. It was so hot she couldn't talk or swallow, but it was so gooey she couldn't spit it out.

"Ye right, lass?"

"Here you are," Col handed her a napkin.

Ondine dabbed at her lips and madly waved her hand in front of her mouth, as if that would cool things down.

"Hold on a minute." Hamish reached for another napkin and held it up so everyone could see the printing. *Fried Cheese Balls. Brugel's National Treasure.*

Then he grabbed a marker pen, crossed out the first three words and wrote "Duchess Anathea".

Ondine nodded. Anathea making private wishes was one thing, but maybe they could help her popularity in other ways too? If people thought of their Duchess as a National Treasure, they'd be on the way to loving her to bits.

"You're brilliant!" Ondine smothered Hamish in far too many cheesy kisses than was socially acceptable in public.

"Careful kids, you don't know what people might be wishing while you do that."

"Of course." Ondine pulled herself away from Hamish and scoffed another cheese ball.

"We have another problem." Old Col said. "How are we to pay for this advertising?"

"Anathea will. Won't she?" Ondine asked.

"She's broke," Old Col said.

That stopped Ondine in her tracks.

"I should clarify." Old Col split open a cheese ball in her fingers and blew on it to cool it down. "It's not quite at the 'selling off the family silver' stage yet, but it's getting there. That's why she can't afford to hire a public relations company."

Ondine bit into another cheeseball, but the fun of it grew cold. The task ahead of them felt insurmountable.

CHAPTER 9

Heading home, Ondine replayed Old Col's words in her head as they trudged through the snow-lined streets. The train took them back to the station across the road from *The Duke & Ferret*, their family pub. But the lights weren't on, not for them, nor for *On The Fang*.

Every single streetlight was out. Through the foggy restaurant windows, she could see candles burning for light on the dining tables. The donut of darkness she'd seen from the top of the Ferris wheel was now all around them.

Hamish – clever, thoughtful Hamish – had a torch in his satchel to guide them across the street.

Inside, they found Ma and Da re-using the wedding dinner candles to help customers complete their meals in comfort. It added a warm glow to the room, complimented by the roaring fire. She waved to Thomas as he fed two more logs to it.

It took an effort to remove all their layers of hats and coats and scarves in the dark, in the private room behind the kitchen. Ondine lost her balance taking her boot off and fell backwards into a box of extra thick plastic food wrap. The cardboard split open and the contents rolled out.

Hamish shone his torch on the roll and Ondine had a closer look. There was something printed on the plastic. Which was odd, because food wrap was usually clear, because you're meant to see the food beneath it. This was opaque and as she unrolled it, and Hamish shone the torch to help them see better, she found herself looking at a keyboard layout.

"That's nae clingfilm," Hamish said.

"Cybelle!" Old Col said, her voice full of purpose. "I'll bet Brugel to a brick this is one of her schemes."

Schemes? What schemes did Old Col know about that Ondine didn't? Mind ticking over with possibilities, Ondine immediately wondered if these 'schemes' meant extra money coming in.

Being Christmas Eve, they found Cybelle and Henrik in the kitchen, frantically cooking and serving meals. Except they had the added problem of no electricity. Henrik and Cybelle were adapting to the situation, using every single gas burner to keep things cooking along. The ovens weren't working, as they were electric, but they could still boil and fry their way out of trouble.

The overhead fan wasn't working, so a fair amount of smoke billowed from the frying steaks. Ondine opened a window and a gust of snowy wind came in and blew the smoke clear.

There was still some hot water left, but it grew tepid so it would require even more detergent to break down the grease from the dirty plates in the sink. All the while she couldn't stop thinking about how on earth she and Hamish could help Duchess Anathea.

How would they pay for the advertising campaign to increase the Duchess's popularity? If it had been a normal year, her family might have been flush from the pre-Christmas trade. [1]

---

1. The jewels and pretty shiny things they'd found under the floorboards in book one were well and truly spent on renovations and the wedding. The ones

But this year, thanks to Pavla's untimely demise, they'd had to close during the busiest, most profitable time of the year.

"We could re-name the pub after her, couldn't we?" Ondine wondered out loud.

"What's that dear?" Ma asked.

It would take too long to explain so she shrugged and said, "Don't worry."

Old Col came over with a hot saucepan full of steaming water to top up the sudsy sink. "I know we're desperate for ideas, but we're not *that* desperate," Col said. Then she tested the water with her fingers and decided it was far too cold. She wafted her hands over the water and muttered incantations. The water grew hot and steamy, then it boiled. The extra sudsiness bubbled over and dripped onto the floor.

"You've overdone it," Ondine said, not daring to put her bare hands anywhere near the boiling water.

"Sorry, must have had a senior moment. You know how it is. Or you will one day, at any rate."

"Don't worry about the water, I can always add some cold. How about you focus on zapping the power back on?" Ondine asked.

"You think I didn't think of that?" Old Col shot back, but judging by the guilty look on her face, she most likely hadn't.

Oh dear, maybe she really was having a senior moment.

Old Col held her hands towards the window and flickered her fingers, chanting under her breath.

"The window?" Ondine wondered why she aimed her magic that way.

"I'm gunning for the power supply on the corner pole," she

Ma had been able to keep, of course. The rest she'd taken back to the creators at the Hera Collection.

said, wiggling her fingers afresh. She sang words under her breath and the lights came on in the kitchen.

"Yay!" Ondine said. The lights flickered on and off, then crackled and snapped out. The smell of burnt elements filled the room. "Oh dear," Ondine said, feeling terrible for her great-auntie.

"This isn't one of our regular winter blackouts," Col said. "There's magic behind this loss of power, I guarantee it. Only the witch that made a curse can break it." [2]

"I bet Lord Vincent's behind this," Ondine said.

"Don't be so content to pick the low-hanging fruit," Old Col arched her brow.

"Who else could it be?"

"Oh, I agree, Ondi, it most likely is Vincent, but he's not magic, so someone else is doing his magic for him."

With a sigh, Ondine guessed, "Mrs Howser?"

"There you go again."

Ondine grew frustrated. "Yeah, but I bet it is her."

Old Col creased her mouth in thought, then said, "Low-hanging fruit or not, I think you might be right."

A sheen of perspiration glistened on Ma's brow as she carried a stack of dirty plates from the dining room towards Ondine's sink.

"After we're done here, tell me everything the Duchess said. And Aunt Col? Josef needs a hand at the bar."

At that point, the lights in the restaurant suddenly came on again. Instead of popping out like they had in the kitchen –

---

2. Brugel is one of many countries in Europe that has intermittent power supply during winter, on account of large amounts of snow, frozen connections and people being unceremoniously disconnected because they cannot trudge through the snow to get to the bank to pay their bills on time. They could try internet banking, but this requires a reliable electricity supply.

which was still dark – these stayed on. A cheer floated in from the dining room.

"Better late than never," Ma said as she wiped her hands on a tea towel. "How many more meals do you have to go, Chef?"

Henrik looked up. "This is the last one."

"Typical!" Ma threw her hands up and let out a frustrated sigh.

EXHAUSTED from the enormous night before, Ondine didn't wake until nearly ten o'clock on Christmas Day. In normal circumstances she'd be mad keen to open her presents. Instead, she luxuriated in the warmth of her bed and the serenity of Cybelle not being in the bed next to her, snoring up a storm.

Every few years the family closed the pub for Christmas Day so they could have a slodgy-slow day as a family. Considering they'd closed for Margi's wedding, then been forced to close in respect to Pavla, Ma was grabbing any opportunity to get customers. Unfortunately, they were still short-staffed because Margi and Thomas hadn't returned from their honeymoon.

"There's a pile of dishes with your name on it," Cybelle said as Ondine made her way to the kitchen by eleven.

Blurble went her tummy.

"Just kidding!" Cybelle said, "Have some sausages and marmalade. That'll perk you up."

"Thanks." Ondine inhaled the food on her plate. Only after she licked her fingers did she spare a thought for anyone else. "How many are out there?"

"Only twelve for brunch. Practically doing it in our sleep," Henrik said, looking so tired he might still be asleep.

"Merry Christmas Ondi," Hamish said as he came back in with empty water jugs to refill. She beamed at him and returned the greeting. Then they had a little smooch and didn't care that there were other people around.

Ma filled her arms with plates of food to take out. "Hamish, could you grab the dessert menus for me?"

"Dessert? For brunch?" Ondine boggled.

"It's Christmas!" Ma said.

Desserts were the most profitable items on the menu. Small serves, high prices.

"I'll tempt them Missers G," Hamish said with a wink.

"Be careful," Ondine said.

"Of what, lass?"

"The work inspectors," she said.

"Ye really think they'd be working on Christmas Day?"

"We are." Ondine couldn't help grumbling.

SURE IT WAS CHRISTMAS, but for the de Groot family, it was another workday to get through. Nothing remotely interesting happened until they'd seen off the last of the lunch crowd and were taking a breather in the private room before first dinner began. [3]

Da walked in with his arms full of take-away food. "Merry Christmas all!" he said, handing out hot boxes with sauce dripping out the sides.

"What's this?"

"Noodles from *Fang's*."

"I thought they'd closed." Ondine remembered the night when their staff had been hauled away.

"They're only making it look like that, so the inspectors don't come back. Dig in, smells delicious."

---

3. The first dinner, followed soon after by the second.

"Merry Christmas Ondi," Hamish said, handing her a book-shaped present.

She tore the wrapper off and grinned. The second book in the series about Elmaree.

Oooh, the sequel. I'm going to love it. Here, this is for you." She handed him the little box wrapped with a flat bow. Not a frilly bow, because that would be too girly and she didn't want to embarrass him. Her breath stalled as she watched him open it. The little voice in her head said, *I hope he likes it, I hope he likes it.*

"It's brilliant," Hamish said as he took the broad silver ring from the box and held it. For a second Ondine wondered if he noticed the inscription she'd agonised over. Did it say too little? Did it say too much? Would he wear it?

In silent answer, Hamish slipped the ring on the last finger on his right hand, then he whispered the same words she'd inscribed on the ring. "You have my heart."

"What does it say?" Ma asked with a complete lack of tact.

"Something that means the world to me," Hamish said giving Ondine one of his heart-meltingly lopsided smiles.

They tucked into their food, a happy mood settling over them. Ondine saw how relaxed Cybelle looked and figured this might be the best chance they had to raise the issue that had been niggling at her.

"Belle, how are the keyboard covers going?" Because her mother heard everything, Ondine deliberately kept her voice as light and innocent as she could manage. It came out far too light, far too innocent and all too completely needy.

Cybelle froze, mid mouthful. "What do you mean?"

Gulp. "I accidentally knocked a box over and one of the rolls rolled out. It's a very clever side business. You've always been very clever."

Cybelle's eyes slitted with suspicion. "It's nothing."

"Oh, I'd never say anything to anyone else about it." Ondine backtracked as fast as she could.

"We're not making any money, if that's what you're after," Cybelle said.

Mercury's wings, that's *exactly* what Ondine was after. "I'm sorry it sounds like I'm fishing . . . but I was just saying I think it's really clever and I wish you and Henrik all the best with it. Sheesh, no need to get defensive," Ondine said, sounding mightily defensive.

Hamish chimed in, "We were hoping to get extra funds together, on account of the fact we need to do a job for Anathea and it's goin' tae cost us. And the tips are down on account of being closed for so long and –"

"We don't have any money." Cybelle's expression froze.

Henrik looked at the ground and kept his hands clasped together. A little too tightly, judging by the whiteness of his knuckles.

Ondine looked to Hamish. He squished her hand in support.

Ma let out an exaggerated sigh behind them.

Ondine tried again. "Belle, what you and Henrik have done is nothing short of incredible." Too flowery? Too verbose? To bluffy? Thinking she'd said too much but not enough, Ondine ploughed on. "I know I should help you more than I do, and I will after this, I absolutely promise."

"You help out plenty," Henrik said, his eyes still downcast.

Cybelle elbowed him in the ribs.

"What's all this?" Da said.

Henrik, Cybelle, Ondine and Hamish all said, "Nothing!"

Da crossed his arms over his chest. "Oh really?"

Henrik spoke in a soft voice. "This goes no further than this room."

As one, they nodded.

With a sigh of defeat, Henrik revealed all. "Back in November, just after Anathea took over, they made a new law about buying Brugel-made computers, which have to have the Dvorak keyboard on them. But everyone knows where the letters are on a QWERTY keyboard. Nobody wants to swap over. But they want to *look* as if they're complying with the laws. So we started making slipcovers with Dvorak layout on them. Put them over your existing keyboard and away you go."

Da's eyebrows shot upwards.

Ma dabbed at her eyes with a handkerchief. "My little entre-preneurs."

"OK. Here's our problem." Ondine brought it back to the big issue at hand. "Once Anathea is popular, she'll give Hamish his papers and he'll be free to work for us without fear of inspectors."

Ma sat up a bit straighter at that. They needed Hamish's free labour.

Ondine had everyone's attention. "We tried using magic yesterday in Savo Plaza. We're not sure if it worked. And in the meantime, we have some more ideas. Well, Hamish has a really good idea. But we need money to get it started and we're a bit broke except I was hoping Cybelle, that you and Henrik might lend me some of your money *and I'll pay you back.*"

She had to take a deep breath to recover from such a big explanation.

Henrik sighed and looked to Cybelle.

A pleading tone stole into Ondine's voice. "We don't need much. Just enough to get started."

Hamish gave her hand a squish of support.

Henrik cracked. "How much are we talking about?"

Cybelle groaned.

"I'm sorry love," Henrik said to Cybelle. "You've seen how poor the tips are when Hamish isn't out front."

Cybelle groaned again. "But it's our future fund!"

"I know." Henrik gave her a hug. "But . . . our future does kind of rely on Hamish being out the front."

Ondine beamed at the vote of confidence.

"Fine then!" Cybelle threw her hands up in defeat. "But if we're handing over money, I want a say in how it's used."

"Aw yeas!" Hamish cheered. He quickly explained his idea about putting Anathea's face on napkins.

"That's stupid," Cybelle said.

An invisible hammer whacked Ondine in the head at Cybelle's slapdown.

"It is?" She and Hamish said together.

The corner of Cybelle's lip curled. "You want people wiping their dirty faces on the Duchess? It sends the totally wrong message."

"Oh," Ondine and Hamish said together.

"Sorry, I didn't mean to sound so harsh. But if you think about it, napkins are only one step up from toilet paper."

Ondine instantly wished she could get the visual of Anathea on that kind of product out of her head.

Cybelle again. "Here's what we do. We make a stencil of Anathea's face and stamp it on the keyboard covers."

Ondine's forehead scrunched in confusion.

"As an inside joke," Cybelle said. "The covers are how people get around the new laws, which *she* made. Every time people see her face on the cover, they'll smile because they'll be happily using their old keyboard, yet they'll be complying with the law."

"It . . . sort of makes sense." Ondine said, wishing they could go back to the napkins idea.

Cybelle was ignoring Ondine's look of pain because she kept right on talking. "Think about all the things that make you smile."

Too easy. Hamish made her smile.

Cybelle groaned. "A *product*!"

Whoa, she could read her mind? Ondine guessed her love for Hamish must be writ large on her face anyway.

"Chocolate?" Ma suggested.

"Aye, that's good," Hamish said. "How about a warm open fire?"

Henrik grabbed a notepad and wrote the ideas down as they kept brainstorming.

Everyone began talking at once.

"Flowers?"

"Ginger biscuits."

"Hot soup."

"Tea."

"Fluffy kittens?"

"Hats with ear flaps?"

"Now we're getting somewhere," Cybelle said. She too grabbed a piece of paper and began scribbling. Before long she had some sketches of the Duchess's face and the hexagonal flag. "What we do is make some small posters, maybe half a page size. Small enough to fit on the curve of a lamppost, without getting distorted. We paste them up near where people buy things that make them happy. There's a florist down the street, we put these on the lampposts or the walls or street signs near that. [4]

"But, will anybody notice them?" Hamish asked.

"Possibly not, at first," Cybelle said. "That's the beauty of it. It's in people's peripheral vision. They won't make a direct connection, so they won't think it's propaganda. If we put an ad in the paper saying how much everyone loves Anathea, it will turn people off because they'll see it as a blatant add. This way is heaps better."

Henrik gave Cybelle two thumbs up.

---

4. Cybelle is the Banksy of Brugel.

Two days after Christmas, the de Groot household became a flurry of non-food-related activity as Ondine, Hamish and Cybelle woke extra early to gather their half-page posters to slap all over town. They divided up the bundles of papers and everyone grabbed a pot of glue and a thick brush, then headed out to the shopping districts. Being Sunday, many shops were closed for the morning and the cold kept the crowds away. All the same, they had to work quickly. Not because they'd be spotted, but because the glue kept freezing in the pots.

One of the best spots Ondine found was the side of a hot soup caravan. She slapped a poster near the "Hot Soup For You!" logo.

Feet entirely frozen, she, Hamish and Cybelle scarpered home for a hot second-breakfast. Then she spent the rest of the day washing dishes, as was her lot. Between meal services she and Cybelle collated posters and marked out maps of where they'd slap up posters the next morning. Hamish worked upstairs with a vintage photocopier to make enough posters for them to paste onto walls and lampposts.

The printing left chemicals on his hands and sometimes the results came out a little blurry. But it gave the images a retro-look, which was so on-trend.

They stopped their subversive advertising program to deal with the New Year's Eve dinner crowds and then they gave themselves a rest on New Year's Day because they deserved it.

When January came around, Ondine had to go back to school, which meant getting up even earlier to get some copying and pasting done and keep the campaign rolling out.

It was cold, miserable work, especially when she had to trudge through snow. But it was also great fun to be doing something a little subversive and – in Ondine's mind – for a good cause. A good, secret cause.

CHAPTER 10

In the middle of January, more snow came to Venzelemma, followed soon after by the arrival of hundreds of witches attending CovenCon. CovenCon garnered the largest gathering of witches and pre-witches in Eastern Europe. [1] This annual conference was to have been held in Norange, but Old Col had been instrumental in getting the location switched to Brugel.

The organisers were lured to the atmospherics of the Brugel's not-quite-world-heritage-listed Massa-Kuche, on the coastal side of Venzelemma. The direct translation of Massa-Kuche is 'Bulky lump on the hill'. Part castle, part ruin, Massa-Kuche has magnificent views over the Black Sea and is serviced by a funicular tourist railway and four-star hotel. [2]

Stepping from the funicular railway that brought them to the top of the hill, Ondine's nose tingled as she breathed the cool wintery air. Ahead of her was the castle, built on a ledge that she

---

1. People who are not-yet-witches, but believe they one day will be.
2. A funicular rail line is so steep the carriages must be hauled up the incline with sturdy cables. The two carriages are always attached to each other, so while one goes up, the other comes down, thus minimizing the energy required to reach the top.

could see – now she was up this high – was part way up a larger mountain range.

The castle had a classic medieval-style drawbridge over a running river. To one side of the river was a tumbling waterfall that churned into white froth, which then charged under the drawbridge and fell dramatically down another waterfall which took a huge plunge down the sheer side of the mountain. As they walked over the drawbridge, the timber creaked and shuddered. Several staff members stopped more people from walking on it at the same time, lest it collapse under the weight. From the groaning drawbridge they walked into a hallway already heaving with people.

Many people have a traditional idea of what witches look like, but true Brugelish witches wear warm hats with orschlappen, and wouldn't be seen anywhere without their multi-pocketed travelling cloak and knapsack. They all wear strong boots and sturdy pants, even the gentlemen.

Here was where Ondine, Hamish and Old Col figured they'd be able to help Anathea become popular. *Properly* popular. If Anathea could behave herself – big if – and not irritate the tripe out of people – bigger if – their newly-minted Duchess just might endear herself to the crowds here. Because if Anathea charmed the witches, she'd be well on her way to winning over the rest of the country.

"I was always going to bring you to CovenCon," Old Col said to Ondine as they picked up their registration kits at the reception desk. "Ignore everything Birgit Howser told you."

Being told to ignore something is like being told not to think of pink motorbikes. The moment Old Col said not to, all Ondine could think about was Mrs. Howser and her persuasive words about how she could instruct magic far more effectively than Old Col could.

She rubbed her elbow at the memory of the tug of love.

Taking in the atmospherics of this centuries-old castle helped distract Ondine from less pleasant things. The solid stone walls – now sealed and polished and not at all dusty – were a lasting testament to the way Brugelers used to build their castles. 'Build' is probably not the right verb. 'Excavate' is more accurate; as they used to begin on the top of a mountain, then dig away until the castle emerged. [3]

"No matter what she says, child, you are far better off with me," Old Col said, interrupting Ondine's deliberate 'not thinking about Mrs Howser' thoughts. "Now stay close. I don't want her getting – heavens above, I can see her across the room. And she looks like she's looking for you."

Mrs Howser had come dressed for the occasion, in her 'look at me' luxurious purple hooded cloak with gold trim over a royal blue dress. Compared to the humble brown travelling cloaks the rest of the witches wore, nobody could miss her.

Before they could get a better look at Howser, Old Col pushed them sideways and dragged them through a nearby doorway, where they found themselves in an auditorium.

An empty auditorium, but one with the power to intimidate its hundreds of guests. Heavy velvet curtains draped behind the podium, while the walls were decorated with richly detailed tapestries.

"Quick, get under the lectern." Old Col shoved Ondine in the back and pushed them towards the stage.

"But the curtains?" Ondine started. They'd be a much more comfortable place to hide.

"Too obvious," Old Col said, shoving them closer to where she wanted them.

---

3. Which is one reason why Brugel has so few mountains of any repute. But they do have some wonderful castles.

"We'll nae fit in that unless ye turn our bones tae rubber," Hamish said. "Ye nae gontae turn our bones tae rubber are ye?"

"Not in it, under it," Old Col said. Another push in the back, a push down this time where they could see the crawl-space under the stage. Plenty of room. For a ferret maybe. But a grown lad and girl?

The complaint was on her lips, then Ondine shut right up. It was the *perfect* place for squishy canoodling. So she didn't dare ask another question, such as why they had to hide from Mrs Howser when it had been Mrs Howser who had wanted to bring her to CovenCon in the first place.

"Now stay there and don't make a sound. Birgit's giving the keynote address and she cannot know you're there."

Ondine and Hamish wedged themselves into the small space. The only light came through the gaps in the floorboards above. Lying on dusty boards would have been uncomfortable enough, but they also had a spaghetti pile of cables and extension cords to contend with.

Gradually the auditorium filled with people who brought extra noise in with them.

"This is just like old times, eh lass?" Hamish kept his voice low as they crouched together under the stage. Ondine pressed her finger to her lips to indicate they should keep quiet. In return Hamish grinned at her. She couldn't help grinning back, especially when he bussed the tip of his nose against hers. Her insides turned mooshy.

Footsteps clomped above them. The timber boards creaked. Conversation in the auditorium lowered to a murmur as people noticed Old Col reach the dais and tap her finger to the microphone. An echo rang out, then the whiney pitch of feedback as she said, "Dobra." [4]

Not everybody hushed. Some were so caught up in themselves they forgot they'd paid good money to be here and kept gabbing on, their murmured words sounding like 'watermelon and cantaloupe' to Ondine's ears.

Old Col cleared her throat. "Her Lordship Duchess Anathea, Madam First Minister Cebotari, Lord Vincent, distinguished guests, ladies . . . and I see we have some gentlemen. Dobra and welcome to the twentieth annual CovenCon!"

Frustration knotted Ondine's tummy. Lord Vincent was out there too. Who gave him an invite? Desperate to find out, she found a gap in the boards and peeked through, looking for her nemesis. She didn't have to look hard. There he was, sitting in the front row next to the First Minister. He was dressed in his usually elegant city clothing with a touch of witchy-ness about him, like a travelling cloak instead of his suit jacket, so that he would fit right in. [5]

Bad boy charm oozed from his every pore as he flicked his dark blonde hair off his forehead.

Tosser.

As much as Ondine tried to listen to her great aunt's introduction while keeping an eye on Vincent, she found it hard to concentrate because nestling into Hamish proved so distracting.

It was silly to waste what precious time she'd have with Hamish by spying on Vincent. He wouldn't be going anywhere.

She and Hamish snuck in a few kisses. Warm kisses that made things flip in her belly.

Kisses that turned her head and made her forget about every-

---

4.   Literal translation is, "Welcome to Brugel, don't mind the mess the maid has the day off."

5.   Just like the way politicians wear a cattleman's hat and blue work shirt when they visit 'the country folk'.

thing else. Kisses that made her bones sigh. Kisses that made a wet *shmack* noise as their lips came apart.

Pure magic.

Above them, Col cleared her throat and clonked her substantial heel on the floorboard, reminding them they had an audience.

Oops, better behave then.

On the other hand, if they became loved-up, it would make Old Col's wishes come true, which meant she'd be wishing thoughts along the lines of making Anathea as popular as possible.

They were kissing for Brugel!

Oh those kisses. Ondine could never get enough of them. Maybe it was the cramped space, maybe it was the rare moment of privacy, but she needed Hamish's kisses more than she needed her next breath. Despite trying desperately to have a normal life with him (after all the mayhem they'd been through in the late Duke's Palechia) they never had time to truly enjoy themselves and wallow in their love for each other. Deep down she knew this suited her parents just fine, but it only served to frustrate her all the more. One metaphorical foot was pressed hard on the accelerator while circumstances kept an anvil on the brake.

Emboldened, Ondine pressed herself into his strong body, her fingers playing with the short hairs at his neck. Their lips were made for each other, they fitted so perfectly. When he coaxed her lips open – not that she needed much coaxing – the touch of his tongue against hers sent firecrackers off in her belly. He felt so, so right. His hand moved in lazy strokes over her back and rounded the curve of her hip. New and wonderful sensations took hold. The smell of him, a mix of soap and his earthy skin felt glorious as her heart staggered behind her ribs and her breath came in soft gasps. Her senses were in a tailspin. What freedom! A naughty thought flitted through her head – no wonder Margi and Thomas got married!

Above them, Old Col coughed again and stomped the floor. The muffled sound of applause burrowed through the floorboards. Was that Col's way of letting them know the magic was working? Should they keep kissing, just in case?

It took all her willpower to pull back from the kiss. She pressed her ear to Hamish's chest in an effort to slow down. His erratic pulse thumped against her skin, proving he was just as intoxicated as she.

She made the universal 'shush' motion in sign language, then pointed to the boards above them. Heavy boots clomped over their heads, the long skirt of her cloak swished about.

"Thank you Miss Romano for that excellent and *lengthy* introduction." The voice belonged to Birgit Howser at her sarcastic best.

Oh dear, Ondine thought. They should stop the lovefest while Mrs. Howser was so close. Who knew what she might be wishing at this moment?

"Dobra and welcome," Mrs. Howser said with a wavering alto that reverberated through the speakers. "I'm so impressed to see so many people here after the last-minute change from Slaegal to Brugel. Our motto this year is *Feel The Magic*, and I'm sure you will." [6]

Polite applause spread through the auditorium.

Ondine mentally tuned out. She returned her attentions to

---

6. The official story was that the hotel in Norange, Slaegal's capital, had run into 'financial difficulties', what with the economy and employees stealing from their workplace. A pen and notepad here, a complete 1,000-thread sheet set there. But in this case, management was stealing from staff, stripping their homes while they were at work and selling the ill-gotten goods online. The real reason was that there was so much whacky magic happening around Brugel, they simply had to move to that magical epicentre.

Hamish, lying beneath her. How sweet of him to rub her back. She closed her eyes and let his warm strokes soothe her. But not so much that she'd become distracted and start kissing him again. Oh all right, just one more kiss.

He delivered another of those devastating smiles, which filled her with more mooshy feelings. Slowly his warm hand stopped rubbing her back and he pointed to his eye, pointed to his heart then pointed to her. The gesture made her feel so loved she could have melted into him. With her free hand, she returned the sign language, then buried her head into his chest, content to lie with him in a cocoon of love, listening to his heart beating.

Through a crack in the timbers above them, Ondine could see Mrs. Howser standing at the podium, bobbing her right heel up and down. Her heel didn't make contact with the floor so it didn't make a sound. It looked like a classic case of nerves. But then something blurred behind the woman. A strange, shadowy shape moved out of her, then back into her.

Blinking, Ondine turned to Hamish and his eyes the colour of mischief. Had he seen it? Were people playing with the lighting and making shadows appear behind Mrs. Howser's back?

But, hang on. Shadows appeared on the ground, not in the air directly behind a person. This shadow was like a dark entity moving in and out of Mrs. Howser's body.

When it happened again, Ondine felt sure it was no trick. Mrs. Howser had an independent shadow moving in and out of her. A moment more staring and the shadow moved to stand directly behind its master.

". . . We call it many things, but the most common is 'Dark Magic'," Mrs. Howser told the crowd. "A name that has the power to frighten and make us wary. But if we look at it another way, with compassion and understanding, education and a fair amount of common sense, you'll see there truly is nothing to worry about. I call it 'Deep Magic' as its origins are from deep within our history. Deep Magic is a part of us; it is part of who we are."

She paused to take advantage of everyone's attention.

"Deep Magic is the shadow to sunlight. It is part of our everyday lives." [7]

Every time Mrs. Howser said the word 'magic' the shadowy shape ebbed and flowed from her body. Hamish held her tightly, indicating he'd seen it as well.

With the lights directed at the stage, and Mrs. Howser standing behind a lectern, the shadow was something only Ondine and Hamish could see.

The shadow that turned and twisted, then changed direction and came straight for the spot where Ondine and Hamish were hiding.

---

7. Brugel has been on the receiving end of great waves of migration as life in other parts of the world became unbearable.

In the fifteenth century, witches and warlocks fled the Spanish Inquisition; in the seventeenth century, people escaped the Salem Witch Trials, and in the late 20th Century, it was music lovers deserting the Eurovision Song Contest.

CHAPTER II

Fear turned Ondine's belly to lead. While Mrs. Howser extolled the virtues of 'Deep Magic', the oily shadow stretched and flowed out from her in an egg-whites-from-the-yolk kind of way. Then it folded and twisted into something low and menacing, making no sound as it sank to the floor. Ears straining, Ondine heard no gasps from the crowd; the audience could not see what was going on.

The shadow had to be using the lectern as a shield.

Ondine and Hamish froze together, hardly daring to breathe. Like a sniffer-dog picking up a scent, the dark shape moved as if seeking them out. It found a gap in the timber and oozed through, pouring itself into their cramped space.

Moments earlier, lust had made Ondine's heart race. Now she felt the organ catapult against her ribs in terror as the shadow pulsed and leeched through the timber crack. At first a worm shape to get through the tiny space, the head of it spread out into something not quite human but entirely grotesque. It was featureless but it had rounded pits where its eyes might be. Coldness spread through Ondine as those pits turned directly at her. Hamish's body rippled with tension as he held her tightly.

Neither of them dared breathe. She couldn't move a muscle from fear. The transparent oil-slick of darkness swayed hypnotically left and right. Tendrils moved outwards from the bulbous end, creating a Medusa head of tentacles only a hand-span from Ondine's face.

The one thing that stopped her from screaming was the way Hamish held her. No sooner had that thought filtered through her brain than – *boomph* – he was gone and she rolled into the space where he used to be. Plumes of dust flew up her nose, but she didn't dare cough for fear of being found out.

Wait, what? Where was Hamish?

He'd turned into a ferret!

Fine then, he could run off for help. Good man!

The black . . . *thing* . . . didn't flinch. Its faceless head with dents where eyes should be and writhing tentacles for hair stayed focused on Ondine.

Just as she thought she couldn't be any more grossed out, the tentacles grew like pea-sprouts, curling and wrapping around the floorboards and beams for support as the rest of its octopus-body poured through the crack. Through another gap in the boards, she caught a glimpse of Mrs. Howser. The shadow was still connected to her, leeching out of her, stretching like elastic but not breaking.

All the while Mrs. Howser kept on with her speech, her voice reassuring, calm, and considerate. "We cannot have day without night, light without shade or a summer without winter. This Deep Magic is not to be shunned or feared, it is to be embraced. It makes us whole."

So believable.

So hypnotic.

Fresh panic shot through Ondine. Was Mrs. Howser mesmerising the entire gathering of witches?

Shambles. Where *was* Shambles? Had he run to get help?

Run to warn everyone? Her ears strained for the sound of scurrying claws on timber. Instead, she heard something that sounded suspiciously like . . . eating?

What?

Turning her head, she saw Shambles chewing on wires.

Buzz-bzzt! Lights flickered. Sparks flew. Every hair on Shambles's body bushed out in shock. He chomped down.

An ear-cracking "Bang!" rang out.

"Aaaarrrrgggghhh!" screamed Shambles in shock. He shot through the air, twisting and writhing, his furry body twice its normal size.

A new fear took hold of Ondine at the sight of the electrocuted, airborne ferret. One more twist, his body transformed back into Hamish in mid-air.

Landing squarely on Ondine, knocking the wind out of her.

The black shadow slurped out of sight, like liquid up a straw.

The lights went out. Ondine couldn't see a thing.

"Have I hurt ye, lass?" Hamish asked.

Ondine shook her head. But in the dark, Hamish couldn't see her, so she wheezed out a, "No".

Screams and panic broke out in the auditorium.

"Just a power cut," Mrs. Howser said, her voice no longer soothing and hypnotic. If anything, there was an edge of panic.

"Everyone relax," they heard Auntie Col say. "Let's make our way out in an orderly fashion. Try not to bump into anyone. Let your eyes adjust. Follow the green glow of the exit signs, that's the way."

Hamish rolled off Ondine in the darkness. She knew he didn't have a scrap of clothing on. Any other time she might blush furiously, but she was too terrified of Mrs. Howser above them to think straight. A booted foot stomped down hard on the boards, showering them with dust and the odd spider. Torchlight shone through the cracks.

"You!" Mrs. Howser's angry voice cut through. "I knew it!"

The auditorium lights came back on. Heat stole over Ondine's face as she tried desperately not to ogle Hamish in his birthday suit. Grabbing his clothes, they snake-crawled out of their hiding spot and crouched down behind the back of the stage. As much as she wanted to gaze upon Hamish, she averted her eyes while he dressed.

"What do you think you were doing?" Mrs. Howser said, hands fisted on hips.

"Um . . ." Ondine's mind turned blank. They were well and truly sprung. Also, the old witch must have seen him naked.

"We were checking the electrics," Hamish said as he pulled his shirt over his head.

Brilliant! Ondine thought, then immediately wished she'd soaked up more of Hamish without his shirt on.

"We didnae realise the time. The place filled up so quickly, as it did. We didnae want to disrupt things so we just figured it was best to stay there until you were finished, so we did."

"Sure you did." Mrs. Howser didn't sound like she believed them.

Oh would you look at that. Hamish had his shirt on inside out, so he had to take it off and put it back on the right way.

Take your time, no rush.

"There you are!" Old Col said too loudly as she approached. "You're not still checking the wiring are you?"

"Give it up, Colette." Mrs. Howser turned her full attention to Ondine. "This is what she has you doing? How is any of this helping develop your magic? You could be achieving so much with your life but she's got you crawling under floorboards. Spying on me? I could have you arrested! [1]

Old Col brushed past Birgit. "You'll have to bully them later. I came to let Ondine know Her Lordship Anathea requires an audience." [2]

"She does not," Mrs. Howser shot back. "You're bluffing."

"I assure you, she does. I'm sure Her Grace wouldn't mind if you tagged along, Birgit, just to see what it's like to be in the presence of greatness," Old Col said.

"Melody!" Mrs. Howser turned her attention to the front row of seats. "Wake up!"

There Melody sat, her eyes more glazed than a doughnut.

"I said, 'wake up'," Mrs. Howser shouted.

In the snap of a finger, Melody came out of whatever trance she'd been in.

Had she been sitting there the whole time and they hadn't noticed?

"Stop lazing about. Our Lord Duchess needs us."

Mrs. Howser was going to gatecrash their meeting with Anathea? That couldn't be good.

Col's stricken look proceeded some hasty backtracking. "After lunch."

"What?" Hamish said out loud, verbalising Ondine's thought.

"Beg yours?" Mrs. Howser said.

"After lunch. If we meet before lunch, we'll get all the wafty smells from the kitchens . . . er . . . wafting through, and driving us to distraction. Best we meet after lunch, when we're all fighting fit and ready to face the afternoon."

---

1. In Brugel, there is no right to remain silent if you are arrested. There is, however, the right to respond to all questions in haiku.
2. Your Lordship is the correct address to the head of Brugel, whether Duke or Duchess.

"I don't believe it. You *were* bluffing!" Victory shone on Mrs. Howser's face.

"Not in the slightest. I'm merely looking out for your protégée. Poor Melody here looks like she'll fall over the next time she sneezes."

"She's perfectly hearty," Mrs. Howser said.

Old Col wrapped her fingers and thumb all the way around Melody's upper arm. "She's *starving*! You dare accuse me of not looking after Ondine's magical interests. In turn, you're not looking after Melody's health and welfare. If you'd studied under me, dear girl, I could guarantee you four meals a day. First *and* second dinner."

"It always did come down to food with you," Mrs. Howser said. She clicked her fingers. "Melody, we're leaving."

There could be no stronger indication of the hold Mrs. Howser had on Melody than the way her fingers wrapped tightly around the girl's upper arm to draw her away.

If they didn't break the hold soon, Ondine knew by the tightness in her belly that Melody would grow physically weaker and Mrs. Howser would grow magically stronger.

Which added up to things going very, very badly for Duchess Anathea and Brugel.

CHAPTER 12

With no idea what to do next, other than follow her great-auntie's lead, Ondine joined the queues at morning tea. Standing in line, she and Hamish piled sweet biscuits on their plates and waited for their turn at the urns brimming with tea, coffee, hot chocolate and an overly optimistic pot of chicory. [1]

"What d'ye mean we're not meeting with Anathea?"

"Hush, Hamish," Old Col hissed between her teeth.

"I can't believe you were bluffing," Ondine said.

Old Col glared at her.

Ondine didn't like being glared at.

"Keep your voices down," Col said, "The walls have ears." [2]

---

1. A coffee substitute that came into its own during the Soviet Coffee Crisis of 1976–79. International price hikes made it near impossible for Bruglers to get their hands on the proper stuff. Farmers in Slaegal and Craviç sowed thousands of acres of chicory, in the hope of satisfying local demand. By 1980, fresh supplies of coffee beans from Vietnam made its way west, and the crisis was over. This in turn lead to precisely zero demand for local chicory and the crops ran to seed. To this day, their blue flowers grow rampant across the landscape.

2. And potatoes have eyes.

"Just asking," Ondine said, looking over to the wall to make sure there were no body parts stuck to them.

"Don't worry, everything is well in hand," Old Col said.

The queue moved slowly. Eventually it was Ondine and Hamish's turn. The tea and coffee urns were empty by this point, so they drained the last of the hot chocolate into their cups.

A collective groan sounded behind them.

"Sorry." Ondine looked at the untouched pot of chicory and then to her three-quarter-cup of hot chocolate. "Here." She gave her cup to the witch in line behind her.

"Yer a good lass," Hamish said, offering her a sip from his cup.

"They should just make two pots of coffee, then everyone would be happy," she said as they took a seat. [3]

Everyone else at CovenCon was taking a mental break at morning tea, catching up with friends or furiously networking. No such luck for Ondine and Hamish, as they spotted Mrs. Howser walking off somewhere, with Melody in tow.

This small event would not have been so noticeable if not for the fact that at the exact same moment, a waiter wheeled out a trolley with two fresh urns of coffee.

Witches swarmed for the caffeine hit. Except for Mrs. Howser.

It could be entirely possible for Mrs. Howser not to like coffee. But that didn't sit right with Ondine. The woman was strange, but she wasn't *that* strange.

"Where do you think she's off to?" Ondine asked Hamish.

"I have a feeling we're aboot tae find oot!" he answered back with a cheeky grin.

---

3. Everyone except the chicory farmers would be happy. They are still trying to claw back their decades-old losses.

As they stood up, they saw Lord Vincent walking off in the same direction. A flash of blue caught Ondine's attention and she saw Lord Vincent still had that blue stain on his hand. The one she and Hamish had given him the night he'd tried to burgle their restaurant.

"Ye dinnae think they're in cahoots?"

"I have no idea," Ondine said, not knowing what cahoots meant, but knowing it couldn't be good.

Following at a safe distance, they came to a set of glass doors leading to the outside swimming pool.

Unless both Mrs. Howser and Lord Vincent were certifiably bonkers, it was a safe bet they weren't taking a dip at this time of year.

Through the glass, they made out the shape of Mrs. Howser standing near the potted palms that had withered and grown manky in the cold weather. Melody was close by, her witch's cloak wrapped tightly around her as she leaned against a lamppost.

They also saw the shape of Lord Vincent. Three sets of footsteps in the snow. Even if they found a place to hide out there by the pool, their footsteps would give them away.

Time for plan 'D'. [4] "Let's try approaching the pool from the other end," Ondine said.

They wouldn't have to walk through those doors and they wouldn't be seen. On the other hand, they would have to go outside, and it was freezing.

"Aye, we'll need our coats."

"Good thinking."

---

4.   D is the second letter in the old Brugelish alphabet. In Soviet days, if plan 'D' failed, there were thirty-one more letters to fall back on.

IN NICER WEATHER, they might snuggle together for fun, but as they crouched under the shrubbery next to the terraced wall beside the swimming pool, Ondine and Hamish huddled together out of a desperate need to stay warm. Which only strengthened Ondine's belief that Mrs. Howser was truly horrid. At this time of year, a sensible woman – a *nice* woman – would have held her secret meetings indoors. It took every effort to not shiver and remain as quiet as possible to hear what Mrs. Howser was saying.

" . . . considered, I might not need your help after all." Which was Lord Vincent talking, not Mrs. Howser. It sounded to Ondine's ears as if he were rejecting whatever she'd offered him.

Then Mrs. Howser spoke, dripping with such sarcasm it figuratively ran down the walls. "Sweet, yet stupid. Your grandfather tried that tactic as well. It didn't do him a lick of good."

"I assure you Birgit, it's no tactic. What's two years' waiting in the long run?"

"Deluded as well. You think you can sit back and wait and it will simply come to you? That never got anyone anywhere. It won't get you anything either, not while Anathea's growing more popular by the day. If you want it, you have to grab it with both hands."

Vincent didn't sound convinced. "You're empire building and you're using me to do it."

"I'm getting things done. You might like to try it some day."

A pause in hostilities made Ondine wonder if one of them had walked off, but just as she thought about taking a peek through the shrubbery, she heard Vincent again. "You enjoy sharpening your teeth on the hand that feeds you, don't you."

"It gives me no pleasure. But I'll give you this for free: Promises ring hollow if there is no follow through."

"Promises? More like blackmail."

"Oh dear. Now we've resorted to name-calling. Listen to me, you jumped up bludger, you owe me –"

"– I don't owe you *anything*," Vincent said, his voice stronger, angrier. "Whatever deal you had with my grandfather is long gone. Don't think you can use *me* to collect."

Listening to them reminded Ondine of two dogs fighting over the same bone. They were circling and bristling their fur. Any minute now the snarling and biting would begin. It made Ondine fret for Melody, who must still be somewhere near Mrs. Howser, but had added nothing to the conversation.

Perhaps she'd been smart enough to go back inside?

"You are so lazy. You really think you can sit back and . . . and . . . *wait* for someone to *hand you the keys*?" Mrs. Howser said. "You do that while Anathea gets the laws changed to favour her daughters over you. Do you honestly think by the time you're twenty-one she'll step aside and just . . . give it to you?"

A nasty pause took hold. Ondine furiously held in a sneeze.

It may have been freezing, but Vincent's words carried plenty of heat. "Don't speak to me like I'm naive."

"Hah! Somebody needs to. Anathea's got what she's always wanted. No way will she let go of it. Have you seen how close she is to everyone that matters? Not just the First Minister but also half the Dentate? Give it six more months and she'll have charmed the other half. That's why you have to move now, while things are unstable."

"And in return, I'll be utterly beholden to you. I'm nobody's puppet, *witch*."

Ondine could have sworn she heard Mrs. Howser growling before she spoke. "Do you think magic grows on trees? This is a lifetime's work and I've yet to see a scrap of compensation. You *owe* me!"

"What?!"

"You heard me. If I hadn't used my . . . *talents*, your father would never have been born, which means *you* wouldn't be here either."

That shocked Vincent into silence. Ondine and Hamish were shocked into silence too as they huddled together in mute worry. It sounded awful. It also reminded Ondine of the conversations she'd had with Anathea back at the Autumn Palace. About the age Anathea had reached by the time her baby brother, Duke Pavla was born. Anathea was Duchess Presumptive until Pavla came along. But . . . how did Mrs. Howser have anything to do with *that*?

After what felt like the longest pause, Vincent said, "What . . . did you . . . do?"

Mrs. Howser made a scoffing noise and her hands gripped the railings with a rasp of dry skin on cold metal. It sent a flurry of snow falling below.

Ondine and Hamish smushed themselves further into the shrubbery to stay out of sight.

"I made sure your grandfather got what he wanted," Mrs. Howser said. "He wanted a son more than he wanted his next breath."

"Please tell me we're not –"

"– Related? Don't look so pale, boy. Trust me, I'm *not* your grandmother." Mrs. Howser made a shuddering noise and said, "Perish the thought! Although your grandfather was rather charming in his day . . ."

Hamish's eyebrows sat up so high they might fly away. Ondine felt her eyes grow wide. Her mouth dropped open, as if that would help her to hear better. [5]

Mrs. Howser said, "It wasn't like that. It was the most difficult thing I'd ever done. I had to call on every power I possessed

---

5. Listening with your mouth open does widen the ear canals so you can hear more clearly. Alas, it makes you look like a slack-jawed yokel.

to make sure it worked. It wore me out, but I did it for Brugel. I did it for your grandfather and your father. And for all that work, he didn't give me so much as the lint from his pockets. So whether you like it or not, you owe me, and I'm going to collect."

A beat of silence.

The wind howled.

Vincent broke the tension. "Or you'll stir up trouble I suppose?"

Mrs. Howser scoffed again. "I am giving you an incentive to help me."

Vincent said, "It's called blackmail and I don't want anything more to do with you."

At which point Mrs. Howser's voice softened. Ondine missed the next bit of dialogue so she dropped her jaw all the way down to open her ears properly.

" . . . It's called showing your true nature. You will soon show yours, so let's not mince words. You need me. I can help, for a fee."

"Don't touch me!"

Hello, Mrs. Howser must have gotten too close, Ondine figured.

"Get your hands off me. I don't need *anything* from you." Vincent sounded royally annoyed.

There were some footsteps, and a spray of snow flew over the terraces and landed on Ondine's legs. Were they having a scuffle?

A door opened. One of them must have gone inside to the hotel. A chill spread through Ondine, and it wasn't merely from the snow. The chill froze into fear as she and Hamish looked up to see that oleaginous, black shape ooze across the swimming pool, freezing the surface as it swayed and travelled over the water. Frozen thick enough for Mrs Howser to walk across, her heels cracking the ice but not breaking through.

Howser looked directly to where they were hiding. "You two are so predictable! Well? Don't just sit there. Run along and tell Colette everything you heard. That's what you're meant to do, right?"

In mute shock, Ondine and Hamish looked at each other for a second, then scarpered off in a flurry of snow.

CHAPTER 13

Their long spell outside had left them shell-shocked, numb from the cold and starving. They had the dual task of trying to find Old Col to tell her what they'd heard while also avoiding Mrs. Howser. As they walked inside, the delegates were moving into the banqueting hall for lunch. Lunchtime already? They *had* been outside a long time.

This part of the castle looked recently built, but decorated to look as old as the rest of the place. The textured plaster panelling almost looked real, if you squinted, and you ignored the repeating block pattern.

As rotten luck would have it, Old Col and Mrs. Howser were standing side-by-side in the lunch queue. No chance to talk to one, no chance to avoid the other.

Hunger ruled the moment, so Ondine and Hamish joined the line for hot food.

Mrs. Howser was in fine voice. "Dear me, moving CovenCon from Norange to here . . . You had to make it all about you, Letty."

"We moved it because this is where the magic is. And if you call me Letty again I'll call you Limpy," Old Col said.

"I don't walk with a limp!"

"Not yet."

Hamish gave Ondine a worried look. The two old witches clearly had a lot of bad memories to hash out.

"Ondine!" On hearing her name, she turned to find Melody standing there. Or rather, leaning against the edge of a table. Somebody bumped her and she nearly went flying. Despite the food nearby, Melody didn't have a plate in her hand. She barely looked strong enough to hold a plate, let alone pile it with food.

Ondine forgot her appetite for a moment. "Melody, it's so good to see you." The lie flowed too easily, considering how pallid her friend looked. Cracked lips, strings for muscles and sticks for bones. Hugging her felt like embracing a lamppost. "Come and sit down with us and have some lunch."

"Oh, no, I'm fine," Melody said. "Can we . . . have a chat?"

Hamish gave a nod, indicating he'd get their food for them rather than lose their place in the line.

"Sure." Ondine looked around for a quiet place to sit. They spied a table way over in the corner. From the look of Melody, she might not have the strength to walk that far. The chairs by the wall would have to do. It was so noisy nobody would overhear them at any rate.

Scratch that. Ondine could barely hear Melody either, her voice was so soft. "I'm worried about you," Melody said.

Double-take time. Clasping her friend's papery hand in hers, Ondine said, "I should be the one worrying about you. You're fading away!"

At which time, Hamish presented Melody with a plate groaning with carbs. Pasta salad, potato salad and hot chips on the side. With a lemon wedge and pepper sachet.

Melody fell upon the plate. Mouth stuffed with chips, she said, "Mrs. Howser is taking an unnatural interest in you. *Mmmph*, this is delicious. She talks about you all the time. I don't know what you've done to get her attention but she's fixated. Thanks, more please." She handed her empty plate to Hamish but kept talking. "She's got me using magic night and day. So much of it is about finding out where you are, what you're doing, who you're with, and where you go afterwards."

Panic froze Ondine's limbs.

"Is she not feeding you?" Hamish presented Melody with a second plate, which she ate with the same speed as the first.

"Oh yes, you should see the food bills. But it's exhausting; she's working me so hard I have nothing left in the tank." Fat tears sploshed down Melody's cheeks as she shovelled the food away. Her words came out in a rush. "I'm so sorry sometimes I wish I never had this gift. I just want to sleep."

Ondine moved the second empty plate away and hugged her friend again. When they broke apart, Melody looked to the buffet. Some guests were piling their plates high; others were keeping to the salads and grilled chicken. "You can always tell the ones who really have magic. They have to eat like walruses because it takes so much out of you."

"Aye, like in the pub, eh Ondi?" Hamish said, "Licking the plates clean, so they are."

"Oh dear, then it really is spreading," Melody said.

"Or folks got tapeworm," Hamish said.

Lucky Melody had nothing in her mouth, otherwise she would have spurted all over Hamish as she laughed. Ondine didn't feel like laughing. She wanted to cry at the sight of her friend looking so poorly. And shiver at the thought of Mrs. Howser being so interested in her. And what was spreading? Magic? But everything she knew about magic said you were either born with it or not. You didn't catch it.

"I don't get it. Aunt Col says I have magic, but I'm not that hungry. Well, no more than usual in the middle of winter." Meanwhile, others nearby ate like there was no tomorrow.

"Jupiter's moons, I just realised what this means!" Relief poured through Ondine like a geyser. "I can't have magic if I'm not hungry all the time."

Melody's tired eyes lit up. "Oh but you do. You have loads of it. But you're different because you're a carrier, not a subject."

"A what!?"

Melody kept her voice low, leaned in close and said, "Mrs. Howser put the spell on Hamish when he was living with her as Shambles, back at Psychic Summercamp. It was designed to start spreading as soon as he bonded with someone and became human again."

Ondine and Hamish shot each other looks.

"You lived with Howser?" Ondine asked.

"I had tae," Hamish said, getting defensive. "She took me in sharpish after the big dance when Old Col lost her temper."

"Oh yes, of course," Ondine shook her head with confusion. "I knew that. It's just that it happened such a long time ago, I'd forgotten that I knew it."

Melody rushed in, "Anyway, it's not your fault, Ondi. It could have been anyone. You're spreading magic, but you don't have any signs of it yourself. Just like Black Sonja." [1]

Ondine reeled in horror. "But she killed people!"

"OK, bad comparison. It's a bit like that. You're . . . oh, what did Mrs. Howser call you? A symptom . . . an *asymptomatic* carrier. You've got magic oozing out the yin-yang but you don't feel a thing. In the meantime, everyone's catching it from you."

Ondine gulped and said, "But that's horrible!" The word

---

1. Around 1346, Black Plague spread from Asia to the Crimea, which is very near Brugel. Sonja of Yersina was a tea and spice merchant whose travels brought her into contact with the plague. Although she did not develop any symptoms herself, she passed it on to her customers and then some. This could have been terrible for business if not for the fact her parents were undertakers. She inherited the thriving family trade in 1348 when her parents popped their clogs

'oozing' reminded Ondine of the gelatinous black shape they'd seen coming out of Mrs. Howser. Could she too have something similar to Mrs Howser's shadow?

"Is there any more pasta salad?" Melody eyed the buffet.

"Mel, you need a break from Mrs. Howser."

"But she is helping me get better at magic."

"Yes but, look at you. You're fading away to nothing. Come and stay with us and rest up." Her offer was two-fold. Chef's food would return Melody to health and the break would get her away from Mrs. Howser and her oozy black shadow.

Melody sighed. "That's a really sweet offer, but I can't."

Hamish returned with a plate of Singapore noodles. "Get some meat on ye bones. Ye turn sideways and ye disappear!"

The noodles looked delicious. Ondine's tummy rumbled, but she wasn't as ravenous as someone burning their energy with magic all day. "Why don't you ask your parents if you can –"

" – It's very kind of you, but no," Melody said.

"Why not?" Ondine fidgeted with worry. Had Melody's parents seen how ill she looked? She didn't need magic lessons; she needed to get to a fat farm. [2]

"She must know you're talking to me," Melody said while she shovelled in more food. A chunk of noodle flew out and hit Ondine on the cheek. Melody had that panicked look about her, as if she were in trouble. "She knows everything."

Ondine's words brimmed with sarcasm. "Kind of like, she's psychic then?"

Deadpan from Melody. "There is that."

Ondine stood up and made sure Hamish stayed with her friend while she headed to the buffet. Witches, pre-witches, seers

---

2. At Bruglish fat farms, you go in thin and come out looking normal. As opposed to the ones elsewhere in the world, where you go in fat and come out a little less fat, before abandoning all your promises at the first plate of hot chips. Mmmmm, hot chips.

and pre-seers crowded around the tables, piling their plates high, then getting sidetracked with talking to people and standing about, blocking the food Ondine wanted. [3]

"Excuse me," she said. "Sorry." She budged the person in front of her. "Can I get to the beetroot salad please?"

The chatty coven moved a few centimetres over, allowing Ondine access. So much to choose from. Sandwich points, pickled squid, pasta salads, slices of rare beef with horseradish cream, stir-fries, fruit and cheeses. At the allergy table they had sandwich fillings on rice cakes, leafy salads, fruit and more fruit and steamed vegetables with sweet chilli dressing. The vegetarian and vegan tables looked so colourful Ondine's mouth began watering afresh.

"Bingo!" someone said.

"Eggplant stack!" another said, at which point they burst into giggles. Ondine didn't get it. [4]

Armed with a good spread of lunch, she made her way back to Hamish, where Melody was mopping the last smear of dressing from her plate with a wedge of bread.

With several mouthfuls of food in her belly, Ondine didn't feel so hopeless. Another thought soon chased that away. Was she hungry from natural causes or witching ones?

Hamish helped himself to some of Ondine's rare beef.

Feeling full, Ondine put the plate to one side.

"Are you going to eat that?" Melody said.

"Give it laldy." Hamish handed it over.

"He means you can have at it," Ondine translated for her friend's benefit,

---

3. At CovenCon, they allow non-witches and non-seers to call themselves pre-witches and pre-seers, so that those on the way to witching and seeing feel as if they are really on their way.

4. It's a lay-down misère, if you tick the 'vegan' box on your conference registration, you'll get an eggplant stack.

"There you are." Old Col and Mrs. Howser stood in front of them. Standing together. Like old friends.

Ondine gulped past the boulder in her throat.

"Time for our audience with the Duchess," Mrs. Howser said.

"Ye mean, all of us?" Hamish asked.

"Yes, of course," Mrs. Howser said. "Come along Melody."

CHAPTER 14

Standing in the state receiving room, Ondine gulped hard as she and everyone else waited for Duchess Anathea to grace them with her presence. Guilt and fear swirled in her tummy, making her light-headed and lead-bellied. Guilt that they hadn't done enough to make Anathea popular. Fear that Hamish might never get his work papers and be arrested and deported.

Or be forced to spend the rest of his years as a ferret.

Every corner of the room dripped elegance. From the art deco light fittings to the towering vases of flowers on the side tables, this was a properly decorated room. Right down – or more accurately, up – to the glass dome above that flooded the room with natural light.

Not an ordinary urn of coffee on a table for this room. No. It had a proper coffee-making machine. One that warmed the cups, ground the beans, percolated the coffee at exactly the right temperature and steamed the milk. [1]

---

1. The correct temperature for making espresso is between 88 and 95 degrees Celsius (at sea level). Tea, of course, needs to be made with boiling water that is 100 degrees Celsius (at sea level). It's not about being fussy, it's about doing

If it had been only her, Hamish and Old Col meeting the Duchess, she would have been nervous. But Ondine had even more worries because Mrs. Howser was in the room. Based on what she and Hamish had overheard by the pool, Mrs. Howser wanted to work for Vincent. She was also dead against Anathea becoming more popular.

Why had Col allowed her nemesis to come to the meeting?

So many questions swirled in Ondine's head she felt a thumping ache coming on. It started at the back of her neck and grew up the left side.

Howser-shouldn't-be-here-thump-thump.

How-do-we-let-Anathea-know-this?-thump-thump.

Why-isn't-this-meeting-more-secret?-thump-thump.

Maybe-Aunt-Col-is-losing-her-mind?-thump-thump.

Speaking-of-Aunt-Col-I-don't-seem-to-be-learning-very-much-magic-Bong!

The clock struck one as Duchess Anathea walked into the meeting room with her fluffy white dog, Biscuit-of-the-half-grown-teeth, trailing after her. Something had changed about Anathea since they'd last met at the Ferris wheel. Her face shone with more gloss than usual. She looked haughty, more commanding. Her blonde hair glowed with vibrant health. Being the head of state clearly agreed with her.

Hamish slipped his hand in Ondine's, partially dissolving her worries and head thumps. As one, everyone bowed their heads to show their respect. In the corner of her vision, Ondine couldn't help notice Mrs. Howser didn't bow as deeply as everyone else.

As Anathea sat, Biscuit leapt into her lap and made himself

---

things properly. We must uphold our standards or the savages will win (at sea level).

comfortable. The lapdog yawned to reveal a curved row of pointy teeth buds.

"Told you his teeth would grow back," Old Col said.

The Duchess craned the dog's jaw around to have a look. "Getting there."

"That would be Ondine's doing," Old Col said. "She's developing the most agreeable talents."

Locking gazes with Ondine, the Duchess said, "That is appreciated."

"Thank you," Ondine said, then silently thought, *I think.*

A flute of sparkling wine sat on the table in front of Anathea. She dipped a finger in the bubbles and held it out as Biscuit licked it off. Then she dipped her finger back in and did it again, before she had a sip.

Ondine's gorge rose.

"That's mockit." Hamish said.

Ondine squeezed his hand to silently plead for his . . . well, his silence, really.

"How goes the task that was set for you?" Anathea asked.

"Very well thanks," Ondine said, being careful not to mention the type of task Anathea had set, because if Mrs. Howser found out she'd –

"If I may be so rude as to interrupt," Mrs. Howser said, taking a step forward. "You need some special magic, and you need it rather quickly. I believe I and my protégée, Melody – stand up Melody, don't be shy – will be only too happy to help in any way you see fit."

A broad smile – one might almost call it warm – spread across Anathea's face.

"Naw, ye dinnae want that," Hamish blurted.

"Don't," Ondine said under her breath.

"Oh really?" Anathea said. "And why would I not want to use any help that might be made available?"

"Because it could dilute the magic, of course," Old Col chimed in. "Your Lordship, I'm not one to blow my own trumpet, but you'll get your very best results from Ondine and Hamish, I assure you. Mixing the magic with other spells could end up . . . ah . . . well, it could make something of a mess, you see."

"If I may speak freely?" Mrs. Howser said.

Anathea nodded.

"The original magic between Hamish and Ondine was *my* creation. As well-meaning as she might be, Colette Romano is misleading you if she thinks she can control it."

"I beg your pardon?" Auntie Col's hands landed hard on her hips.

Mrs. Howser continued as if everything was fine and dandy, when in reality Ondine was stomach-churningly nervous. "I mean no disrespect," Mrs Howser said. "But if you want results – real results – then allow me to humbly offer my services."

"Uh," Ondine started, but didn't know how to go on.

"There is an objection?" Anathea asked, her gaze locking with Ondine's. "Is Birgit Howser the originator of your magic or not?"

Ondine squeaked out, "Well, yes, she probably is." Then she cleared her throat and tried to explain. "At least, she put the spell on Hamish and then when he bonded with me it set off a chain reaction thingy, but please, Your Grace, let us keep working for you. It's working so well. The people love you more than ever." That last bit was a desperate attempt by Ondine to remind Anathea that they were doing their best to make her popular. Because if Anathea started thinking she didn't need them, what incentive would she have for granting Hamish his citizenship?

Anathea looked directly to Mrs. Howser. "You mean to say it's the spell made by you that makes people's wishes come true?"

Mrs. Howser made a bow to affirm this.

"Excuse me! I was the one that turned him into a ferret in the first place!" Old Col snapped.

It brought the room to a sudden and horribly uncomfortable silence. This could only get messier. Old Col looked weak and watery while Mrs. Howser looked more confident by the second. Mercury's wings, why did Col agree to let Howser join the meeting?

"It was one of *my* spells, Your Grace," Mrs. Howser said. "Of course, Colette here added her . . . *contribution*. But it's no idle boast when I assure you the mutating magic is all of my making."

"A ferret?" Anathea said, her eyes growing wider as she looked from Hamish to Old Col and back again.

Ondine wanted to bury her face in her hands. The cat – or ferret in this case – was well out of the bag. Now that Anathea knew of his other skills, Ondine would bet her life on Anathea wanting him to stay that way and spy for her. Just as the late Duke had done.

"Aye," Hamish said.

Biscuit the dog pricked up his ears.

Anathea looked from Old Col to Hamish again. "The night you made Biscuit's teeth fall out. You had a ferret spying under the dining table, didn't you?"

"Please, Your Grace, do not upset yourself with trifling matters," Mrs. Howser said, sounding as slippery as her greasy shadow. "It is enough to say that Colette Romano has been trying to impress you with another witch's magic. But as I am here now, and I forgive Colette for her transgressions, please consider me a convenient replacement for your magical requirements?"

"I have not been claiming credit for your work," Old Col

said, her voice wobbling and her expression frail and senior. "That's not what's been happening at all."

Anathea raised her palm to shush them all. "A ferret you say? This is something to be seen."

Ondine and Hamish gulped in unison.

"Go on." Old Col sounded defeated. "You may as well show her."

"Aye." Hamish kissed Ondine on the forehead and let go of her hand.

The grimace on his face made Ondine ache for the pain he had to endure. This transition was slower than his flash-change under the stage, but no less shocking for Ondine to see her true love reduced in such a way. At first his face turned dark, then fur sprang out all over the place, even from his ears. His nose turned pointy as long whiskers sprouted from his cheeks. His ears shrank away into furry triangles. A moment later he vanished under a pile of lifeless clothes.

"What an interesting thing to be seen," Anathea said.

Shambles the ferret poked his pointy, furry face out from under a shirt. The ring she'd bought him for Christmas slipped free and rolled on the floor. An ache started up in Ondine's heart from the pain of seeing him like this.

"How very interesting. And how very, very useful," Anathea said.

"I was like this for dozens of years, until I met Ondine," Shambles said. "And when I finally came round, I was still fit-like, on account of the spell Col made. So ye see, she is a great witch, sure she is."

"How loyal he is," Mrs. Howser said. "He would have found it hard to expose Miss Romano's lack of usable magic, probably based on some kind of gratitude towards her. I'm sure they meant no harm in deceiving you, Your Grace."

Ondine protested, "It's not like that!"

Biscuit the dog shot out of Anathea's arms and charged at Shambles.

"Not again!" Ondine cried. In a flash, she scooped Shambles into her arms, away from the marauding dog. His teeth might be tiny buds, but she wasn't taking any risks. [2]

Ru-ru-ru-ru. Biscuit leapt at Ondine, then dug his claws into her pants. *Riiiip!* Those same claws tore an ugly gash in the fabric on the way down. Defying gravity and lack of fitness, Biscuit leapt even higher. Chomp! His teeth closed around Shambles's middle.

"Arrrrrghghghghghghghg!" Shambles cried out.

"Stop it! You're killing him!" Ondine screamed.

---

2. The last time Biscuit had taken a bite out of Hamish, he'd had all his teeth and Hamish was a Shambles ferret. And Ondine hadn't been there to protect him. Some quick thinking from Col saved the moment. She had magicked all of the dog's teeth out, so he couldn't do any harm.

CHAPTER 15

"Naw, naw, ahahahahahahah!" Shambles garbled.

It sounded like he was . . . *laughing?*

"Awwww, his teeth are so wee! Best tickle fer ages!" At which point Shambles burst into a fresh bout of ferrety giggles.

With a quick tug, Ondine pulled Shambles away. Biscuit slipped off him and fell to the floor in a puddle of fur. Shambles was covered in slobber, but at least it wasn't blood. Silently, she chanted, 'Don't kick the dog, don't kick the dog'. No amount of grovelling could make up for that. [1]

"I can see now why my departed brother wanted to have you around permanently." Anathea said. "I would like you to perform the same kind of services for me as you did for the late Duke."

Shambles said, "Ye honour me, Yer Grace, but I cannae leave Ondi. She's me life."

Such sentiment would ordinarily make Ondine grin with happiness, but not in this kind of atmosphere.

Anathea shrugged. "I hardly see what difference this makes.

---

1. Be nice to animals, because you never know when you'll be turned into one.

You are already supposed to be working for me. I propose it becomes more of a formal arrangement. Where you stay of an evening is entirely your business."

"So ye mean, ye want me to work for ye, here in Venzelemma?"

No, Hamish, you're supposed to stay with me. We're never going to be apart again, Ondine wished.

Anathea's brows made the slightest crease. "I'm not going back to Bellreeve, if that's what you're thinking."

Biscuit barked freshly at Shambles, desperate to gnaw his belly again. Ondine didn't trust that dog for a second. "Your Grace, it's not safe for Hamish and Biscuit to be under the same roof. Things will only get worse when his teeth grow back."

"Your Grace, thank you for this audience," Old Col said in a tone that told Ondine it was time they ended this meeting.

A commotion by the main doors distracted them. As one, everyone turned to see the cause of it. Ondine's stomach did that hideous dropping away thing as Lord Vincent sauntered in, blue hand and all.

Did he never wash?

Shambles crawled up her back to settle on her shoulder. "He doesnae look so good."

Understatement of the year. Lord Vincent looked like he'd been turned inside out and shaken a few times, then shoved back together in a rush.

"Dearest nephew," Anathea said with an imperial tone. "To what do I owe this interruption to my busy schedule?"

His said in a growly rush, "You are in grave danger." Perspiration gathered on his forehead, as if it took every ounce of strength for him to be here.

Like watching a tennis match, Ondine's eyes shot back and forth between Vincent and Anathea.

"Really? From whom?" the Duchess gave her return volley.

"From me!"

Terrible didn't even come close to describing how Vincent looked. He staggered forward and drew breath. His face turned grey. Had someone poisoned his food?

In his next breath he fell to his knees, his eyes rolling back into his head.

Morbid curiosity took hold. Ondine stepped closer, to get a better look. Vincent's head snapped forward. He jumped to his feet and thundered at full strength, "You! This is all your doing!"

Ondine leapt backwards.

Shambles whispered, "Ondi I think we should –"

"Die!" Vincent pushed his palm out. Time and space rippled before Ondine's eyes. A rolling shockwave knocked her to the floor.

"No!" It was Aunt Col's voice this time. Dizzy and half-concussed, Ondine saw her witchy great-aunt rebuffing the advancing shockwave. In the next heartbeat Duchess Anathea scooped Biscuit into her arms and hid behind Col, using her as a human shield.

Where had Mrs. Howser gone? What was she doing all this time? Saving the Duchess? No. She stood there, arms crossed, watching it unfold.

Melody crouched against the wall, her hands over her ears.

Thick, heavy pounding reverberated inside Ondine's head, as if she'd put her ear to a speaker at a rock concert. Shambles flailed about on the floor, moaning and groaning like he was about to revert to human form. He had the worst habit of changing at the exact wrong time. It would be an absolute disaster if he . . . Mercury's wings, he started changing.

"No Hamish!"

Vincent heard her. He stopped duelling with Old Col.

"Perfect!" In two steps he reached Shambles, drew back his foot and kicked.

Hard.

His boot made contact with Shambles, sending him soaring across the room.

"No!" Ondine screamed.

Shambles's body wobbled and twisted through the air until he hit the wall with a sickening crack, then slid lifelessly to the floor.

Ondine scrambled to his side, but something tripped her and she hit the ground again, smacking her chin on the tiles. Pain shot through her. She shut her eyes hard to ride it out. Tears sprouted anyway. Jupiter's moons, it hurt!

"Vincent! This madness must be stopped!" Anathea said, cowering behind Old Col.

Ondine tried to get up again, but she slipped on something wet and smelly. Biscuit piddle. She nearly threw up in her effort to move away.

Hamish, I must get to Hamish, she thought. But when she turned to where he'd fallen, he wasn't there. Had he crawled off. Had someone taken him away?

"He's possessed," Old Col said of Vincent, to nobody in particular.

"Help me!" Vincent called out, even as the magical assault continued.

Col yelled out, "Who's pulling the strings?"

Vincent made garbled sounds.

"Where's Hamish?" Panic constricted Ondine's chest. "What have you done with him?"

"The boy's mad," Anathea said. With a burst of panic, she ran for the door and pulled it open. "Security! Security!"

Meanwhile, Old Col and Vincent were still holding each other steady with equal measures of magic and bluster. Sound waves reverberated around the room turning everything hazy and blue. Noises crashed inside Ondine's head, giving her the biggest thumper of a migraine she'd ever experienced.

Mrs. Howser stood there with a satisfied look on her face.

Col's voice came out strong and sure. "Give up!"

"Help me!" Vincent yelled.

Anathea slipped out the door to safety.

"Where is Hamish?" Ondine pressed her hands to the sides of her head and staggered around the room.

"What?" Vincent lost his concentration for a split second.

Old Col seized her chance. "Stop!" The boom of a jet engine breaking the sound barrier pounded through the room. Light fittings exploded. The large dome above them shattered, showering everyone with broken glass and sending magic into the snowy sky like fireworks.

The thumping inside Ondine's head fell away. A piercing ringing took its place. Maybe, just maybe, if this had been an ordinary day without the spying and plotting and scheming, she might have the strength to make sense of it. Instead she felt twenty-seven kinds of wrong. Confusion held her in its grip. Vincent lay slumped on the floor. It looked like Old Col was saying something. Her lips were moving but nothing came out.

Gradually the piercing noise faded away, replaced by the buzzing of wasps. Through the buzzing, Anathea came back into the room, flanked by security.

"He's gone crazy. He's possessed," the Duchess said.

Old Col agreed. "He was fighting something, but he wasn't strong enough to hold it back."

Ondine leaned against the wall, waiting until the room stopped spinning. Turning, she saw Melody curled in foetal position.

Looking completely at ease, Mrs Howser turned to the security people and said, "Something is very wrong with that boy."

Anathea gulped as she looked at the slumped form of Lord

Vincent. "He's always given me the creeps, that child. I truly fear for Brugel when he inherits."

Mrs. Howser stepped forward to help the Duchess. "There's plenty of time to declare him insane before then. Now, careful where you walk, there's broken glass everywhere."

Col's top lip curled in contempt as she looked at the security people. "Your Duchess could have used you a few minutes ago."

"Apologies, My Lord Duchess." The security guard dropped to one knee. His eyes sprang open as a glass shard punctured his skin.

For the next few minutes, Ondine regained her balance and ignored the confused talk and apologies. She only had one thing on her mind. "Auntie Col, did you see where Hamish went?"

His dishevelled face appeared around the doorway, along with a naked shoulder and bony knee. "Ondi, would ye mind grabbin' ma clothes, I'm fair freezing."

Relief surged through her. "Uh-huh." Ondine nodded and grabbed the bundle of clothes she'd dropped at some point. Unfortunately, she'd dropped them too close to the lake of Biscuit piddle so they had that unforgiving acrid smell. It would have to do until they got home and could wash this horrible day down the drain.

CHAPTER 16

Back at the family pub, Chef approached Ondine, Hamish and Old Col with a cheerful smile. He caught one whiff of the dog-wee smell, scrunched his face up and ushered them towards the back room. "Get cleaned up, I'll get you some to-faux-fu soup." [1]

After they'd showered and changed and properly cleaned themselves up, Ondine and Hamish met up with Ma and Old Col in their private room behind the kitchen. The soup arrived and they slurped it down while they debriefed after an insane day.

But why did Ma need to be in here? "Aren't you busy?" Ondine asked.

"Have you ever known Tuesday nights to be busy?" Ma shot back.

"Good point."

Ma pressed on, keen to find out everything. "Will you tell me what's wrong? Was it the run-in you had with Lord Vincent?"

---

1. An incredibly popular tofu substitute, made from chicken.

At which point Hamish began rubbing her back in a sign of support and love.

"Auntie Col told me," Ma said. "She filled me in on everything that happened."

"That would be everything except what we heard by the pool, eh lass?"

"You went swimming?" Great Aunt Col shivered at the thought.

"That's the bit we haven't had time to tell you about. We came back inside to find you but by that point Mrs. Howser was with you and we couldn't say anything."

Old Col huffed. "That woman! No wonder she stuck so close. She knew the more she stuck by me, the less you could say."

That may have been the case at CovenCon, but now they were home, they had plenty of time to relay everything, so that's exactly what they did. Everything they overheard and saw from their morning of spying on Mrs. Howser, including the black oozy shadowy thing.

A shiver spread through the room.

"No wonder you two didn't say much during our meeting with Anathea." Col said, shaking her head. "I knew Birgit was up to something. I thought an audience with the Duchess would expose that. Which, of course, it did. It's all falling in to place now. She met with Vincent and transferred some kind of controlling spell onto him. To do that she would've had to be close enough to touch him. Did you see whether she touched him? Shook his hand? Patted his head? You see, the higher up the body, the more powerful the spell."

Hamish piped up. "Weil, we didnae see anything, but we heard him say 'don't touch me,' so we did."

"He sounded really annoyed about it," Ondine added.

"Oh dear." Old Col sucked in her cheek in thought. "If she patted him on the head, it explains his lack of control."

"Maybe that's why he sounded so annoyed. Maybe he thought she was being patronising or something, when instead she was getting close enough to cast a spell," Ondine said.

Ma drummed her fingers on the table. "Couldn't have happened to a nicer person. He's caused you no end of grief. I would have thought you'd be glad to see him suffer."

"No Ma, not even Vincent deserved that. He was completely possessed. He was crying out for help. I felt . . . sorry for him."

Ma crinkled her brow. "Sorry?"

"Yeah. A bit."

"Must have been *really* bad," Ma said.

"I wonder, hmm," Old Col said. "When he said we should die, I thought it was rather extreme. But perhaps he was directing that to Howser and not Anathea?"

"That's kind of painting a nicer picture," Ondine said. "I don't want to think nicely about Vincent. He doesn't deserve my sympathies."

"True lass," Hamish said.

"But what I don't get," Ondine said, completely not getting it. "One moment Howser is trying to sweet-talk Vincent into joining her, the next she's sending him insane. What's all that about?"

"Motivation, dear child," Old Col said. "It's her way of showing Vincent 'you're either with me or against me.' There is no middle ground with Birgit."

It was Hamish's turn to crease his brow. "So she throws a witchy tantrum if she disnae get her own way?"

"That's about the sum of it. Today she's shown Vincent what a powerful enemy she can be. He can continue to defy her and pay the consequences, or join her and reap the rewards. It's a surprisingly persuasive argument," Col said. "And another thing, she's lying about not getting paid. She was paid, and handsomely. How do you think she got the money to start that psychic school of hers?"

That made Ondine blink with surprise. "You knew about her helping the previous Duke have a son?"

"I was there," Old Col said in a huff.

"Eww!" Ondine said.

"Not in that way! Honestly!" Old Col huffed.

Ondine stifled an inappropriate giggle. When she unscrambled her thoughts, she turned to Old Col again. "Why would Mrs. Howser lie to Vincent? About the money and all that?"

"Keep up, child." Old Col rolled her eyes. "Because she's greedy, that's why. Mind you, she wouldn't have considered it a lie. Knowing her as I do, she merely thinks she wasn't compensated *enough*."

All eyes turned on Col, waiting for the rest of it.

"Oh all right. You wouldn't think it, but we used to be close friends. We both worked for the late Duke. Or the later one, I guess. Pavla's father. Anyway, Birgit came into plenty of money but she never told me where it came from. I was too polite to ask at the time. Don't look at me like that; I can be polite when the mood takes me. Anyway, I thought maybe she had a wealthy lo – . . . uh . . . patron or something. I kept thinking she'd tell me who'd stumped up the money, but she never did.

"Things really fell apart after the Debutante Ball, and the rest, as they say, is lies and conjecture. [2] A few days later, when I'd calmed down, obviously, I searched for Hamish to reverse the ferret spell I'd put on you dear, but I couldn't find you. Or Birgit for that matter. I didn't know she had you, you see. And years

———————————

2. The infamous Debutante Ball so many decades ago, where Hamish had taken his first taste of plütz, tripped on Col's dress, ripped her hem and called her a witch. Oh, and Col had then turned him into a ferret.

later, when our paths would cross at CovenCon or at Halloween, she never let on. That must be why I've never been able to reverse the ferret spell for good, because she put another layer on top. Only the witch that placed the last spell can remove it."

Silence cloaked them for a while, until Old Col spoke again. "By the way. There's something you're all overlooking about today. I'm not bragging or anything, but it was *my* magic that held Vincent back. Birgit spent the whole meeting bringing me down, but when it came to it, I was the one that sorted things out."

"Thank you, Auntie Col," Ondine said. "You really came through." Which was as close as Ondine would admit to nearly being swayed by Mrs. Howser. Because Mrs. Howser had very nearly made Ondine wonder if her great aunt had started to lose her grip . . . on magic and other things.

She had to acknowledge a certain amount of jealousy over how far Melody had come in six months' tuition with Mrs. Howser. Compared to how little Ondine felt her great aunt had been able to teach her. On the plus side, Ondine could make other people's wishes come true; that was pretty amazing!

If only she knew how to control it. Then she'd *really* have magic.

Sadness swamped Ondine, because she had to acknowledge the magic had come about because of Hamish being under Mrs. Howser's extra spell, not the original spell from Auntie Col.

Which had Ondine's conscience juggling all kinds of disloyalty.

On top of those worries, Duchess Anathea now knew Hamish could be a Shambles-ferret-spy. To a paranoid Duchess, her beloved Hamish made the perfect package.

"Ondine, pay attention!" Ma snapped her fingers in front of her face.

"Oh yes, sorry." They were all looking at her.

"Ye must be tired, lass." Hamish rubbed her back again.

"Yeah."

"We're talking about where we go from here. Auntie Col and I were saying you and Hamish will need to work even harder to make Anathea popular."

"Uh-huh." Ondine nodded. "Um. No. Hang on. Why would we do that? The more we work for her, the more she'll want Hamish working with her all the time as a ferret. How does that help anyone?"

By 'anyone' she meant 'me'.

"Yes, but if you don't, she'll be unlikely to grant Hamish his papers." Old Col said. "*Quid pro quo*, and all that." [3]

Ondine thought out loud. "If we stop helping Anathea, we're going to lose Hamish, aren't we?"

"If you need to repeat things to help the world make sense, by all means carry on," Old Col said.

Frustration bloomed in her heart. "Yeah, but, don't you see? If we do keep helping her, I could still lose Hamish because he'll be ferreting around for Anathea. She said as much herself."

"You mean 'we' could lose Hamish," Ma corrected.

"Isn't that what I said?" Ondine mentally swatted away a whiny little 'why me?' buzzing about her head. No way. She would *not* give in to a fit of the sulks.

Hamish rubbed her back again. "I'm nawt going anywhere, I promise."

"I'm not sure we have any other options," Old Col said.

Ondine thought of plenty more options, all of which involved running away with Hamish and leaving Anathea and

---

3. Old Brugelish Latin meaning, "pound for pound".

the rest of Brugel to sort itself out. But in the end, she knew there was only one path she could take.

"We have to help Anathea to save Hamish," Ondine said, determined to not sniffle despite her vision blurring. "We're going to uphold our end of the bargain, come what may."

That familiar twinkle shone in Hamish's beautiful green eyes. "Aye, weil keep snuggling and making magic, fer the good of Brugel."

Well, there was *that*.

CHAPTER 17

Considering the mayhem and trauma of the previous day, Ondine didn't particularly feel like going back to CovenCon the next morning.

Old Col told her in no uncertain terms they had to. "Life is full of things we don't particularly feel like doing, but we do them and we get on with it."

Thanks for the support and understanding.

When they arrived at the convention, security had been beefed up since the day before. There were extra people standing by the doors and checking nametags.

No sign of Mrs. Howser. What was the old witch up to now?

After the early plenary session and motivating speeches, it was time to split off into the various workshops on offer. [1]

Ondine and Hamish's job for the day was to stay close to Anathea, so that they could keep canoodling, so that Anathea

---

1. In any conference there will be at least three workshops you really want to attend. And as fate will have it, two of them will be on at the same time.

could keep wishing she were more popular than fried cheese balls.

Their magic had to be working because so many people were looking at Anathea with admiration. Every session the Duchess visited became congested as so many wanted to be exactly where she was.

"Perhaps our work here is done," Ondine said as they grabbed a spare seat in the back row of *Harvesting Magical Ingredients*. Duchess Anathea was in attendance, so it was packed. *Oh, what a shame*, Ondine thought with a smile; there was only one seat left so she had to sit on Hamish's lap.

"Doin' it fer Brugel," Hamish whispered as he wrapped his arms around her.

The workshop itself provided nothing of interest for Ondine, not that she could hear much from way up the back. The guest witch invited the Duchess to take a quickly-vacated seat right up the front.

That earned Anathea a round of applause, merely for taking a seat.

Relief cascaded through Ondine. She whispered to Hamish, "I think it's working?"

It would have been disrespectful to the presenter to sneak out mid-workshop. Not that they could get out with the crowd pressed in so closely around them. So they sat quietly together playing 'handies'. This involved tickling each other's palms until the other person couldn't stand it any longer and had to pull away. All the while they had to be utterly silent. If you made a noise, you lost a point. If you pulled your hand away with the first tickle, you lost three points. If you squirmed, minus four points. And so on.

After five minutes, Ondine was losing far too many points and having a fantastic time. A woman in the next row turned around and shushed them. The woman beside the other woman murmured something about being catty.

Ondine had to bite the inside of her cheek to stay quiet, because Hamish kept moving his hands towards hers – but not touching. Merely the threat of a tickle had her silently shaking in fits of giggles.

Gasp! The woman in front of them grew a tail that grew out the back of her. Then the woman next to her grew a tail too. It was tan with orange stripes and altogether quite becoming. Down the row, every single person grew a tail. Thick furry ones, spotted ones, thin ones and even a ratty looking one with a kink in it.

Ondine looked to Hamish and whispered, "Did we do that?"

"I don –"

He never finished the word, let alone the sentence. Pandemonium broke out. People screamed and wailed as they suddenly noticed their new appendages.

"Ouch, you stepped on my tail!"

"Watch it!"

"Mind your own tail, this one's mine!"

"It's horrible!"

"Get it off!"

In the *mêlée*, Ondine grabbed Hamish's hand and scarpered, caught between laughing her head off and crying in panic.

In the hall, Hamish gave her a calming hug. "I've seen some weird things since coming tae Brugel, but ye *goat* to admit, tails on folks isnae something ye see every day."

Their tummies rumbled in unison as the conference staff set the buffet for morning tea. Any minute now people would swarm the tables, tails and all. Ondine grabbed a plate to beat the rush. Behind them, the noise from the workshop became too loud to ignore. Worried convention staff and volunteers pulled the doors open to see what was amiss.

People ran out, screaming and wailing and . . . *miaowing*? Yes, definitely cat noises coming from the crowd. Ondine piled the chocolate slices on her plate, feeling perplexed and fearful. Would she and Hamish grow tails as well?

Old Col's crepe-paper-thin fingers clamped around Ondine's wrist. "Did you and Hamish do that?"

"I didn't do anything. We were just sitting in the back row, minding our own business." A pile of bricks called 'guilt' filled her tummy that she and Hamish might have caused it. They were merely being loved up so that people's nice wishes about the Duchess could come true.

So many thoughts assaulted her. Mrs. Howser. Magic virus. Spells. Conspiracies. Lord Vincent. Chaos.

The fire alarm blared. Staff ordered people to evacuate. Sirens wailed and emergency lights flashed.

Reluctantly, Ondine put her plate of morning tea aside.

They followed the crowd to the assembly area outside, with many standing well clear of everything over by the funicular station. To one side was the waterfall, which flowed into the river running underneath the drawbridge. It would have been a lovely place to stop and take photographs, if not for the incessant sirens and bumps and shoves from running, panicky people.

To judge from the ominous creaking sound beneath Ondine, they should get off the drawbridge. Emergency vehicles pulled up at an alarming rate. Police, Ambulance, Fire Brigade. Even a mobile coffee shop pulled over near the funicular, on the off-chance they might make a quick schlip. [2]

"What did you do?" Old Col demanded as she stared at Ondine.

---

2. Brugelish currency.

They were still standing on the drawbridge. Safely out of the evacuated castle, but not out on the snow-covered lawn where the delegates were assembling. Ondine gulped. The timber whined and whimpered in protest beneath them.

Hamish defended Ondine. "We did what we were supposed tae!"

With a groan of frustration, Old Col glared at them.

"We were . . ." Ondine's mind went blank with the stress.

Hamish slipped his hand in hers for reassurance. "We were only holding hands, Col. I swear on my life we didnae do anything."

"Holding hands?" Old Col creased her forehead at them.

"Aye, it's nae crime," he said, at which point he caressed his thumb against Ondine's hand. They may have been standing outside in the depths of winter but his touch made her feel warm and loved.

Adding one more level of craziness, Ma arrived, her breath steaming in huge puffs as she tried to steady herself. "Please don't tell me the Duchess has a tail?"

What in the name of all the planets was her mother doing here?

"Where was the Duchess in all of this?" Old Col's stare drilled holes in Ondine.

"We were all together," Ondine said.

"The whole time?" Old Col asked.

"Yes! We stuck close to her like burned cheese on a casserole dish. We were doing our job!"

"And you were close to her the whole time?" Old Col's interrogation technique was seriously impressive.

"Of course we were – ooooh!" Ondine gasped and clapped her spare hand over her mouth as she realised. "Until she went up the front."

Ma's eyes widened. "You were separated?"

"Why are you here Ma? Don't you have a pub to run?"

"Cybelle and Henrik have it under control," Ma said. "Now don't change the topic, this is serious. How close were you to the Duchess?"

"Now, Messers G, don't take it out on Ondi. It wasnae her fault. The room was packed tighter than movie night cheap seats. We had tae share a seat and there were people standing all around us so we were hemmed in, so we were. And everyone was treating Anathea like royalty and they offered her a seat up the front, like."

"She is royalty," Ondine corrected him.

"Och, yes."

"Then you should have gone with her!" Old Col said.

Ma covered her face with her hands and muttered, "I knew this would happen."

"But we couldn't move it was so crowded," Ondine said. Honestly, why did her mother have to show up now? It's like the woman had some kind of magic to appear right when things got complicated.

Old Col crossed her arms over her chest. "Then you should have stopped!"

At which point a passing mailman dropped his trolley and began barking like a dog.

Fresh hell broke loose.

"There's your proof," Ma said as they scooted away from the fresh outbreak of screaming.

"Oh naw, that's too cruel." Hamish looked from Old Col to Ma to Ondine and back again. "Ye cannae blame us, it's naw our fault!"

"Ondine dear," Old Col began. She hardly ever called her 'dear', which meant things couldn't be good. "I wish, just this once, you could think beyond your feelings for Hamish and look at the bigger picture."

"And how exactly do I do that?" Ondine could have sworn angry steam poured out of her ears, to match the steam from her mouth as she spoke. "I don't know what the big picture is. This magic is all new to me. I can't even feel when I'm using it. I don't know how far it reaches or how to control it or who's wishing what, when!"

Hamish tightened his grip on Ondine. "Dinnae take it out on Ondi, she's done naw wrong. So what if a few folks have tails? It's naw tha end of tha world, is it?"

"Ondine I'm so very sorry. You're going to hate me for this," Ma said.

Heavy sickness filled Ondine. Swallowing took so much effort she thought she might throw up.

Ma took a calming breath. "I thought perhaps you could control it –"

Old Col interrupted, "People are getting hurt. Innocent people."

Ondine opened and closed her mouth a few times. "It'll wear off . . . won't it?"

"It's naw as if we can control it," Hamish said.

"This is exactly my point. I thought you *could* control it, but you can't. Birgit Howser has truly excelled herself, creating a spell like this. Can't you see she's using you to create chaos? Sure, making people's wishes come true is wonderful, but that's only the good wishes. What of the bad ones? What if someone wishes something truly malicious? Someone near the two of you has wished someone else into a cat and look what it's done?"

Tears blurred Ondine's vision. "It's not my fault! I can't control what other people are wishing for!"

Ma stepped forward and embraced her. "I know that, love. That's why we have to do something about it."

The words sounded horribly ominous. It also gave Ondine

an inkling of why her mother was here. Things were about to get horrible.

Ma continued. "You see now what Mrs. Howser is capable of. She's using the pair of you to create instability and fear. If it goes on, it will only destabilise Anathea and all of Brugel for that matter."

All breath left Ondine. The corners of her vision turned black and she clung to Hamish as if she were drowning. She sucked in a deep breath. "Use your magic to stop it then, Col!"

"I've been trying to dear, but your virus is spreading beyond anything I imagined. Just yesterday four of the Duchess's staff began sneezing in unison."

Hamish scoffed. "So they've *goat* colds. It's hardly chaos!"

"It is when they sneeze fire and burn down the connecting walls. The fire brigade arrived, blocking the streets. It was peak hour so that caused traffic snarls."

Ondine gasped in fright. She'd caused that? "Was anyone hurt?" Then she looked to Hamish for support. He looked even more worried than her, which didn't help one bit. One last attempt to blame someone else. "But it couldn't have been us. We weren't anywhere near Anathea's staff."

"It appears you don't have to be," Old Col said. "Other people are catching your mutating magic and infecting others." Her shoulders slumped, Ondine braced herself for more bad news. "I hate to admit it, but Birgit's spell is one of the best. The magic is making people's wishes come true all over the place. It's mayhem."

"Catching the virus like a second wave?" Ma asked.

"Exactly. Ondi and Hamish are 'patient zero'. They're passing it on to unsuspecting victims; in turn they're passing it on to more people. It's strongest at the source, at the epicentre."

Had Ondine heard right? "It's spreading?"

Sadness filled Old Col's weathered face. "I'm sorry Ondi, but yes, it's spreading. All the witches of Slaegal worth their salt are here, yet mutating magic is being reported in Norange."

Red mist clouded Ondine's eyes at the news her uncontrollable magic had reached Norange, the capital of neighbouring country Slaegal. "Then why did you drag us out here in public? Why did you let us spread it when you knew it was contagious?"

"I didn't know, I only suspected." Old Col looked defeated. "And I . . . thought I could contain it."

Tears blurred Ondine's vision. "Then Mrs. Howser was right all along. Your magic is rubbish!"

Ma grabbed Ondine in a bear hug. "Hush, darling, let's not say anything we might regret."

"But it's true," Ondine pulled away from her mother, stepped too close to the edge of the drawbridge and righted herself before she fell in the drink. "We all know who's got the real magic around here and it isn't any of us!"

Hamish squeezed her hand in support. "Ondi, love, I hate tae say it but . . . I think ye need tae hush."

"Don't tell me to be quiet!" The moment she said it, she felt sick to her stomach.

Nobody said anything for a long beat.

Hamish said in a low voice, "Mebbe we should be apart –"

" – What!" Ondine stared at Hamish.

"Just for a wee time. Until this settles down and we can get rid of tha spell."

Ondine stepped back in shock and again came perilously close to the edge of the timber. A large icicle dislodged from the drawbridge and splashed into the water below. "Stars! You've already talked about this behind my back, haven't you? Hamish, what are they making you do?"

The delay – just long enough to see his Adam's apple bob up and down on a swallow – gave him away. "Naw lass, it's nae conspiracy."

Ma grabbed Ondine away from Hamish, held her in a fierce hug and said. "We have to do this like ripping off a bandage. Get it over with quickly."

"No, Ma –" Stars and suns, that's why her mother was here. To take Hamish away from her.

Old Col latched on to Hamish's arm, to drag him off.

The drawbridge groaned as the boards warped beneath them.

"Wait!" Hamish stood his ground. "Ye said we'd be able tae say goodbye. Proper like."

Ondine fought free of her mother and threw herself into an embrace with Hamish. The drop to the river below was right at her feet. If they leapt to freedom, would they be all right? All the while she begged Hamish, "You're not leaving me. Tell me you're not leaving me."

"We have tae give it a try, for the greater good."

Head squished to his chest, she felt his heart thumping to break free. In an act of desperation, she locked her hands behind his back and refused to let go.

"I thought this might happen," Old Col said.

From out of nowhere, a new group of people appeared, blocking Ondine's escape. She looked for a way out, anywhere to run, but she was blocked in. The castle, Ma and Old Col behind her, the strangers advancing from the front of the drawbridge, and the steep drop into the water beside them. The advancing strangers wore those all-in-one hazardous material suits. They grabbed at Ondine's hands and peeled her thumbs apart, forcing her to release her grip.

"No! Ma! Make them stop!"

With a sickening wrench, they pulled Hamish away. Ondine kicked and flailed but somebody held her from behind.

"Nae like this!" Hamish yelled. "Ye lied to me, Col!"

Col's voice sounded thin and creaky. "I'm sorry. This is how it has to be."

"Sorry my ar- *armpit*!" With a burst of strength, Hamish broke free.

Hope surged through Ondine like a beam of sunshine as he ran back and held her. He may have forced his captors off him with the ferocity of a lion but he held her tenderly, as if she were made of glass. His chilled hands cupped her face, but when his lips touched hers she felt warm all the way through. If only Ma would let go of her arms she could embrace him properly.

That's when something seriously crazy happened. One of the haz-mat people grew octopus tentacles, wrapping them around Hamish like prey.

Hamish cried out, "You said it wouldn't be like this!"

Was he speaking about Old Col or Ma? It didn't matter. "Hamish, my love!" Ondine strained against her captors to press her lips back to him.

She met with nothing but air as the mob dragged Hamish away from her. The octopus tentacles gripped him. He couldn't move.

With a desperate shove Ondine broke free and hurled herself towards Hamish, the force breaking him free from his captors. The next moment, the man with the tentacle for an arm closed in on them. She grabbed Hamish and looked at the rushing water below.

Closing her eyes she jumped. Lurch! They both went sprawling over the edge and into the icy drink below.

Hamish's voice broke through the freezing water as he screamed in pain at the cold. He splashed and flailed and pushed Ondine further under. Daggers of ice stabbed Ondine as the water rose over her head. She screamed. Nothing but bubbles came out.

The current dragged them towards the next waterfall. She

hadn't given a thought to how far it would drop. Desperate for air, she fought against Hamish to get to the surface. Wet clothes and shoes dragged her down. If she didn't get air she'd drown.

But if they went over the waterfall they'd die.

On a determined push, she broke through the surface and gasped for breath.

"I cannae swim!" Hamish cried out.

"Mercury's w –" Ondine almost said as he pushed her under again. He wasn't trying to drown her, not on purpose. He couldn't be. But in his panic he couldn't know what he was doing.

Churning water lay ahead of them. The edge of the water-fall, which landed who knew how far down. Strength failing her, she tried to push Hamish towards the bank. His clothes weighed him down. He flailed. She flailed and they both went under again.

The current took them over the rocks into freefall.

CHAPTER 18

Screaming, they slipped over the edge. No longer submerged in freezing water but in freefall. Any second now they'd crash onto the rocks below. Closing her eyes hard, Ondine clung to Hamish. She tried to say 'sorry', but the air stole her breath.

The wind blew furiously around them, turning her body to ice. She'd had her eyes closed for so long now, surely they'd hit the bottom soon? Daring to open one eye, she gasped in shock as their world turned blue and green and swirled with magic.

"Hamish, we're OK!" She cried out. They were in a bubble of enchantment holding them steady, floating above the waterfall and, most importantly, alive.

Not warm, though. But at least they weren't drowning any more, or tumbling down a waterfall. The magic bubble holding them wobbled through the air and brought them down towards the snowy lawns. Gasping and shivering, Ondine looked through the skin of the bubble to see Mrs Howser, her arm raised up, glowing magic dust streaming from her hand as she guided them in their bubble of safety to the icy ground, depositing them with a wet 'splud'.

"Thank you Birgit, we'll take it from here," Old Col said, her face grey like thunder as she and Ma bustled over.

Shivering, wet and miserable, Ondine tried to comfort Hamish. "I'm so sorry, darling, I just wanted to get us away."

All Hamish did was chatter his teeth.

"That's enough Ondine," Old Col said as she sat down beside her.

At which point, the hazmat people were back. They grabbed Hamish from under the armpits and hauled him to his feet. Mute and exhausted from shock and despair, she could only watch them drag Hamish away. Away from the convention. Away from her family.

Away from her arms.

Nothing worked in her body any more. Neither bones nor muscles held as a guttural cry rang from her. Pain consumed everything. They'd taken Hamish away, and all because of her love for him.

NUMB WITH HEARTACHE, Ondine shivered in front of the little fire in her bedroom hearth, feeding it bite-sized chunks of wood and watching said wood burn down over the hour to nothing but glowing coals.

It was dark outside; it could be dark forever for all she cared. No sunlight could pierce her miserable soul. Her ankle throbbed in pain. She must have sprained it as she tumbled off the draw-bridge, but in the craziness she hadn't noticed at the time. The logs on the fire crackled, spitting sap from the wood. The flames, smoke and embers lulled her into nothingness as she sat there, knees tucked under her chin, arms wrapped around her legs.

The slow, hypnotic effect of the fire made her eyelids close. A second later, her body shuddered awake, gasping for air. Weird buzzing moved through her; mild electrical shocks that made her tremble and shake. Like the time Cybelle dared her to hold a light globe in one hand and press a nine-volt battery to her tongue.

Orange and yellow flames danced before her eyes. The next moment she fell asleep, her body fizzed all over, then jolted awake. Doze, fizzle, jolt, wake. The cycle kept going; Ondine had neither motivation to properly go to bed, nor willpower to keep her eyelids apart. Over and over again her body cycled through the weird sensations, sleep, buzz, jolt, wake up!

Saturn's rings, she was losing her mind.

Her warm bed waited for her only a few steps away, but as much as she wanted to crawl into it, her body stayed exactly where it was. At least she wasn't sharing a room with Cybelle. She could be properly miserable in private tonight.

More wood burned down to glowing coals. More time passed. All the while her heart ached to a familiar refrain.

Oh Hamish! I miss you so much!

Deep, wracking sobs broke through. All those platitudes she's heard over the years, about time healing wounds, did her no good at all. This pain was so fresh and raw.

And time took so darn long to come around.

She missed him so much, she imagined his hand on her back, rubbing slow circles and making everything all right.

"I'm sorry lass, I shoudnae come, but I hadtae see ye."

It had to be her mind playing tricks. Hardly daring to breathe lest she break the moment, she turned her head.

And felt her heart freshly breaking when she realised the only company she had was her overworked imagination and grief.

WHEN ONDINE WOKE, stark reality stabbed her heart. Cold ash sat in the hearth where the fire had burned last night. At some point she'd crawled into bed but she didn't remember. She still wore last night's clothes. Her bedroom door yawned open as everyday household noises carried up the stairs and down the hall. Regular noises from people going about their everyday normal routine.

As if this were any normal day.

As if the planets hadn't stopped spinning yesterday when they took Hamish away from her.

A twinge of soreness kicked her ears and throat. A vague headache caught her between the eyebrows. When she swallowed, it felt like sandpaper rubbing her throat. Her nose didn't work. Sure signs a cold had set in. Normally she'd chew on olive leaves to fight it off but today she didn't care. Let the virus do its best to make her miserable.

"Ondine, are you up yet?" Ma's voice carried down the hall.

"Nope."

Ma's head poked around the corner, a strained smile on her face. "I need your help in the kitchen, love, can you come down in a minute?"

"No."

"Right then. It's not really a request. I need you downstairs because we need a hand."

"I'm sick." She pulled the covers over her head.

Her mother's soothing tones disappeared as she switched to cold steel mode. "Stop moping and get up now."

Ondine barked from under the blankets, "No!"

Rip! Ma tore the covers away and exposed Ondine, "I know you're upset, but life goes on. Now get downstairs and get to work!"

This time she screamed, "I said no!" It killed her throat to do it too.

Ma's voice dropped low and deadly. "I gave you time off work last night because I felt sorry for you. And you repay that with rudeness? Now get downstairs and get to work!"

CRUMPLED CLOTHES, crumpled hair, crumpled heart. Ondine didn't bother with any kind of morning routine as she shlubbed down the stairs.

"If you fall and break your legs, I'll make you work in crutches," Ma said.

Did she have to be so brutal?

"Time's against us." Ma grabbed a napkin, dabbed it against her tongue and wiped the sleep from Ondine's eyes. "Take table four's order, there's a good girl."

"Don't we do buffet breakfasts?"

"Yes, love, we do. But it's lunchtime now. Table four, off you go, there's a good girl."

It was lunchtime already? Wow, she really had slept in. Ondine poked her head around the corner to see how many people were sitting at table four. Just the one. But it was the one person Ondine never wanted to see again in her life.

Urgh, what's she doing here? One look at Mrs. Howser seated in the dining room and Ondine wanted to run back upstairs and never come down again.

"Mrs. Howser is being an absolute delight and giving everyone a reading," Ma said in a too-bright tone.

Ondine kept her voice low. "But she's mental."

Ma shook her head and annoyed Ondine with a sage cliché. "While our friends watch out for us, we watch out for our enemies." [1]

---

1. The Brugelish translation of the classic line: "Keep your friends close, but

Everyone else is allowed to swan about and have a wonderful life. But not me, no, I get my heart ripped out because of what that witch did to Hamish and I have to keep working. And they expect me to carry on as normal!

"Out you go, there's a girl."

Did her mother have to be so . . . annoying? Of all the people in Brugel, why had they let Mrs. Howser into their dining room?

"Can't we ban her or something?" Ondine asked.

"Only if she gets drunk or rowdy. And she did save your freezing soul yesterday. We should at least be grateful for that. But don't let Auntie Col hear me say that. Out of all the witches at the convention that could have saved you, it had to be Howser."

With a soft push in the back, Ondine felt her legs bringing her closer and closer to her nemesis. Old Col must have put her feet under some kind of spell, because no way would she voluntarily go anywhere near Mrs. Howser.

Before she could run back to the safety of the kitchen, she'd reached Howser's table. Pen and pad in hand, she poised, ready to take her order.

"Sit down, Ondine dear, we need to talk," Mrs. Howser said. "I see you've recovered since your slip in the river."

It wasn't a slip, she'd jumped.

"Uh . . . I can't really fraternise with the . . . I mean, we're really busy."

"Yes. I can see that. Not." Mrs. Howser waved her hand at all the empty tables nearby. With her foot, she pushed the opposite chair out. "Now sit down and let's talk like civilised people."

Ondine pulled the chair out a little further and sat.

---

your enemies closer". A good half hour of Google searching will show this quote is usually misattributed to Sun Tzu or Niccolò Machiavelli, yet the first record of it is from Michael Corleone in *The Godfather Pt II*, (1974).

Mrs Howser raised a brow. "You think I'm going to lay a curse on you?"

Staying out of arm's reach, just in case.

"You are a smart girl. Smart enough to work out who has the real power here. Smart enough to know you want more from this life than working non-stop for a family that doesn't appreciate you."

If Ondine had been the kind of girl to keep a diary, she could have accused Mrs. Howser of reading it.

"Oh Ondine, what are we going to do with you?" At which point, Mrs. Howser made one of those smiles that made her muscles crack.

"I'm fine, thanks," she lied. Conflicting emotions fought for dominance. The woman could not be trusted, yet she'd saved Ondine and Hamish from a watery grave.

"I am sorry about what's happening, dear," Mrs Howser said. "It doesn't need to be this way, of course. If only people would be more understanding, none of this need happen."

Why did she have to sound so *reasonable*?

"You are loyal to a fault," she continued when Ondine said nothing in reply. "As you should be. Family comes first, and all that. But at some point in your life, all the sacrifices you're making have to be worth something, don't they?"

"I'm . . ." *Rummage, rummage. Nope, still nothing.* "I'm fine, really."

"And yet, you're staying at the table. You're hearing me out. Is it so you can run back to your great-aunt and tell her everything I've said?"

"Course not." *Yes, actually.* "Ah, do you mind if I ask why you're here? Of all places?"

"I wanted to check on your welfare. And a woman has to eat. Your chef! He's magic, that one."

Speaking of eating . . .

"You're wondering where Melody is, aren't you?"

The witch was good!

"She's resting. Coven Con quite wore her out, the poor love."

"She looked exhausted," Ondine said.

"Looks can be deceiving, dear one. Magic is tiring, but I'm not making her do anything she doesn't already want to do. Nobody's magic is powerful enough to override free will."

"Then what happened to Vincent the day before last?" Because he sure seemed to be out of his mind and had no connection with free will.

Mrs. Howser didn't even blink. In her calming, sing-song voice, she explained, "He was merely giving his deepest wishes free reign. If he looked concerned, it was only because he surprised himself by how powerful his deepest wishes truly were."

It all sounded so . . . reasonable. That word again. It kept popping into Ondine's head. Had Mrs. Howser leaned forward and touched her hand or something? No. Had she put another spell on her? Not that either. Ondine shook her head, trying to make sense of it all. If she stayed here talking too long, she'd end up falling under this trance of complete *reasonableness*.

Disloyal thoughts set seed. Her great-aunt's magic wasn't really up to snuff, and her family had ripped Hamish away from her. Maybe Mrs. Howser could teach her some useful magic so that she and Hamish could be together again. "So um, now that you're here, um, what can we get you?" Ondine picked up her pen and paper.

"Why don't you surprise me? Bring me out a little of every-thing. I'm in a sampling kind of mood." It didn't seem possible, but the old witch's eyes tinkled with lightness and merriment. As if nothing untoward were going on at all.

"The soup is good," she managed.

"Yes, I'll have that, with the canapé floaters. And the prawn and avocado salad. And the filet mignon, rare as rare can be. That should make a good starter."

"Thanks, I'll get this back to Chef." Ondine rose from her seat.

Mrs. Howser leaned forward a little. "Is this really what you want to do with the rest of your life?"

For a morbidly curious moment, Ondine wondered if Mrs. Howser might make some kind of offer. Perhaps magic training. Real magic. Perhaps a way to bring her and Hamish together again. Because the only thought that filled her head and made any sense at all at the moment was Hamish.

Would it be disloyal to ask Mrs. Howser what she had in mind? It didn't mean she was taking sides, or turning her back on her family. Did it?

"I don't know," Ondine eventually answered with complete honesty. "All I want is Hamish." The moment his name left her lips, heat burned behind her eyes and she had to get back to the kitchen before she blubbered like a lost lamb.

In the kitchen the tears sprang free. Wordlessly, she handed Mrs. Howser's order to Chef before retreating to a corner to blow her nose. The radio was on, as it often was. Through the fog of her brain she registered that Venzelemma International Airport was closed because of too much snow. It made no sense to Ondine, because it snowed every winter and it didn't look or feel any worse than usual.

The news item finished with the words:

"Authorities are refusing to confirm or deny the closure is related to the spread of a virus that has spread from Brugel to neighbouring Slaegal."

A hand tapped on her shoulder, startling her. Chef's voice said, "I made your favourite pudding."

She turned to see him offering an espresso cup filled with

chocolate mousse. "Donwannit," she sniffed. Silently, like an ungrateful child ready to strike with a serpent's sting, she started to think she didn't want anything to do with her family any more.

"I'm really sorry about everything," Cybelle said, moving in for a hug.

Ondine shrugged off her sister's advance. Her wrist caught on a nearby tray, sending it, and the tea set that had been on it, flying. A spectacular noise filled the kitchen.

"Look what you've made me do!" Ondine yelled. Tears spritzed all over the place and she couldn't hold them back.

"Calm down all." Da stuck his head in the kitchen. "They can hear you out front."

"Don't care." Ondine snivelled. Anyway, it was only Mrs. Howser out there, so what did it matter if she overheard?

"Fine. You've made your point." Ma's hands balled into fists and rested on her hips. "Ondine go back to your room and sulk. It's all you're good for."

It was the first sensible thing anyone had said all day.

CHAPTER 19

Ondine couldn't get to her room soon enough. Resentment frothed and boiled inside her as she mentally listed the horrible things her family had done to her. Not just recently, but ever. In the past she'd never questioned working for her family, but she hated it now.

Her parents had grounded her the moment she'd got home from the late Duke's Autumn Palace.

Then they'd made a pantomime of forgetting her Name Day.

But the absolute worst punishment they'd exacted was in ripping Hamish away.

She could never forgive them for that.

Every bone ached as she flung herself on the mattress. To her continued dismay – and despite her most fervent wish – Hamish did not appear out of thin air. For the next half hour she failed spectacularly to go to sleep. The radio offered no company, it kept reminding people of poor traffic conditions, bad snow, closed airports and pleas for people to not visit overcrowded hospitals except for medical emergencies. Frustrated, she picked up the book on her bedside table. The one Hamish had given her on her name day.

Everything reminded her of Hamish.

As she read about the tribulations of Brugel's first Grand Duchess, Elmaree, fat tears sploshed her cheeks. Just like Ondine, Elmaree's heart was set for the shredder.

When Ondine reached the part about Elmaree having to marry the war-mongering Prince Faddei of Slaegal, it became all too real and raw.

Poor Elmaree. Such huge responsibilities at such a young age. Trying to get elder statesmen to take her seriously, while they patted her on the head and told her to be a good girl. Ondine saw plenty of herself in the headstrong Grand Duchess, as Elmaree made her horrible choice: Give up her country or give up the man she loved.

THEY STAND THERE, that wall of wickedness dressed in human flesh, watching me lift the quill to sign my life away. The oleaginous diplomats. The serpentine maids-in-waiting. Willing me to give my country and my lifeblood to them for the price of a line of ink on parchment.

Oh cruel fate that has cast me into such depths! What is this thing they call free will, when the only choice I have is whether to lose my heart or lose my country?

For I cannot have both.

Does it make me a terrible person to put my heart first? I am so afraid I do not think a true decision is possible. Why, if we have a heart, are we not free to bestow it to our person of choosing? Why did the maker give us such feelings if we were not meant to use them?

They are staring at me, waiting for me. I dip the quill deeply into the blue ink and lift it, watching the thick drops fall from the nib. The drops remind me of blood. Royal blood that will be spilled no matter how events from this moment unfold.

Follow my heart, I will lose Brugel.

Follow my head, I will lose the only man I will ever love.

I cannot give myself to Faddei. The suitor whose knuckles are caked in blood from dragging them on the cobblestones!

He terrifies me. He towers over me. He ignores me.

He could snap me like a twig.

The decision comes to me, like clear running water washing all away. Clarity of reason says Faddei will destroy Brugel whether we are married or not. If I refuse to sign, he will declare war. If we marry, he will dispose of me and consume my country.

They are holding their breaths, waiting for me to sign. My face gives nothing away as I lower the quill into the ink once again. My heart is racing as never before. I look to Faddei and execute the only weapon in my arsenal before all is surely lost.

That weapon is defiance.

I snap the quill. Dark blue ink spreads over my hand and blots the paper.

The room is in uproar. Everyone is shouting, questioning, crying, gasping.

All except Faddei, who looks at me with his face of stone. He must have known I would refuse. As if he were waiting for it. He will lasso the moon and use it to crush the house of Brugel, of that I am certain. But the act is done. I cannot take it back.

My actions may spell death for everyone in this room and yet it is the only choice I had.

We are all doomed.

And yet.

Somewhere, amongst this noise and mayhem, my heart sings.

. . .

THE STORY ABSORBED and frustrated Ondine. She wanted to tell Elmaree to stop being so scared all the time, that things would work out. But then she had to admit maybe she was telling herself that. Every time she came to a scene where Elmaree and her secret lover stole time together, she couldn't help seeing the characters as herself and Hamish.

It made her ache for him all the more.

Another thing she noticed was Elmaree's ink-stained hand. It was only a coincidence that Vincent's hand bore a similar splash of colour. All the same, she couldn't help thinking they'd inadvertently done Vincent some kind of favour by linking him back to Elmaree.

Eight dirty tissues later, she had to stop reading. It was too upsetting and far too real.

SOME TIME in the night she woke up, her mind racing. As the fuzzy half-world of dreams evaporated, so did her hopes. Hamish was not coming back.

A fresh wave of resentment roared through her like a big roary thing that wouldn't stop roaring. [1] Somewhere inside, Ondine knew it was wrong to entertain ideas of ditching her family in favour of siding with Mrs. Howser. The trouble was, everything Mrs. Howser had told her made a strange kind of sense. Whereas her family made no sense at all. All they did was punish her.

What had Aunt Col said? Only the witch that laid a curse could remove it.

Therefore, Mrs. Howser had to be the one to remove the

---

1. Lions are not native to Brugel, so Ondine has nothing with which to compare the noises in her head.

mutating magic from Hamish. But why would she want to remove it, when it was working so well for her? A little more instability in the country and both Anathea and Vincent would be begging her for help. Everything was playing perfectly into Mrs. Howser's hands.

A new idea shone through. Maybe if Ondine sided with Mrs. Howser, she might gain the old witch's trust. Then she would remove her spell from Hamish and they could be free.

Trouble was, Ondine couldn't think of a single reason why Mrs. Howser would want to do this.

Self-loathing settled in her heart. She shouldn't be thinking of abandoning her family, but if her family had been nicer to her, she wouldn't need to be thinking about joining Mrs. Howser, would she?

So really, it was their fault, not hers.

The pub, so busy from dawn to dusk, lay eerily silent at this time of . . . whoa, her bedside clock said two forty-three in the morning. No wind howled outside, the only noise she heard came from a goods train down the line.

And a weird squeak.

At first, she thought it might be a tree branch rubbing against her window. But with no wind, the branch wouldn't be moving itself.

Then a heavy thump and a creak of wood.

From above.

This is the top floor. Why does it sound like someone is on the roof?

Because someone *was* on the roof. There had to be. The more she listened, the more certain Ondine became that somebody – or maybe two somebodies – were on the roof.

Pushing the covers back as quietly as she dared, Ondine stepped out of bed. Her feet froze on the floor, which made her wonder how anyone could survive the arctic conditions outside.

Grabbing a dressing gown, she ran to her sister's room. "Belle?" Ondine nudged her in the shoulder.

No response, just the steady snorfle of a heavy sleeper.

She walked out to the hall, towards the sound of a rattling tractor. She snuck her head in her parents' room. There was Da, squished right over to the side, while Ma lay like a starfish, hogging the whole bed. Snoring just like Cybelle.

"Ma, wake up." Ma snored even louder. Ondine nudged her shoulder again but got nothing. Her mother was out for the count.

She crept around to the other side and pulled out one of her dad's earplugs. "Da, wake up. Something's on the roof."

"Hmm," he said, sticking his finger into his ear to block his wife's snoring.

"No, seriously, you've got to have a look. Please."

Nothing. Not even holding his eyelid open could rouse him. No trace of alcohol on his breath either, so he couldn't have been at the plütz. Should she activate the smoke detectors? That would make too much noise and alert whoever was on the roof that they were on to them. In any case, they might have guests staying the night and they needed their sleep. Maybe Chef could help, but it didn't feel right waking him up because he worked such insane hours. She'd have to try Belle again.

It was a tough gig trying to run and stay deathly quiet so that she didn't alert the people on the roof, but she did a pretty good job and raced back to the room she shared with Cybelle.

By this stage, Belle had rolled on to her back and put her mother's snoring to shame. Cold aches tugged Ondine's heart. If only Hamish were here! He'd know what to do. At the very least, he'd be able to scarper up the drainpipe to see what was occurring on the roof.

Then a new thought struck. Maybe the noise *was* Hamish;

maybe he'd come back to her after all. Maybe he couldn't find a way to sneak in? Yes, that had to be it. It had to be him.

It *must* be him.

She charged out to the garden, her feet becoming lumps of ice as she skidded to the shed to grab the ladder. The ladder was so heavy it nearly ripped the sockets out of her shoulders. But what did she care for discomfort when Hamish needed her?

"I'm coming Hamish," she said as she pulled the ladder back up the flights of stairs and dragged it through her parents' room to their small balcony.

If she'd been thinking straight, she would have wondered why the sound of someone dragging a ladder up the stairs and out to the balcony hadn't roused her parents. In fact, she hadn't roused *anyone*.

Alas, she was beyond thinking straight when it came to Hamish.

The old wooden ladder made a heavy clonk as she hooked the extension clips onto the top of the building. She couldn't feel her feet or her hands as she climbed the steps.

Her poor darling Hamish was up here, possibly freezing to death. A few more steps and she reached the last row of bricks that formed the parapet.

She peered over the top.

Instead of gazing into the eyes of her beloved, she found herself staring at Mrs. Howser.

"Looking for your boyfriend?" she said.

CHAPTER 20

In her entire life, Ondine had never felt so cold as she held on to the ladder, staring at the old witch. Any thoughts of defecting to 'the other side' cracked like ice as the most horrible fear made her stomach churn. "W-what are you doing on our roof?" In the chill, she had to fight her jaw to get the words out properly.

"Taking back what's ours," Mrs. Howser said. She at least had come prepared for the cold night, wearing a fur-lined coat with matching hat. [1]

"Here it is!" Ondine heard another voice say. A male voice. She could have sworn it sounded just like –

Lord Vincent.

He'd come prepared for the elements, with heavy shoes and a thick fur-lined long-coat. Saturn's rings! Mrs. Howser must have got to him. He didn't look out-of-it like the last time she'd seen him.

The confident expression he wore told Ondine he knew exactly what he was doing, which was even more frightening.

---

1. With extra thick fur on the earflaps.

The two of them had to be hatching some kind of plan against Anathea. Although what it had to do with the pub roof was completely beyond her.

Lord Vincent climbed down from the top of the chimney with a large shoebox in his arms.

Their stares locked.

"It's all perfectly above board. My grandfather hid them here for safekeeping. He used to frequent the pub in the old days."

"They're stolen." Ondine said.

"You can't prove that. Now, get out of my way!"

Mrs. Howser's claw-like hands dug into Ondine's shoulders to pull her up.

Desperate to get away. Ondine gripped the sides of the ladder and lifted her feet away from the rungs. She slid all the way down to the balcony below. Screaming non-stop.

Thump! She landed on the balcony in a smacking rush, knocking the wind out of her. Surely her caterwauling would wake everyone? Hobbling to a standing position, she looked up to see Mrs. Howser climbing down the ladder towards her.

Head first like a spider crawling down her web to her prey.

Sick with fear, Ondine ran into her parents' room, slammed the door and locked it. Her parents didn't budge.

"Wake up!" she screamed.

Nothing.

"Sorry Da." She pulled the covers back, rolled his flannel pyjama top to expose his rounded belly to the early morning air . . .

And stabbed her frozen left foot on his warm skin.

"Aaaarrrrrggghhh!" Da screamed himself upright.

"Mrs. Howser's on the roof with Lord Vincent and they're stealing something." She looked through the glass door to the balcony. Bold as you like, Mrs. Howser stood there, one eyebrow raised.

Da rubbed his eyes. "She'll catch her death of cold out there." He rose from the bed to open the door and let her in.

"No Da!" Ondine pulled him back. "You have to call the police! She and Vincent were up there and they've taken something from inside the chimney."

Da tried to get up but lost his balance and fell back into bed.

He closed his eyes and drifted back to sleep.

"See you later." Mrs. Howser gave a finger wave from outside, then, with a swoosh of her hand, she created a slide made from ice which she and Vincent glided down.

"Fine, I'll call the plods." Ondine left her dazed father and snoring mother where they lay and ran to the kitchen.

When she picked up the phone, she heard Mrs. Howser on the other end. "Don't worry dear; your telephone will be working again soon. No need to make a fuss, we're merely taking back what's ours. Now go back to bed and forget everything you saw tonight. I do wish you'd had some tea, then I could have spared you the trouble."

Tea? A quick look at the drying racks by the sink showed a dozen washed teapots, all resting upside down. The witch must have read everyone's leaves and added something to the drink.

Well I'll be! Throwing a fit of the sulks helped me dodge a bullet.

If she could just work out what Mrs. Howser meant by 'Taking back what's ours,' she'd have the whole thing figured out. Taking back what? The small glance she'd had of Vincent only showed he had some kind of box. He'd said his grandfather had left it for safekeeping. Which didn't surprise Ondine, because they kept money in a safe under the kitchen floorboards, on account of Brugel's banking system being so unreliable.

But why had a Duke needed to use the roof of a pub to keep things safe?

Unless it was Vincent's *other* grandfather, on his crazy mother's side? That could make more sense.

Think, girl, think!

But all her selfish brain could come up with, as she stood there on the kitchen tiles, stomping her feet in a futile attempt to get the circulation going, was, *Why does all this craziness keep happening to me?*

Which was, by a circuitous route, exactly the kind of thought she needed to have. Because strange things *did* keep happening to her and she refused to believe they were the result of coincidence. It simply could not be coincidence that everything bad in her life had happened after she ran away to home, from Psychic Summercamp, all those months ago.

She made a hot chocolate to warm her from the inside and help her think. Chocolate made everything better. She also filled a soup pot with warm water and placed it on the floor, then stood in it. The heat flayed her skin and prickled her nerves. Slowly – painfully slowly – she wiggled her toes. The next sip of chocolate reminded her of Draguta Matice, the rail-thin laundry master from the Autumn Palace. Which reminded her of Draguta's teddy bear stuffed with trinkets. Then her mind tripped her back to the box of jewels they'd found under the dining room floorboards way back in summer. The same box Lord Vincent had tried to steal.

Mrs. Howser had said she was taking back what was hers. No, not hers, 'ours'.

Thoughts churned like cream into butter, until, to Ondine's utter surprise, one thought became more solid.

Mrs. Howser.

She was helping Vincent. Or using him. It didn't matter which; it only mattered that every event kept coming back to her. Mrs. Howser had to be in on everything.

Even the times when it seemed like Vincent was acting on his own, he had to have had help, and that help had to have come from Mrs. Howser.

Nothing else made sense.

The more Ondine thought about it, the more she became convinced Mrs. Howser and Vincent had been (or maybe still were) using the deGroot family pub as a personal bank. That had to be why they kept coming here.

Every visit one of them had made would have coincided with some kind of jewellery or cash deposit, secreted somewhere about their pub.

The private banking details she and Hamish had found in Duchess Kerala's private rooms in the Autumn Palace immediately came to mind. But now that Ondine thought about it, the banking couldn't have been for Kerala's future; but for Vincent's.

Meanwhile, the present Duchess, Anathea, had to save her pennies and use Ondine and Hamish as her private – and unpaid – public relations company because the royal family was broke. Well, they weren't really broke, it was simply that Kerala, Vincent and Mrs. Howser had siphoned so much away, there was nothing left.

Mrs. Howser had come to Margi and Thomas's engagement party, back in summer, but she'd retired early. At the time Ondine hadn't paid much attention to that fact, but she'd bet her next hot meal Mrs. Howser must have been snooping around for jewellery and other goodies while everyone else was distracted.

Great Pluto's Ghost, I have to tell everyone, right now!

Slap, slap, slide. Her wet feet splashed on the floorboards as she raced down the hall, all the while wondering what Mrs. Howser had been looking for – more jewels? Probably. Cash? It must have been in the chimney for decades because her parents had never mentioned it. They probably never knew anything about it.

She took the stairs two at a time and charged back to her parents' room, where they were both snoring.

"Get up! Mrs. Howser's drugged you!"

Nothing.

"The money!" she yelled, ripping the covers off their bed and exposing them to the cold night air. Ma and Da flinched and wailed and, yes, yes! Eventually they came round! "Mrs. Howser and Vincent have the money. It's why Anathea is broke, and it's why they kept coming here, why things kept happening to us. Because they used this building for all their stolen jewels and cash!"

"Coffee," Da groaned.

Ma reached for the duvet to pull it back over her, but Ondine ripped it away.

"The old coot drugged the tea so she could burgle us. She and Vincent were on the roof."

THREE BLISTERING cups of wake-up-juice later, Ondine's parents were finally catching on to the enormity of the situation as they sat in the kitchen.

"It all makes sense," Ma said. "Ondine I'm so sorry. We should have seen this coming. Howser must have planned it for so long. I was ever so grateful that she had a spot for you at Summercamp. But it seems . . ."

They all took a sip from their respective cups. Now was not the time for Ondine to admit she'd entertained thoughts of joining Mrs. Howser. Thank goodness she hadn't!

" . . . She set us up from the start." Ondine rubbed her

temple. "On the plus side, maybe now you'll believe me when I say I'm not psychic?"

"There is that," Ma said.

A quiet 'hooray' sounded in the back of her mind, but she'd celebrate this personal victory later, when things weren't so crazy. At this point, her parents believed her. That would have to be enough for now. "Mrs. Howser and Vincent must be panicking that Anathea is becoming too popular. We need Aunt Col. And we'll have to tell Duchess Anathea because she needs to know what's going on."

"You sound like a field marshal," Ma said.

Ondine beamed at the compliment, and then acknowledged that the coffee had made her more talkative than usual.

"I'm calling the police," Da said.

"If the phone's working." Ondine remembered what happened earlier.

"Hooray for small mercies, I have a dial tone." Da put the receiver to his ear.

"Ma? Once we get through all this, maybe we can find a way to help Hamish?"

A patronising smile crossed Ma's face and she patted Ondine on the head. "Dear girl. I know you miss him, but in time you will move on."

Ondine slapped her mother's hand away. "Don't say that!" Heartache burned afresh. "I love Hamish with all my heart."

"But you're so young."

"You're one to talk! You were already married by my age!

Tense silence filled the room as they stared at each other in mute shock. She could hear her father's voice as he spoke to the police, reporting the thieves on the roof who stole a deposit box from the chimney.

Finally Ma said, "I'm sorry love. I was about to say, 'Things were different then,' but that would have set you right off."

Ondine muttered, "Got that right."

Ma moved in for a hug and Ondine gladly accepted it. It was a warm, squishy, rocking-back-and-forth hug offering comfort and a big dollop of nostalgia. How many times had her mother cuddled and rocked her as a baby, as a little girl, as a big girl? Even now she still needed hugs to make everything right again.

"Thanks Ma. Your hugs are better than magic."

Ma sniffed and kissed the top of her head. "Thank you, love."

The hug chased away just about everything bad that had ever happened, if only for a moment. "Magic's stupid. Hugs are better."

Ma kissed the top of her head again as Da finished his phone call.

"The police will be here in a few hours, so we can make our statements. It might save time if we write them down beforehand." He looked at his watch. "Maybe we should try and get some sleep before breakfast?"

"I'm wide awake," Ondine said.

A few minutes later, Chef and Cybelle walked in with drag-along shopping trolleys in preparation for heading to the markets.

Cybelle said, "You're up early. What's going on?"

"We had a break-in during the night," Da said. He relayed the events of the past hours.

"You can't let the cops in!" Cybelle looked to Henrik with panic in her eyes. "They'll find the keyboard covers."

"Then you'd better shove them somewhere the police won't see them," Da said.

Ondine buried her face in her hands. This was going to be the longest day ever.

CHAPTER 21

It would have been much easier on everyone if the police had come the next morning. Or even the day after that. To Ondine's continuing frustration, they took three days to arrive, turning up in the midst of lunch service, which threw the family into panic.

Not Ondine, of course, who in her misery of missing Hamish, nothing much panicked her. Nothing cheered her up either, but as she had to pull herself together and get on with it, she did just that.

Henrik and Cybelle had moved the rolls of cling film into the kitchen, hidden in plain sight. Ondine and Da took the police to the surprisingly-spacious-now-the-wedding-was-over private room out the back for the statements.

"You saw what they stole?" one of the officers asked.

The answers had to be to the point. No "I'm not sures" or "I think sos" allowed.

"Correct," she said. "I saw Vincent taking a box from inside the chimney. A small chest, a bit bigger than the size of a shoe box. I'm positive it's full of money from his mother Kerala's secret stash. She was hiding money from the Late Duke, you know. How's the investigation going into that by the way?"

"Er, we're not involved in that," the officer said as he looked to his partner for backup.

More note taking from the officers before one of them asked, "This box was a shoe box?"

"About that size, yes."

"For sandals or boots?"

Boggling, Ondine tried not to show contempt for the question. "Probably a box big enough for boots, because it took Vincent two hands to carry it."

"So you're telling me Lord Vincent, the heir to the Duchy of Brugel, is stealing boots?"

Her eyes rolled all on their own. "No. He stole something that could fit in a box that would be large enough for boots."

"So you don't actually know what was in the box in the first place?"

Deflated. "I don't have x-ray vision. But why else would you go to all that trouble to steal a box from a chimney, in the middle of the night, in the middle of winter?"

The police officer looked at her and shrugged. "Unless you can tell us what was in the box, we don't really have much to go on."

There was no point learning the officers' names because Ondine had the sinking feeling she would never see them again. Their attitude didn't match the importance of the crime. Squashing down her frustration, she said, "Officer, I saw two people: Mrs. Birgit Howser and Lord Vincent. They also saw me. So even if I'm not sure what they stole at the very least they should be charged with trespassing."

"Duly noted. Thank you for your statements. Unfortunately, we can't prioritise this case."

"Why not?" Ondine bristled.

"If you've been paying attention to the news, it's a really bad 'flu season. All units have been called in to assist in hospital waiting rooms, what with people making threats to staff. That takes a higher priority to trespassing on a roof. We'll be in touch if we have anything further."

They would so not 'be in touch', Ondine thought. Then another horrible thought landed. Police needed at hospitals? She hadn't heard anything about the 'flu ... unless it was . . . "Do you mean the mutating magic?"

"Do you know something about that?" The other officer asked.

Ondine clamped her mouth shut and shook her head.

As the afternoon wore on, things went badly wrong. Customers sent their meals back, barely touched. As the week wore on, things became dire. And not just because Ondine missed Hamish as if her heart had stopped working.

"Is everything all right?" Ondine asked as she took a diner's plate. They had shifted the food around but barely eaten a mouthful.

"Yes, it was fine, I just couldn't get through it," he said.

"I can get you something else if you'd rather?"

"No, truly, it was delicious. The serving was too big."

The rest of the customers on the table nodded.

"OK," Ondine said, taking his word for it.

Inside her head, a small light began to beam. If the customers weren't licking their plates clean, they weren't starving from using magic they might or might not know they had. This could mean the mutating magic was wearing off. Which lead her to the next step in this logic ladder – that she and Hamish could be together again.

She took the uneaten meals back to the kitchen. "They're saying they're not hungry enough."

Chef and Cybelle exchanged worried looks.

Ma bustled over and tasted an untouched portion of the food herself. "It's perfectly good."

"We know that." Hope lit a match inside Ondine. "It's a good sign, isn't it? The magic must be wearing off."

Ignoring her discovery, Cybelle picked up a fork and had a taste, also from an untouched section. Because eating something with somebody else's saliva? Eww! "It's a crying shame to send back food this good. What's wrong with them?"

Ma tasted the trout from another quarter-eaten plate. Her eyebrows clamped together and she made a soft groan. "That. Is. Divine." She had another mouthful and made little noises of pleasure.

"Of course it is. Was in the tank only an hour ago," Chef said.

Ma finished another mouthful. "Belle darling would you pop that in the fridge so I can have the rest later? At least we know there's nothing wrong with the food. Should we cut back on the bread rolls on the table? Have smaller servings?"

Cybelle and Henrik set the next order onto plates. Steam rose from the vegetables as Cybelle handed them over. "Table five is ready."

Da came in with the takings from another table. "They paid at the bar. Said they had to leave early. Didn't even leave a tip."

That really crushed the mood. Magic wearing off was one thing, but people not leaving a tip? It was downright miserable.

Ondine said, "If Hamish were here, we'd have better tips."

"Don't make me roll my eyes, dear," Ma said.

"I said table five is ready," Cybelle said.

"Oh! Sorry!" Ondine picked up a tea towel and grabbed one hot plate, balanced the second on her forearm and picked up the third in her free hand. As she walked towards table five, her heart sank.

They'd gone.

Confusion made knots in her tummy. Back in the kitchen she double-checked the order with Ma and Cybelle.

"Definitely table five. Four adults and two teenagers," Ma said.

"Not any more. They left," Ondine said. "Has anyone else ordered the same meals Belle? I could take these out to them."

"Pop them in the *bain marie* while I check."

Henrik rubbed his temple. "This is seriously weird. Did they see the police and run off or something?"

"Ma? Can I talk to you for a minute?" Ondine thought of a plausible reason and it always came back to her one true love. "This never used to happen when Hamish was here."

"Oh Ondi, we all miss him. But I doubt even Hamish could help if people don't want to eat at all."

It was worth a try. "Something is *really* wrong though. People don't leave three quarters of their lunch. And they don't leave before it even gets to the table. There's something else going on, there must be."

"We're having a bad day, that's all."

"Ma, come on. This is *beyond* bad. This is . . ." a light bulb went off in her head, "Mrs. Howser must have put a spell on us!"

Ma's shoulders slumped. "I wouldn't put it past her."

Ondine jumped in with, "Then we must get Hamish back."

"That's all you can think about, isn't it?" It was Ma's turn to roll her eyes. "Sweetheart, I know you miss him, but I think you're clutching at –"

"Ma please! We never used to have half-eaten plates when Hamish was here. And if Mrs. Howser has put a spell on us, then surely when Hamish comes back, he can help fix it."

With less to do than usual, Henrik took a moment to turn

up the volume on the TV. More traffic snarls and jammed inter-sections, and now the trains weren't running because of too much snow.

"*We get snow every winter, why is this year different to any other?*" a frustrated commuter complained to the camera.

"*Woot! I can't get to work, so it's a day off for me!*" another said, looking really happy.

"*No school tomorrow.*" A student beamed. "*Snow day, yeah!*"

"*I blame the Duchess. Too busy throwing parties to get the trains running on time.*"

Ondine put it all together. "Ma, people have been wishing for snow so they don't have to go to work?"

"That's a no-brainer darling," Ma said.

"Yes, but think about it? Hamish and I are nowhere near them, and their wishes are still coming true."

"Ye-es, I thought we'd gone over this?" Ma's brow creased.

"Yes but," Ondine had to slow her brain down so that she didn't trip over herself, "bad traffic, no trains? The magic is out there anyway and we can't stop it. Meanwhile, people don't realise they're wishing for bad things that stuff the place up. Everyone's going to blame Anathea and it's not her fault. She's going to become even less popular! Unless Hamish and I can fix it, Anathea's polls will nosedive and Vincent will take over! And he'll probably have Mrs. Howser as his closest advisor. But if Hamish and I are together, we can use Mrs. Howser's magic against her and make everything better in Brugel." Great Pluto's Ghost, she'd never felt so clever for working it all out.

"Heavens girl, I know you want to be with him but we can't have people growing tails and causing even more craziness."

"Whoa!" Chef yelped as he pulled a trout from the tank. "We've got a live one!" The fish put up a fight, slipping from his hands and flip-flopping on the kitchen bench. For a bizarre moment, the fish flexed so high it was practically standing on its tail fin.

"Well I'll be. There's a fish dancing on the table," Ma said.

Ondine cried out, "Woo hoo! Does that mean I'm not grounded anymore!"

"Don't try to take advantage of me when I'm confused," Ma said, her eyes round as she watched the flipping fish.

"But Ma! You said!" Ondine felt desperate.

"Maybe."

A "maybe" was better than a "no", but not as solid as a "yes". It gave Ondine hope.

Down the end of the kitchen, Da rolled his sleeves up and began washing dishes.

"Why aren't you at the bar, love?" Ma asked.

"They've all gone home."

Meanwhile, from the TV, everyday people complained to the reporters about how hard life was. Everyone kept shooting the blame home to Duchess Anathea.

Ondine and Ma looked at each other, then Ma said, "I think you're right, Ondi. We might need Hamish back."

Mercury's wings! She was glad to hear those words. How hard did she squeeze Ma in delight and relief? No idea, but when she let go Ma almost passed out.

"Sorry. Got a bit carried away."

Everyone turned as two new arrivals walked into the kitchen. They were tanned and glowing and happy. Everything Ondine wasn't.

"Darlings!" Ma called out at the sight of Marguerite and Thomas. She embraced them in a three-way squish.

"It's so quiet out there, I've never seen the like," Marguerite said when Ma eventually let go of her.

"You both look wonderful!" Ma gushed. "I told you the Sun

Bubble Resort would agree with you." [1]

"Mrs. Howser's put a spell on us." Ondine said.

Marguerite's eyebrows disappeared under her fringe as she turned on her mother. "You still haven't paid the Psychic Summercamp fees?"

"I'll fill you in later. It's lovely to see you." Ma gave them another hug. "I'm glad it's quiet out there, you can tell me all about your travels. I love your outfits, I love the colours on your poncho!"

"It's the latest in Sleag-Mex," Margi said.

Da walked up and embraced Margi, then gave Thomas a handshake before pulling him into a hug as well. "Welcome home, kids."

A snort escaped Ondine. Margi and Thomas were married adults, but Da would always see them as children. They should consider themselves lucky because at least they weren't the "baby".

Her parents, sister and brother-in-law vanished into the sitting room in a blur of hugs and giggles and luggage, leaving Ondine feeling empty and left out.

And irritated that she'd lost yet one more chance to ask Ma about when Hamish could come back.

---

1. A resort on the Black Sea, built inside an enormous bubble-dome, with sunlamps glowing fourteen hours a day. It's the one holiday destination where a 'sun guarantee' actually means what it says.

CHAPTER 22

The next morning, still no sign of Hamish. Where was he? Surely if her mother had said he could come back, she'd have passed on the message to wherever he was and he'd be here like a shot.

At least he should be!

He'd better *want* to be!

The rest of the family was huddled around the table in their private room behind the kitchen, passing around honeymoon photographs from the Black Sea. In each photo either Marguerite or Thomas smiled out at them. Sometimes it was both of them at a strange angle, as they'd put the camera on the edge of a banister or tree branch to get a couple-shot. [1]

The photos were so sweet. Smiling faces in every one of them. A spike of jealousy caught Ondine. Her sister had the freedom to be with the man of her choice. And she'd taken a

---

1. In some parts of the world, you can give your camera to another tourist and ask them if they wouldn't mind taking your picture. In Brugel, if you give your camera to a passer-by they will say, "thanks very much" and walk off with it.

holiday with him. Jupiter's moons! When was the last time she'd had a break? Never!

So absorbed in holding her emotions in check and making the right kind of happy noises as she looked at each photo, Ondine didn't hear Great-Aunt Col walk in.

"Margi, you're positively glowing. Marriage suits you. Oh goodie, I do so love photos; let me have a look," Old Col said.

Joy flooded Ondine's system. If Old Col was here, surely that meant . . . ?

"Hello Ondine dear, Colette's filled me in on everything."

Nodding, Ondine tried to smile at her great-aunt, but she was far too interested in who could be behind her.

"You're distracted by something." Old Col giggled as stepped closer to Ondine. "Give me a kiss dear."

Huh? Mechanically, Ondine kissed her great-auntie's cheek, but her gaze stayed locked on the door she'd walked through, her heart kicking against her ribs in anticipation.

The man of her dreams walked in, lugging an old suitcase behind him.

"Hamish!" She nudged Old Col aside to throw herself at him.

Hamish dropped the case and wrapped his arms around Ondine, holding her close. It felt beyond wonderful to be with him again. A gulping sob racked her body as she clung to him.

"Ach, dry yer eyes," he said.

Pulling back, she wiped her face with her sleeve and said, "Where have you been? I think your hair's grown. Has Col been feeding you? Are you OK? Where did Col keep you?"

"Col was doin' her best tae help with tha curse, lass. Dry yer eyes, I want tae see yer smiling face."

"Nope."

"Awww. Then cry all ye want, but ye'll have tae give me a proper kiss sooner or later."

"Gladly!" Ondine wiped her face with her sleeve again and planted a kiss on him. Within the bounds of propriety with her entire family watching.

Immediately the phone rang. Ma raced to pick it up.

"Thank you, Ondine." Margi suddenly wrapped them in a three-way hug. "I needed an album to put all these beautiful photos in!"

Confused, Ondine turned to see that the pile of photos that used to be all over the table were now lovingly arranged in display books. She scratched her head and said, "You're scrap-booking?"

"It's a legitimate craft!" Margi shot back.

Ma came bouncing back in, clapping her hands. "Twelve more for dinner tonight. Thank heavens you're back, Hamish!"

That's when Ondine noticed the clock on the wall sporting thirteen numbers. "Did anyone wish for more time in the day?"

Henrik raised his hand.

"Best we wish that one back I think," Ma said. "No knowing how far that wish might go."

Good point. Ah well, if it meant kissing Hamish again, Ondine would do it.

For Brugel!

"Get a room you two!" Belle said.

"Leave the door open," Ma said.

"Wide open!" Da said.

Henrik snorted with laughter as heat raced up Ondine's neck. Da glared at Henrik so the chef pretended it was a sneeze.

How wonderful to be back in Hamish's arms. A pile of homework beckoned once they reached Ondine's room. She'd get to it, eventually, but first she recharged her emotional batteries with a warm cuddle with Hamish by the window.

He rubbed her back as she gazed out across the street. The Asian restaurant, *On the Fang,* must have recovered from their immigration raid because people were queuing up on the footpath to get in. They had to be serving seriously good food to warrant such a wait in the snow. Not that Henrik was any slouch, his meals were incredible.

Phone ringing sounds echoed up the stairs. That had to be the result of Ma wishing they were booked out every night. This respite from frantic work might be their last in a while.

Ondine kissed Hamish and could have sworn her heart grew to twice its size. How she'd missed his warm lips, they way they melded with hers so perfectly, as if they were made for each other. The way they parted and made her sigh with pleasure. The way his tongue teased hers and made things explode in her head.

Utter, utter bliss.

Such beautiful kisses. The more she took, the more she wanted.

The more she thought about them, the more her head turned to mush and weird sensations took over. The way her head felt lighter but her body felt heavier. The excitement in the way he responded to her, safe in the knowledge they couldn't go very far with the door open.

Hamish pulled back from the kisses, making them shorter, just like his breathing. They were both smiling so much it was difficult to kiss properly. It didn't matter as Hamish held Ondine close and caressed her cheek.

"Aye, this is magic."

Placing her palm to his chest, Ondine felt his heart thumping and had to agree this moment was the most magical of her life. Plus he kept smiling at her, which turned her brain to mush and made her heart race. The soft touches against her cheek, the way he tucked a stray tendril of hair behind her ear.

"Were you all right, all this time? I was so worried about you," Ondine asked.

"Och, I havetae admit, when those folks turned up wearing radiation suits, I thought I was off tae a laboratory or such like."

His accent sounded so thick, on account of not hearing it for a so long.

"But I was at yer auntie's all this time. She was making me take potions and lotions, all so she could work out what other spells I could be under."

"Oh you poor darling!" Ondine kissed him afresh.

"What rot!" Auntie Col said as she passed the open doorway, "You slept most of the time."

Hamish pulled away and defended himself against the witch's accusation. "Aye, because ye made me intae a ferret most of the time." He resumed kissing Ondine, making up for lost time.

A warping, buzzing noise filled Ondine's body like electricity shorting out.

No, not her body. The electricity really *had* gone off.

Across the street, *Fang's* neon dragon blinked out. On the corner, the traffic lights blinked amber. A train departing from the station stopped before it reached the crossing. In the distance they heard a car screech.

"Ondi!" Ma's voice carried up the stairs. "Down here please, and bring candles."

Candles wouldn't make any difference in the middle of the day. Ondine rolled her eyes, knowing her mother was using the power outage as an excuse to call her back to work.

Old Col made a tisking noise, then said, "Just heading downstairs for a cup of tea. Can I get you anything?"

"No thanks." Less talking, more kissing. So much kissing.

"I'll ask your mother to fill me in on everything that's been going on, you carry on dear."

A little more kissing, a few more sighs. Eventually, Hamish pulled away and said, "Come awn lass, there's always work to do."

"Just a few more minutes. The lights will be back in a sec anyway."

Hamish's chuckle rippled through her as they savoured their last cuddle.

Before they had to return downstairs.

Before they had to be respectable again.

"I'm surprised the power's not back on yet," Ondine said as they took the stairs.

"There you are," Ma said. "Hamish? Put more logs on the fire. Ondi? The dishes are stacking up. Your father's off finding batteries for the radio so I've put Thomas in the bar."

To hear her mother's frantic tones you'd think it was a national emergency, instead of a regular Brugel blackout, which they'd worked through plenty of times before. "We're fine, Ma. If the power doesn't come back on we'll put the food outside in the snow. That's just as good as a refrigerator."

"It's all across Venzelemma." Da walked into the kitchen holding a small blue toy monster with a radio in its tummy. It had been one of Margi's favourite playthings and later handed down to Ondine. She remembered how she used to fall asleep listening to it, then waking in the night to a soft hiss of failed reception as the batteries died.

Ma raced over to him. "Any word on how long it will last?"

"Nothing yet."

"How are they able to broadcast if there's no power?" Ondine asked.

"Diesel generators love," Da said, turning the volume up. It made strange squeaks and crackles as he tried to fine-tune to the station's call-sign using the monster's red nose.

... EXPECTED TO LAST SEVERAL HOURS, possibly into the next day. Authorities are asking people to check on their neighbours and make sure they're all right. Temperatures are set to drop to minus twenty tonight. Hospitals and essential services are still open but residents are urged to cut back on electricity usage where possible.

"How can we cut back on electricity, we don't have any?" Cybelle asked.

Sick guilt swirled in Ondine's tummy as she felt responsible for making this happen. She'd been canoodling with Hamish so much their magic must have spread out to the street. Somebody nearby must have wished for a total blackout across the city.

"It's a better reception over here." Da walked a few steps closer to the door, "Right. They're saying there was a fire at the power plant and output is down to twenty per cent. This could go on for days. Shops are closing," he relayed.

"Shouldnae told us how long it would go fer. They'll be looting next," Hamish said. "No security. Tha police will have their hands full."

Ondine's eyes peeled wide at the thought. "It's chaos."

Old Col walked in with her empty teacup and saucer. She must have been having a quiet cuppa in the family room. The teacup was upended, from reading the leaves. "I was planning on heading home later, but I think I'll sit by the fire instead if it's all the same."

"Of course. Can't have you out in this weather," Ma said.

Not that Old Col left the kitchen. Instead she rummaged around for something to eat.

Hamish hugged Ondine. "We'll be fine. Plenty of food and wood fer the fire."

"Speaking of which," Ma interrupted and pointed her thumb to the dining room, "We have customers and there's a job for you out there."

"Aye ma'am."

Niggly, naggly worries kept Ondine standing still. They'd had plenty of power shortages before. Three or four every winter from cold snaps and ice storms. But they only ever lasted an hour or two. Never for days. This had to be deliberate. Coming so soon on top of everything else that had happened. It was too much to be a coincidence.

"It has to be Vincent!" Ondine blurted out to nobody in particular. "I bet any money he and Mrs. Howser are doing this." Mentally she prepared a whole heap of arguments to push her case.

"I think you're right," Ma said with no equivocation.

"Me too," Da said.

"Aye," Hamish said.

As one, her sisters and Henrik nodded their heads and agreed. Considering Ondine had spent the better part of her childhood not being believed or taken seriously, it was a huge moment.

Everyone stood, boggling at each other, until Hamish said, "So then, what are we gointae do about it?"

"Anybody want this last biscuit?" Old Col asked as she held the tin in her hands.

"Call the police," Ma said.

"What?" Old Col looked aghast.

The muscles in Ondine's head prepared to roll her eyes, but Da beat her to it! Her own Da rolling his eyes!

"I mean about the blackouts," Ma said, "not the biscuits. Eat as many as you like auntie."

Old Col shrugged. "Do we have any more, this tin's empty?"

"Colette love, normally I'd say 'That's a good idea' to call the police, but how do you think they're going to solve this when they can't even follow through on a basic break and enter?"

"Oh." Ma's face fell. "Do you think maybe Mrs. Howser has put a spell on the police as well?"

"Aye, filled their heads with treacle," Hamish said.

"I just had a horrible thought," Ondine said, "People are going to say the power shortages are the Duchess's fault. They already blame her for the trains not running on time."

Cybelle chimed in, "Maybe we should let the Duchess sort out her own problems. We have enough of our own."

Ma gave her middle daughter a hug. "Cybelle, under any other circumstances I'd agree with you. As much as I'd love nothing more to do with that family, we are in lock-step with them."

Cybelle didn't sound convinced. "I think you're needlessly getting yourselves involved in things that aren't our concern. If we hadn't gotten involved in the first place, none of this would have happened."

"Belle." Ondine rolled her eyes faster than her father could. "You forget that *they* came here in the first place. They started it. We were just minding our own business when Vincent came snooping around looking for that stash of jewels."

"And why was the jewellery hidden here in the first place?"

"They were using it as their private bank," Ondine explained. "That way they never had to declare anything or put it on record. And where better to hide something than in a public pub where there are always lots of people around, coming and going at all hours."

"I never knew anything about it," Ma said. "And I'm certain my parents never did either."

The pub had been in Ma's family for decades. Her parents had run it until they'd finally succumbed to the lure of the caravan and joined the greying throngs clogging up the roads around the Black Sea. [2] They'd spent many good years of retirement doing this until they had to respond to the call of the nursing home. [3]

Things stayed quiet for a while, until Ma spoke up, "If we are to have any hope of dealing with this, we're going to have to fight magic with magic. Aren't we Ondi? Now, stop slacking about everyone, we have hungry customers to feed."

Yes, of course, *get back to work everyone*, that was Ma's default position. That's when Ondine gave herself a mental slap. They were missing a vital ingredient in their 'fight back against Mrs. Howser' plan. "Hang on everyone! We're going to need Melody."

For a moment everyone stopped and gave their best 'I'm so confused' face, before Old Col declared. "Ondine is absolutely right."

It's always a nice feeling to earn a compliment, especially when it really mattered. With all eyes on her, Ondine pressed home her advantage. "You said only the witch who put the spell can remove it; they need to be her words, yeah? Well, there's no way Mrs. Howser will fix the spell she put on Hamish, not when

----

2. In some sections of neighbouring Craviç they have "caravan only" roads so that the only drivers they hold up are other caravan drivers. Their prettiest roads are reserved for cars, motorbikes and bicycles. Trucks and white vans are restricted to motorways. It's a form of motoring apartheid other countries can only dream of.
3. Otherwise known as God's waiting room.

it's all working so well for her. But Melody, she can do it for us. She's a whizz at astral projection; she can go into people's memories when they're asleep, without them even knowing and –"

"– Get her to reverse the spell in her dreams, and she won't even know she's done it!" Old Col grabbed Ondine in a hug. "My girl, you're brilliant!"

All of a sudden, things were turning in Ondine's favour.

Why did that thought scare her all the way down to her boots?

CHAPTER 23

Ondine was having an awesome dream where she met Melody in Savo Plaza and talked her around to joining their side. The dream felt so real, especially as Ondine and Melody were in their pyjamas and it was snowing something massive in the plaza. Also, Melody pleading with Ondine to, "Save me from this barking mad woman" had an air of authenticity to it.

When Ondine woke up with cold, wet hair, she knew it had been no ordinary dream and that she had in fact been outside in the snow. Melody has gone the full-astral and projected Ondine into her dreams. Or vice versa. Whichever the case, Ondine felt certain her friend needed their help.

Today, they'd get Melody back.

It was one thing to declare a plan of action and feel positive and upbeat about it. It was another matter entirely to put that plan *into* action. Especially when it involved meeting people outdoors, in the depths of winter. Ondine, Hamish and Old Col headed out, mid-afternoon (there was no way Ma would let them leave before the lunch service was over). Being winter, it was already growing dark and it wasn't yet four in the afternoon.

They hoped to find Melody at Savo Plaza, if Ondine had correctly interpreted her dream last night.

One of Ondine's gloved hands held Hamish's, the other gripped a vacuum flask filled with Chef's best soup. It was their first plan of persuasion – lure the girl away with food.

"Don't take it personally if she says 'no'," Old Col said. "Or if she's not even there."

"Ye of little faith," Hamish said.

"Faith is something I have by the bucket load," Col said, "the fact is, we don't know what kind of hold Birgit has over that poor girl. We have to tread very carefully."

With each step, Ondine's confidence shrank. "What if she's not there? What if I only dreamed I'd talked to her last night?"

"I'm confident if she can be there, she will be," Col said. "Trouble is, I'm sure Birgit Howser won't be far behind."

Arctic winds chomped at Ondine's neck as she, Hamish and Old Col shuffle-walked through snow-laden footpaths towards Savo Plaza. The low sun cast long shadows, but the streetlights were not on. It was hard to know if this was part of the blackout, or if it simply felt really dark because it was so darn cold.

"What's that?" Hamish grabbed Ondine and pulled him close.

Ondine heard something as well. Peering around the corner, they saw people furtively sticking to the shadows. Their arms were full.

Full of what?

It was hard to see clearly, what with so much snow falling, road workers had shunted the snow towards the kerb, creating snow walls that now reached shoulder height. It turned pedestrians into mice, negotiating a snowy maze. [1] It also provided

---

1. Figurative mice, not literal ones. Ondine's mutating magic isn't that far out of control. Yet.

looters with something to hide behind.

Several people wearing scarves across their faces huddled near the windows of a technology store. Some unseen command had them placing their hands on the window. Were they going to push it in? The glass wobbled and . . . melted onto the path at their feet. Glowing red, then cooling and cracking in the cold air. The looters climbed in over the windowsill and took whatever they wanted. Arms and shoulder bags bulging with stuff, they walked out the store, calm as you like.

"Mercury's wings, did you see that?" Ondine asked.

"Aye, some folks have no respect for law," Hamish said.

"I mean the way they got in. The window just melted off."

"Now you see why I had to split you up for a while. Too many people making bad wishes come true," Old Col said.

Speaking of bad wishes, they heard a whining engine and felt the ground rumble.

"Uh-oh!" leapt out of Ondine as a tank came rolling around the corner. Not a current model Brugelian Army tank either. Something tricked-out and crazy from a graphic novel.

An eruption ripped the sky apart as the tank fired a missile that sailed over their heads and broke the doors of a bank.

From the sidelines, people rushed into the now-broken bank to loot the contents.

"Some folks' wishes are way out of hand!" Hamish grabbed hers and they ran towards Savo Plaza.

They were three blocks from the fairground when a deep rumbling sound greeted them.

"Not again!" Ondine feared another tank would make an appearance.

"Relax, dear, they're power generators." Old Col said. "Back in my day, every block of flats had them."

The acrid aroma of burning diesel assaulted them as they walked closer. Luckily, this was soon overpowered by the delicious smells of melted cheese from a food van. It was using its own generator to keep the kitchens firing and the hot food coming.

Ondine shrugged and said, "If things go badly, we can console ourselves with deep fried cheeseballs."

The cheeseballs were a highlight of Martisor, a festival that kicked off in late January. The locals called it 'Fat week'. It lasted for ten days and people ate so much they could explode. [2]

Turning the corner, Savo Plaza opened out before them, but instead of glittery prettiness, they found a few stallholders trying to make a go of it and the rest of the plaza in darkness. The generators were loud and obnoxious, casting a pall over the area as they tried to keep the festival limping along. If felt damp, empty and unsafe.

No sign of Melody yet; on the plus side, no sign of Mrs. Howser either.

At least there were still some food booths operating, selling hot food dripping with cheese. [3]

Oh bliss, there was a candy silk van selling bags for a schlip each. [4] Ondine was in heaven.

A few of the same rides were here from the last time they'd visited, defying the cold weather and black-outs affecting the rest of Venzelemma.

"The key is to have a good time and act normally," Old Col said as they walked through the fairground.

Ondine nearly laughed at the suggestion. Could she remember what normal was?

---

2. The literal translation of Martisor is, "March better be here soon, I can't feel my feet any more."

3. Lactose intolerant Bruglers often migrate to Slaegal, where they are much happier.

4. Similar to cotton candy or fairy floss, this confection is made from silky strands of spun sugar, which you eat with a crochet hook.

"Sit yourselves down; I'll get us some cheesy chips," Old Col said.

A pang of guilt shot through Ondine at how wonderful her great aunt could be at times. Not long ago, Ondine had entertained the idea of defecting to Team Howser. They'd only been thoughts though; it wasn't like she'd acted on them or anything.

Hamish sat shoulder to hip with her on the bench seat to share body warmth. The moment Col returned with the steaming chips, they dived in. After two bites, Ondine could feel her arteries complaining and her stomach rejoicing. Warmth won out over good health and she had another handful, the melted cheese forming string bridges between the bowl and her mouth.

"Ondi!" Two wiry arms latched around her and hugged hard.

Ondine yelped in shock.

"Got ya!" Melody said, taking a seat beside her.

"Melody!" Ondine threw her arms around her friend, careful not to rub her cheese-oiled hands on Melody's thick woolly coat.

Considering how furry and dense the fabric was, it was a wonder Ondine could feel Melody through it at all. Part way through the hug, fear settled in. If Melody were here, could Mrs. Howser be far behind?

"I'm so glad you're here," Ondine said. "Here, I brought you some soup." She unscrewed the wide lid of the vacuum flask, which doubled as a mug, and poured out the soup. Steam rose in great clouds. "Careful, it's hot!"

Of course Melody ignored her. She was starving and freezing, and the soup was her salvation. Half her face was obscured by her enormous brown fur hat with the requisite ear flaps for this time of year.

"You'll burn your tongue!" Ondine watched her friend gulp it down.

"It's divine!" Melody held the mug out for a refill.

OK then, Ondine refilled it and took her chance. "Loads more where that came from, it's one of Chef's specials. Why don't we go back to the pub and warm up?"

Melody shook her head, downed the soup and held the cup out for thirds.

"You poor thing, you're so hungry." They'd been counting on her state of famished-ness to persuade her over to their side. "Come and have dinner with us, you can have as much as you want." Ondine attempted to place the emotional wedge. "I'm surprised Mrs. Howser didn't bring you along when she came over to our pub the other day."

"Mmmmm. Wait. What?"

"Oh, I'm sorry, I feel like I've really stepped in it," Ondine said, watching for Melody's reaction. "Weren't you invited?"

"She visited you, and she didn't take me?"

"Er, yes," Ondine said, acting crestfallen on the surface, while privately rejoicing at how well this was going. "Chef's food is always fabulous. She ate a bit of everything, especially the soup with canapé floaters."

"When was this?"

Doing her best to look like she'd put her foot in her mouth, Ondine named the date. "It was after CovenCon. Maybe you had some magic to catch up with?"

Looking deflated, Melody pushed the empty mug back to Ondine. "It's no use. I can't come with you."

Jupiter's moons, the girl was three steps ahead of them. Ondine kept trying. "But you work so hard for her, don't you want a bit of time off? When was the last time you hung out with your friends?"

"Or your parents," Old Col said.

Oh yes, parents, good point.

"She knows." Melody closed her eyes tightly and tapped the side of her head. "She sees and hears everything."

Old Col produced a super-sized bowl of cheesy chips. Melody's eyes sprang open and she grabbed four chips and shoved them in.

"Still *goat* yer appetite then?" Hamish said.

Ondine elbowed him in the ribs. Then she leaned in to Melody. "Are you here by yourself?"

Melody shook her head. "Even when I think I'm alone." Again she tapped the side of her head.

Ondine scrunched her forehead.

Reluctantly, Melody stopped shovelling food in her gob and looked about, as if Mrs. Howser was about to leap out from behind a tree. Then she grabbed the tassels of her fur-lined hood and tied the ends together, pulling them tightly.

Worry burrowed through Ondine. Melody was choosing her words carefully, trying to give them a message that she couldn't say out loud. Could Mrs. Howser hear everything they were saying? In which case, *they'd* have to choose their words with utmost care –

"Ye need tae leave the crazy witch," Hamish said.

Ondine slapped her palm to her forehead.

Melody looked at Hamish, blushed furiously and lapsed into giggles.

Did she have to react like such a girly girl just because Hamish looked at her? Hang on . . . Ondine watched as Melody reached for a napkin and began to write.

Which would ordinarily be pretty *ordinary*, except for the fact Melody didn't have a pen in her hand. Plus, she had her eyes closed the whole time and kept right on giggling as if they were having such tremendous fun.

On the napkin she wrote: *She hears everything I hear.*

Jupiter's moons!

Catching on, Ondine joined in the giggling to disguise her fear that Mrs. Howser was listening to their every word.

Then Melody wrote:

And see.

They were absolutely stumped. If they couldn't talk to Melody without Mrs. Howser knowing everything, the old witch may as well show herself now.

They needed Melody in so many ways. Breaking the bond between Melody and Mrs. Howser was the only way to weaken the witch, and therefore weaken her grip on Vincent. And it would help break the curse Hamish was living under. Oh yes, and they also had to make Anathea the fairest of them all.

It was so hard to think of the big picture when her thoughts were so full of Hamish.

"Have another chip," Hamish said.

Melody giggled, this time there was no matching expression of embarrassment on her face. Instead, she looked at Ondine and mouthed the words, "Help me."

Ondine plastered on a smile. "Of course I'll get more chips."

Mercenary thoughts crept in. Maybe they should simply kidnap Melody and wait for Mrs. Howser to try and get her back? In the meantime . . . no, Mrs. Howser would know what they were doing . . . so it wouldn't work. Also, something else tinkered at the edges of Ondine's thoughts. It would be getting really dark across the rest of Venzelemma, which meant more looters with more bad wishes could be about. They needed to get Melody home with them, and soon.

Frustration took hold. "We need to break the link between you and Mrs. H. Can you hear me you old witch? That's right. This ends now. Let Melody go –"

"– Are you out of your mind?" Old Col cried out.

"I'm sick of waiting. Melody, do you want your freedom back?"

Melody's face crumpled as if she were about to cry. Instead of speaking, she closed her eyes and nodded.

Frustration had Ondine feeling messier than the sick people staggering out of the rides.

Wait a minute. *The rides!*

"Auntie Col, if Mrs. Howser can see and hear everything Melody does, let's use the fairground rides to shake her loose."

"So much for subtle," Col threw her hands in the air.

They were in a fairground, which fairly reeked of happiness – and diesel fumes – while the rest of the city descended into chaos. This could work. "Let's go on that one," Ondine said, pointing to The Pretzel. It spun up and down and twisted back and forth. The most sickening ride in the plaza.

Hamish baulked. "*Noat* that one."

Old Col paled. "Count me out."

"You get a free pass," Ondine said to her great-auntie. Sure, her elderly relative was looking a lot healthier these days than she had been at the palechia, but there was no way she'd subject the dear old thing to The Pretzel. "Come on Melody, I dare you."

"I'll be sick!" Melody protested.

"And so will Howser." Ondine looked directly into Melody's eyes, as if they were a window to Mrs. Howser. "Do you hear me you old witch? Break it now or we'll pretzel your brain."

"Are ye sure, hen?" Hamish's complexion dropped a few shades too.

Ondine shot back, "Don't tell me you're scared?"

"Course I'm nae scared of a wee ride."

Perfect. "Stay here, Col, we'll be back soon," Ondine said, dragging them towards the ride.

To get to the pretzel ride, they had to walk past a group of patrons who'd just got off it. They looked like vomit zombies, which only made Ondine all the more determined to make her plan work. If Mrs. Howser could see and hear everything via a link with Melody, a psychic link with someone spinning round a fairground should mess her right up. This ride had pods on the end of long arms, which went up and down, side to side and could also flip back and forth. A squeeze from Hamish's hand gave Ondine reassurance.

She'd been so caught up in severing the connection between Melody and Mrs. Howser, she'd overlooked a huge flaw in her plan.

She hated spinny-sicky rides.

Because they made her so spinny and sick.

Too late to back out, the woman with the 'Carnie Crew' baseball cap ushered them into their cabin with its scratched paint in lurid colours and showed them how to fasten the five-point harness.

Five points?

Mercury's Wings, how did she ever think this was a good idea?

All the while, she plastered on a smile as the flashing lights flashed around them and the tinny music played, to show the others how fake-excited she was instead of for-real-petrified.

Just as Melody clicked her shoulder strap in, an old woman's hand reached into the cabin. "Not so fast."

Mrs Howser!

Of course the old witch would show up right now.

"You're not going on this ride," Howser yelled at Melody. Then she turned her fury on the Carnie. "Get her out of this, now."

Showing no fear of hysterical old ladies, the Carnie turned to Melody and asked, "Do you want to get out sweetheart?"

For a second Ondine feared Melody would back out and leave her and Hamish twisting like . . . pretzels.

"Er . . . no. I'm fine thanks."

"You are not!" Mrs. Howser yelled.

Luckily for Ondine, the people in the queue were getting grumpy and moaning about how much time they were wasting.

"You are coming with me!" Mrs. Howser climbed into the cabin and sat beside Melody, clawing at the harness to get it off.

Hamish wound his free hand into Ondine's and brought it to his lips. "Isn't it *loavely* that we ken make other people's wishes come true?"

A bell went off in her head. "You're so smart, have I told you that?" She knew if they shared a hug or a kiss, magic would happen – for other people. And right now, Ondine bet her next hot meal Melody would be wishing Mrs. Howser would get out of here.

Ondine leaned forward, but her harness held her back from Hamish's lips.

Mrs. Howser kept tugging at Melody's harness to get it off. "You are not doing this to me, not after all the work I've put in!"

Hamish leaned forward as far as he could. Their lips were millimetres apart.

"Got it!" Mrs. Howser cried out in victory as one of Melody's shoulder straps came free.

The ride started up. "That's against health and safety!" the carnie cried out, as she pulled the emergency shutdown lever. It sparked and smoked, but failed to stop the ride.

Mrs Howser was probably the one making it run. If Ondine could kiss Hamish, she could make the carnie's wish come true. The wish she should be having about stopping the ride. Unless the carnie was having worse wishes that Ondine didn't want to think about.

Pressing forward, Ondine tried to reach Hamish. Their lips remained frustratingly apart.

"I have tae change," Hamish said, pulling back.

The pain would be hideous, but if Hamish changed into a Shambles ferret, he could slip out of his harness. But that would mean he'd be a ferret and Ondine had become so used to him not being one. Plus, if he changed back into human and didn't do it exactly the right way inside his clothes, the ride would lose its PG-12 rating.

"Wait!" Ondine cried out as Hamish's face turned fuzzy and black.

"No!" Mrs. Howser screamed as she noticed what Hamish was up to. In a flash of light and noise, she struck Hamish with a burst of magic to stop him transforming.

"Right, out you get!" Mrs. Howser crowed with victory as she pulled Melody from her seat.

Defiantly, Melody screamed, "I will not!"

Ondine lunged; the momentum caused the harness to slip off her shoulder. Her face smacked into Hamish's almost-fuzzy chin in the least elegant, least romantic kiss on the planet.

Hamish cradled her face with his palms; fuzzy palms that were not-properly-Hamish-like. His face too was gnarled and hairy.

Not the tiniest bit lovely, the way she loved her loveable Hamish.

"It's me, Ondi, and I'll love ye till the day I die."

She looked into his face, a face dark around the edges but not completely transformed into his other persona. Hair sprouted from his eyebrows, ears and nose. She needed to love him with all her heart yet all she could think of was how ferret-like he'd become.

Perhaps, perhaps if she truly kissed him with a pure heart, he might change back? "I love you Hamish." She breathed in, then planted the most beautiful, the most tender, the most emotional kiss she had in her arsenal.

Fireworks went off inside her head.

Mrs. Howser screamed like a kicked dog.

The cabin door slammed shut.

Ondine and Hamish broke away from their most beautiful kiss in the universe and looked at the two seats opposite. Melody was strapped in again, nice and tightly.

And so was Mrs. Howser.

Melody must have wished it!

The ride whirred into action.

"Arrrrrghghghghghghghgh!" Mrs. Howser screamed.

Hang on. Melody was supposed to wish the old witch out of here. Not keep her with them. Unless . . .

"Suck it up!" Melody said, sounding very un-Melody-like as she peeled her eyes wide open. "Set me free or you get a double dose!"

Because of Mrs. Howser's connection with Melody, she would get twice the ride and twice the sickness.

"Melody you're brilliant," Ondine said.

Hamish screamed as they spun and tumbled and fell and rose and lurched in every which way. Much to Ondine's disappointment, their incredible kiss had not cured his face-fur.

Nausea kicked in. Nasty, lurchy, hot-and-coldy nausea that grabbed Ondine in the guts and twisted. Hard.

She clamped her mouth shut.

"Nooooooo!" Mrs. Howser cried.

Ondine felt so proud of Melody – what a fantastic wish under pressure. Having Mrs. Howser with them was the perfect punishment. Her grimacing gave Ondine something to focus on while they dropped and soared and dived and twisted and churned and rolled and rolled again.

It felt like the ride would never end. Just as it slowed it sped up again, sending them through all those hideous motions once more.

Thank goodness they'd left Old Col out of this. She wouldn't have survived.

"Break the link!" Melody yelled.

"Never!" Mrs. Howser's voice cracked but her expression remained defiant.

Melody clung to her shoulder straps in the same way her hair clung to her perspiring face. "The ride won't stop until you break the link. I wished it that way."

Beside Ondine, Hamish moaned. She didn't dare look in case he disgraced himself. Lurch. Shudder. Drop. Rise. Tilt. Tumble. Wobble. Hot sick burned the back of her throat. If this ride didn't stop soon she'd make such a mess. The lurching and twisting plastered her hair over her damp face, but the g-forces pinned her arms back making her unable to clear her vision.

"You are in so much trouble!" Mrs. Howser cried out.

It couldn't be true. Melody was enjoying herself? "That goes double for you!" She yelled back.

Spin. Drop. Twist. Spin. Pike. That was just for Ondine. Mrs. Howser was getting it in stereo.

"Make it stop!" the witch cried.

Melody pressed her advantage and said exactly what Ondine was thinking, "It stops when you break the link!"

An anguished howl erupted from Mrs. Howser. "Nooooooo."

"Do it!"

"Never!"

"Then we stay here forever."

"You can't!"

Determination filled Melody's face. "I can and I will. I'm having a great time, wheeeeeee!"

CHAPTER 24

The ride, would it never end?

Mrs. Howser made a pathetic mewling noise and began to cry.

Ondine's stomach leapt into her throat.

Over and over they tumbled and spun in space, held firmly in harness. No way out for any of them until Mrs. Howser gave in.

The interminable ride rode on. For the rest of Ondine's life if she never saw a fairground again it would be too soon. She resorted to silent begging, as if she had some kind of psychic link to Mrs. Howser to beg her to stop.

Lurch, spin, twist, drop, spin, drop, lurch, lurch.

With a weak admission of defeat, Mrs. Howser said, "Make it stop." A sob escaped and she crimped her eyes shut. "You win."

Suddenly, the ride stopped.

Ondine's stomach crashed back into position.

The Carnie lady opened the cabin door with a huge smile. "All done? Who needs help with their –" Her jaw dropped for a second. Then she called out to someone they couldn't see. "Marko? We're gonna need the hose again."

If the world would stop spinning, Ondine could give Melody a hug for being so very brave and clever.

Mrs. Howser was the last to leave the ride. She staggered out, all crumpled of spirit and damp of face. "You'll pay for this."

As if her brains were still spinning (and lurching and dropping and tilting and rising, then tilting and dropping at the same time) Mrs. Howser's words dropped in to Ondine's brain and flew straight out again. Let the woman say or do what she liked. Nothing Mrs. Howser could magic could possibly make Ondine feel any worse right now.

"Oh you poor thing!" they heard a man call out.

Through the blur of moving buildings and spinning lights, Ondine's stomach clenched harder.

Turns out it was possible to feel worse because Lord Vincent came into view.

He looked . . . he looked concerned and almost, *kind*. How he managed that Ondine had no idea.

"You poor dear, let me help you," Vincent said as he approached Mrs. Howser and held her steady. That blue hand looked bluer than ever. Had he turned it into a tattoo? "Everything is all right now. Here, have some cold water, it will make you feel better."

By this point in Ondine's life, she should have known the expression, "Things can't get any worse," was a total lie. Because right now, Vincent's act of chivalry in offering Mrs. Howser a cool drink in her moment of distress made everything a whole lot worse.

"What a nice man," someone in the crowd said.

"I think that's Lord Vincent," another said.

"Isn't he lovely?"

"So sweet."

"He makes me swoon."

And so on *ad nauseam*.

Hamish's clammy hand held Ondine's. "As if the ride wasnae sickening enough."

Ondine looked into Hamish's handsome face and jumped in shock. His features were still fixed in the starting-to-turn-into-a-ferret phase.

"What's wrong, hen?" Hamish's hands flew to his face, where he must have felt the fur for himself. "Aw naw! I'm ugly!"

Ondine gulped and tried not to admit anything. She felt sick enough from the ride, let alone his messed-up face. "We'll fix it, I promise."

"Let's scram," Melody said as she reached Ondine.

Ondine barely dared hope. "Is the link . . .?"

"Broken? Yes," she confirmed.

"Then let's get oot of here," Hamish said.

Old Col ambled up with extra napkins so they could wipe their faces.

"Don't suppose you've got any water?" Ondine asked.

Old Col tisked. "That was too clever of Vincent. Turning up at the right moment, helping a lady in distress. You can bet it will be all over the news inside an hour. Meanwhile, where's Anathea? What's she doing to make people like her? Hmm? What's she doing to get the crowd on her side? And . . . Hamish dear, what's happened to your face?"

"Can we work that out tomorrow? I need to lie down," Ondine said. No sooner were the words out of her mouth than she fell upon a bank of snow as if it were a bed. "Oh. This is so good."

"That's enough, child," Old Col said. "We need to get home quickly. The rest of the city is probably in lockdown because of the blackout and the looting."

As far as Ondine was concerned, those were real-life problems affecting other people. She had to ice the nausea away before she could even think about walking home. That gave her a new thought. "Old Col, if there's no electricity, how do we get the train home?"

"They'll most likely switch to diesel engines," she said.

THE NEXT DAY they still didn't have reliable power, so they burned candles for light, boiled water in an old gas-top kettle and bought the newspaper instead of listening to the radio or watching television.

The main story in the newspaper featured the "gallant" Lord Vincent coming to a distressed woman's aid in Savo Plaza.

The rest of the pagers were filled with stories of looting and the hospitals being overrun with patients presenting with a viral strain of magic they were calling Ant Flu Hn26. Named not because it was spread by ants, but because it was marching all over Europe like ants on a discarded box of cheeseballs, across Brugel, Craviç, Slaegal and even Wallachia.

Ondine, Old Col, Hamish and Melody were down one end of the kitchen, reading the newspaper and talking over the events of the night before.

Henrik and Cybelle were at the stoves, cooking breakfast, making extra for Melody so she could get back to full strength.

"I think it's safe to say Vincent has magic *and* a PR company helping out," Old Col said. "There's no way this happened by chance."

"The Ant Flu?" Ondine asked?

"Not that, the bit with Lord Vincent being in the right place at the right time."

"Aye," Hamish agreed as he took a plate of food from Henrik. "Vincent and Howser have tae be in this together."

Ondine's appetite was back as she guzzled her scrambled eggs on toast. "How do we compete? We try and make her popular by putting up posters, which costs us money; he gets in the papers for free."

"Why are you helping Anathea?" Melody's brows crinkled.

"She's goat me papers," Hamish said, scratching at his beardy half-ferret face. "We help her hold on to the throne, she helps me stay here and not get deported."

"Oh," Melody said.

"Yeah, Oh," Ondine said. "And it's getting us exactly nowhere." It was hard to look at her lovely Hamish, what with him being stuck mid-transformation. Old Col should be helping more on that front. In fact, Hamish should be doing his best to transform back and forth and fix himself.

Unless he couldn't? A thought which made food stick in her throat.

"Forgive me for asking, but," Melody's voice took on a placating tone. "why *do* you want to help Anathea? Aside from making sure Hamish doesn't get deported."

"Because she should have been duchess all along!" Ondine said, unable to stop the whine in her voice. "And if you got to know her, you'd know she's really nice and she's concerned about people, and she's a darn site better than Vincent."

"Are we done with politics?" Cybelle asked.

"For now yes," Ondine said, feeling incredibly glum about the mess they were in and their lack of progress.

"Aren't you forgetting something?" Melody said as she accepted another plate of food from Cybelle.

Everyone looked at her.

"You've got *me!*" she said with a huge grin. Then she grabbed the last two sausages from the serving dish nearby and ate them straight off her fork without putting them on her plate first. "And thank you so much for breaking the link. I can't tell you how good it feels to be free."

"You're looking better already," Ondine said, "and – and I don't want to put a dampener on our celebrations, but how are we going to help Anathea win hearts and minds when Howser and Vincent have all the resources and magic and loads of money?"

"Too easy." Melody beamed with confidence as she accepted a plate of scrambled eggs from Henrik. "Howser's been linked to me; I've been linked straight back to her. I know all her secrets."

Hamish hugged Melody with glee.

A stab of jealousy caught Ondine by surprise. "What sort of secrets?"

"All of them," she replied. "Her spells, and her stratagems for Vincent. It's all in here," she said, tapping the forked sausage to the side of her head.

Hamish must have seen Ondine's face because he backed away from Melody a little. Which only made Ondine feel more awful.

She shovelled in food to block out these new, nasty feelings. Hamish still looked too ferrety from his half-transformation last night.

Would he be stuck like that forever?

The lights flickered on again, and they had electricity. It was good news for the restaurant, but bad news as the fluorescent lights did nothing for Hamish's hairy complexion.

"Can ye find Howser's spell so I can be meself again?" Hamish asked.

"Too easy," Melody winked, "we'll have you back to handsome in no time."

It had to be battle fatigue. That was the only way to explain Ondine's sour mood when they should be celebrating Melody's rescue. Ondine had read about war weariness in the book about

Grand Duchess Elmaree. Elmaree and her supporters had fought for so long, they never had a chance to simply enjoy a normal day and be themselves.

Like Elmaree, Ondine had a to-do list that stretched to the horizon. Make Anathea popular; get Hamish his work papers; get Hamish back to his gorgeous self; and then defeat Vincent and Mrs. Howser.

"We should have done this last night, but I was too sick and wonky," Melody said. She dropped her dirty plate in the sink and reached for Ondine's hand with her left and Hamish's with her right. "I know you never got the hang of astral projection, Ondi, but I love it. Join up and we'll go travelling."

Ondine gave over her hand and reached for Hamish with her other. Before she could, Old Col wedged herself beside her and took it.

"What are we doing?" Ondine asked.

"We're beating Birgit at her own game. You're coming with me into her memories."

Ondine creased her brow. "You sure you know what you're doing?"

"Of course," Melody said. "Done it heaps."

Not entirely convinced, Ondine asked, "But won't she be up and about already?"

"Doesn't matter." Melody winked. "It works just as well if the person's awake or asleep. They don't feel a thing."

"Are ye sure, hen?" Hamish asked.

Jealousy twisted Ondine's stomach again. "Hen" was his special name for her, not other girls.

"Uh, yep. Quite sure." Melody blushed furiously, making Ondine instantly suspicious about whose memories she'd been visiting. Before she could ask any more questions, Melody said, "Ready? Close your eyes, let's go."

Everyone closed their eyes and squeezed hands. Ondine had

to stay with them or she'd break the chain. Or be left out. And there was no way she wanted to be left out of this.

When she closed her eyes, Ondine saw only darkness and heard only background noise from the pub. Slowly the everyday noises and darkness faded away. Small sparkles of light danced behind her eyelids. Her body grew lighter, until she was little more than a –

"Imagine you're a jellyfish, floating with the tide," Melody said.

– jellyfish. Yes, That's exactly how she felt. Hope unfurled that this experiment might work. She certainly felt lighter and . . . *driftier.*

"The floatier you feel, the better," Melody said. "We're all connected so we'll keep each other floating along. I'm guiding us towards Birgit Howser and we're going to access her memories."

Coldness danced around the edges of Ondine's perception.

Melody said, "Don't worry about the chill. It means we're getting close. She's always been a cold stone, that one. I can't thank you guys enough for breaking the hold she had on me. I thought I was going to freeze to death."

Interesting, Melody seemed to be –

"Reading your thoughts. Yes. First things first, let's fix Hamish's beautiful face, yeah?"

Oh yeah.

In a flash of noise and lights and spinning, Ondine was back in The Pretzel car and everything was going haywire. Memories and nausea from last night came rushing back. Ondine's eyes were already shut, so she couldn't shut them any more. Could they hurry up and –

"Get this over with?' Melody said. "Right, we can see her, and we can see us, but *she* can't see us. We're going to rewind to the point where she . . . ahhh, here we are."

"Is this what you went through last night?" Old Col asked. "I'm so glad I sat it out."

The real life scene flicker-jumped back and forth, as if someone were zapping through the adverts in the story of their lives. Melody reached the exact point where Mrs. Howser cursed Hamish to freeze, mid-transition.

"Gotcha," Melody crowed in triumph. She captured the words in the air between them, then took them to the other side of the picture.

The words hung in mid-air, written backwards.

Instead of saying 'Freeze!' Melody said, "Ezeerf!" She turned to Hamish to reverse the spell. Not the Hamish strapped into his seat in the Pretzel Ride, but the Hamish floating above her.

Melody's hand was still holding Hamish's as she waved it in the air. "Ezeerf!"

Ondine saw the dark bristles over Hamish's face retreating. His whiskery nose smooshed back to his Scottishly handsome one. His eyes morphed from black to sparkly green.

Gratitude overwhelmed Ondine and she nearly threw herself at Hamish.

"Don't break the link," Melody said, giving her hand a reminder-squeeze.

As desperate as she was to throw her arms around her beloved, Ondine held back. As soon as this session was over though, she'd cling to him like an orangutan.

"One more thing," Melody said. The five of them drifted high above the Martisor fairground and bobbed along on the wind. Soon the city fell away and they followed the train lines into the countryside.

It may have been night when they were at the fairground, but by the time they reached the forested hillsides, silver pink dawn dusted the horizon. Behind them, heavy clouds built into ominous anvil shapes.

It looked surprisingly familiar to Ondine.

"We're in Bellreeve," Melody said.

"Aye, I thought I recognised the place," Hamish said. "It looks different too."

"I know when this is," Old Col said. "We've gone back a few years, haven't we Melody?"

Melody giggled and said, "Told you I was good."

"That's enough showing off from you," Old Col said.

As if to punctuate her speech, a flash of lightning rippled through the sky, followed by rolling thunder.

They floated on, above the path Ondine, Hamish and Old Col had taken when they first approached the Autumn Palace. On the rise of the hill they saw the gatehouse. At first Ondine thought the guard on duty was asleep. Then she noticed he was under a spell.

Splattered spots of rain fell.

There, standing by the flagstones near the gatehouse, stood Birgit Howser. She looked much, much younger. In her arms she held a ferret.

Shambles!

Mentally, Ondine worked out the time frame. It had to have been soon after the debutante ball, if Hamish was already a ferret.

"I dinnae remember her doing that. Mebbe I'm asleep. Och, hen, do I look that bad when I'm like that?"

"You have your moments," Ondine said.

Old Col said, "Bit of shush, please."

"It's quite all right. Remember, we can see her but she can't see us," Melody reminded them.

They floated above Birgit as she made ready to cast a spell over the flagstones. Those same stones Ondine, Hamish and Old Col had walked over when they'd arrived at the palace, setting off a chain of crazy events and huge helpings of weird magic.[1]

Hamish said, "Ye know lass, I never did see a Mister Howser."

"Shush!" everyone said.

"Dinnae shush me, she cannae hear us."

"No, but we need to hear *her*," Melody said. "She's about to say the spell."

"When first love and ferret pass this way,
The warning signs will fly and fray
The end will come for Brugel's head
My payment, now, or he'll be dead."

Brugel's head? Ondine wondered. "She means Duke Pavla, right?"

Old Col huffed. "At least she didn't rhyme Duke with puke."

The five of them floated towards the ground so they could stand on the reverse side of the spell and catch every word.

Ondine creased her lips in thought, then said, "Howser set this trap, like some kind of remote alarm system. But why? I mean if you set up magic, wouldn't you want to be around to see it happening?"

"Not necessarily," Old Col answered. "Having strange magic happen when you're not around does give you a certain amount of deniability."

Ondine screwed up the rest of her face in puzzlement.

"It means, dear, that she can have the perfect alibi for when things go wrong. She sets things up to go wrong in the first place, then swans in offering help and nobody suspects her. Very clever, really."

Birgit Howser looked up, her unlined, years-younger face looking no less evil than her old wrinkly one had last night.

---

1. How weird? The moment they'd stepped over the flagstones in *The Autumn Palace* a tornado had appeared. Then it had rained fish. That's how weird.

Her eyes turned hard as stone and she glared at Ondine. Time froze as the old witch's eyes bored holes through Ondine's soul. Lead filled her belly and she had to swallow a few times before she could whisper, "Are you sure she can't –"

Mrs. Howser pointed her finger and screamed. "Get out! Get out of my memories!"

Ondine screamed.

They all did.

She pulled her hands back to cover her mouth. Too late, she'd broken the link.

Flashes filled her eyes. Ondine opened them to find herself back with everyone in the kitchen, gasping in shock.

"I'm nae sure that was supposed to happen, lass."

Old Col sniffed. "I fear we've really upset her now."

"Yeah," Melody said, chewing on her thumbnail. "How did she do that?"

While Melody and Old Col conferred with each other, Ondine found she only had eyes for Hamish. Because he was back to being so handsomely Hamish again.

"Ondine, snap out of it," Old Col said. "Help us think of ways we can fix this."

Huffing and feeling tired, frustrated, emotionally wrought and – despite the enormous breakfast – still a bit hungry, Ondine crossed her arms over her chest. "I don't know how any of this magic works."

Muttering just enough for everyone to hear, Old Col said, "If we can't fix this, Howser will keep making chaos across the country."

Added to that, Mrs. Howser now hated their livers. [2]

It was an absolute certainty that the moment Ondine thought, "things can't get worse" they absolutely would. "Yes

---

2. The Brugel equivalent of hating someone's guts.

but . . . Hamish and I can still make nice things happen." Did anyone notice how desperate she sounded?

"Ondi's right," Hamish said. "I'm glad I'm me again, and we've freed Melody, but we havnae made Anathea the best and fairest, so mebbe it's a good thing we havnae broken Howser's wishing spell, so we can still use it." Then he flashed a smile Ondine's way and made her tummy flip. In a nice way, not in a stuck-in-The-Pretzel-ride way.

"You're right, of course," Old Col said. "We'd best use the magic while we still have it. Let's get close to Anathea and make her wishes come true."

Which sounded remarkably like their earlier plans. Before Old Col and Ma had split up her and Hamish.

Melody put her hands up. "I have an idea. The Snow Maze Festival comes straight after Martisor. Big crowds. The Duke always cut the ribbon and gets to go through first.

Obviously it will be Anathea this year. Loads of people turn up. They should have the power properly back on by then."

"She's a clever one, isn't she Ondi?" Hamish said. "Lots of people there to boost Anathea's popularity ratings."

"If Vincent and Birgit show up, as they're bound to," Old Col added, "we can have it out with them, once and for all."

The lights flickered above them, as if applauding the ideas Melody and Old Col were creating. In the midst of everyone congratulating each other for being so clever, Ondine sighed and thought, *Why didn't I think of that?*

CHAPTER 25

Like an unwelcome guest, winter made itself completely at home and messed the place right up. Where light snow had covered the world with pretty magic at Christmas, the deep freeze of proper-winter slathered everything with a thick layer of hard ice.

Every day, just before lunch and then in between first and second dinner, Hamish, Josef, Henrik and Thomas took a shovel each and headed out to clear a trench through the snow so their customers could get to the front door. They threw the snow into the kerb, adding height to the walls of snow and ice. In the middle of the night, the street sweepers also cleared the streets like some kind of snow-eating alien with a lightning-fast metabolism. Gorging itself at one end, squirting it out the other. The snowspray slathered the walls of icy debris at the kerb, making them higher and wider than before. Snow buried lamp-posts, rubbish bins and bicycles, if they happened to be chained to the post at the time.

Walking the streets felt exactly like walking in an enormous maze of snow. Which conveniently put people in the right mood for the next festival. Between Martisor and Easter, Savo Plaza held the annual Snow Maze Festival. Some people complained about so many festivals arriving one after the other, but they were quickly hushed up with a well-aimed snowball. After all, there was no point in having an empty plaza. [1]

And at this time of year, they had plenty of snow with which to build the maze, which cannot be said for summer.

The sun kept its distance and the heavy white stuff kept on falling as Ondine, Hamish, Melody and Old Col walked the cobbled streets to the Plaza. Banners hung from buildings, groaning and creaking with the weight of snow piled over them.

Despite the cold, it was a much nicer walk than the last time they'd come here, because the power was back on, alarm systems were working and so were the traffic lights.

"Here's how it's going to play out," Old Col said as they shook the snow off their umbrellas. Steam poured from her mouth as she spoke. "When we get near Anathea, Ondine and Hamish will get loved up. That way, Anathea's wishes will come true. It's going to work. I can feel it in my bones."

It would work. It had to. Ondine worried her bottom lip in thought. "Aunt Col? I don't want to be a downer but, are we sure Anathea is going to make the right kind of wish?"

"What is wrong with you? I'm telling you to get sucky face with Hamish, and you're asking questions?"

Trust her great aunt to get to the meat of the matter. "I dunno." She made tracks in the snow with the toe of her boot. Something was missing, but she couldn't name it. As if they hadn't quite resolved all the outstanding issues that had arisen. "I guess . . . I'm worried about what everyone else is going to be wishing for when we do it." Because last time they'd been loved-

---

1. The Brugel Bannermen's Guild takes credit for the series of festivals all lined up in a row, having spearheaded a campaign for such events. They erect banners for "festival z" while taking down the banner for "festival y", thus saving time – but not money, as they are paid only for banners they erect, but not take down.

up in public, people grew tails. Chaos broke out. Worse still, she and Hamish had to break up.

"I'll make sure that doesn't happen." Melody said. "I'll be sending out astrals that put everyone in a good mood and make them think positively."

"Aye, that's Barry," Hamish said, giving Melody a grin. [2]

Jealousy pricked Ondine each time Hamish complimented Melody-With-All-The-Answers. Meanwhile, she slipped further into the sulks and became Stressed-Out-Ondi-With-No-Answers. And that niggling, nagging feeling of having forgotten something pretty huge kept . . . niggling and nagging at her.

Old Col grabbed her by the elbow. "Come along. There's the Duchess. Let's get in close so we can make an impact. Ready child?"

"Not really."

"Love conquers all, my dear, just you remember that," Col said.

Dread filled Ondine as she looked upon the golden carpet near the entrance to the snow maze. The maze was a huge thing; taller than an average person so you couldn't see were you were, and made entirely out of snow.

Light snow drifted and fell on the carpet, but not for long as a worker with a vacuum backpack worked away quietly to keep it clean.

It wasn't the maze filling Ondine with thoughts of failure, but the people standing on that carpet near the front. The First Minister Cebotari stood proudly beside Duchess Anathea, both of them resplendent in heavy brown coats, solid outdoorsy boots and hats with earflaps. Even little Biscuit the dog had a brown

---

2. Barry means good. Or puke. If you have a really good night out, you have a Barry good Barry at the end of it.

coat on and booties on his feet. Standing beside Anathea was the last person in the world they expected to see, Lord Vincent.

Hamish asked, "What's that balloon doing here?" [3]

"He *is* next in line," Melody piped up.

Col shot back, "Not if they change the laws of succession."

Hamish suggested, "Mebbe she had no alternative? She has to be fair and let him tag *aloang*?"

"Of course he'd turn up," Ondine said, her eyes almost rolling in frustration, "He's trying to out-popular Anathea."

Judging by the number of screaming, squealing teenage girls in the crowd, he had that competition easily won. Yes, he was handsome, but only at face-value. Ondine knew the real Vincent, she knew he was ugly on the inside.

But he was young and looked like a pop idol. How could Anathea compete?

"Melody, you have to do something," Ondine said. "We can't make Vincent's wishes come true, because we know what he'll be wishing for and it won't do any of us a lick of good."

"Already on it," Melody said with a look of concentration on her face. "I'm sending blockers. But um, there are a lot of people here and I can't do all of them."

So many *squees* erupted from the crowd; it hurt Ondine's ears. How could an old crone like Anathea compete against a rock star like Vincent?

Old Col coughed into her closed hand. "Do your best Melody. As long as you block *him* and keep Anathea positive, we should set everything to rights."

A voice boomed over the crowd. "My Lord Duchess, Lord Vincent, Her Honour the First Minister, distinguished guests, ladies and gentlemen . . ."

---

3.   Massive insult, in both Scotland and Brugel.

Ondine followed the sound upwards and noticed loud-speakers cabled through the high branches in the trees.

"Better get smooching," Old Col said.

"Not here," Ondine said. They were drowning in a sea of overhyped fangirls who were mentally writing themselves into Lord Vincent fan fiction. "If this lot get their wish, they'll rip Vincent to shreds."

Old Col turned and raised an eyebrow. "You say that like it's a bad thing."

Hamish gave her hand a squeeze. "Yer a good lass for lookin' out for him, even if he doesnae deserve it."

The compliment boosted her spirits and she squeezed his hand in return.

"Over tae the side, weil be closer tae Anathea and away from the squealies."

They pushed and squeezed through the crowd until they reached the very edge of the audience section. At which point Anathea noticed them and gave a curt nod, as if she'd been expecting them.

Ondine was expecting a lot from Anathea as well. They weren't doing this out of the kindness of their own hearts or for the good of Brugel. They were doing it for purely selfish reasons. Ondine wanted Hamish forever, but if he didn't have his work papers allowing him to stay in Brugel, he'd either have to live the rest of his public life as a ferret or be shunted home to Scotland.

No matter how angry and used and tired she felt, she had to push every negative thought aside and kiss Hamish with all her heart. She didn't want to think about the consequences of failing. Of him being deported. Of Anathea getting booed off stage. Vincent triumphant and becoming Brugel's next Duke. Mrs. Howser's shadow casting a pall over everything.

Panic caught in her throat, making her feel even less loved-up and smoochy. Thinking about Mrs. Howser had a way of draining every nice thought from her head.

Hamish's steady hands cupped her face and he winked, but the lovely swirly whotsits that normally swirled in her tummy did not leap into life.

"We havetae kiss, it's fer Brugel," he said, lowering his lips onto hers.

Nothing.

No fireworks. Not even a sparkler or a small candle.

"Mercury's Wings, Mrs. Howser must be here somewhere, sucking all the fun out of me." That was the only way Ondine could explain her lack of gushiness. Hamish's kisses always made her feel loopy and silly and fabulous. They'd never made her feel *nothing* before.

"But we freed Melody from her." Hamish scrunched up his forehead.

"Maybe she's put a spell on me or something and . . . I can't love you any more?"

"Nae possible. Sure'n she's evil, but lass, ye heart's so big, no mangey *spell* can stop our love."

A bony hand clamped hard on her shoulder and dug down hard. "No you don't!"

Everything happened in slow-time. Noises stretched and warped, vision blurred. Hamish fell away from her. Or did she fall from him? Whiplash emotions bombarded her system as Mrs. Howser's face loomed.

"You're not doing anything," she said, calm as you like.

To add bizarre on top of the strange, Mrs. Howser's voice and movements were perfectly normal, while everything else around them moved with the speed of cooling toffee. They were in some kind of time bubble. Ondine couldn't speak or move or even think clearly. Everything in her system started shutting down. Great Pluto's ghost, this was the niggly naggy thing she'd forgotten.

They hadn't dealt with Mrs. Howser directly; they'd merely tried to get around her. Look what good it had done them. They'd chipped away at the edges of their problems but the big one, the bad magic maker, would make their life hell if they didn't deal with her directly, once and for all.

These thoughts surprised Ondine in their clarity. Up until this point, she'd only been able to think of herself and Hamish. Suddenly – and with a fair amount of deep personal guilt – she realised there were some things in this life that were bigger than her.

Every instinct told her to shut down, to collapse under the weight of the negative magic Mrs. Howser bore down on her. But that would be giving up. That would be letting the baddies win.

It wasn't going to happen.

It *couldn't*.

Outside this magic time-bubble, Hamish reached for her, his body moving in slow motion. Inside the bubble, she had to move fast. Mrs. Howser's hand was still clamped on her shoulder, and she was pushing down, making her blend into the footpath.

Ondine said, "No." A single thought, but a powerful one.

"You can't win." Mrs. Howser's words felt heavy and cold, dissolving Ondine's willpower like acid. Drip, drip, drip, they ate away at her resolve. Why did her eyelids weigh so much all of a sudden?

"That's right, you're going to have a nice big sleep," Mrs. Howser said. The worst of it was how sweet and reasonable the woman sounded.

Sleep. Oh sleep, that would be so good right now . . . but

there was something she had to do first. Something about . . . oh that's right. Mrs. Howser was going down!

It took a breath. Then it took a mental image of steel filling her marrow. Then it took every ounce of strength she had.

"NO!" Ondine yelled.

"You're a feisty one."

A tiny victory, but enough to begin the re-group for the next attack. "No," Ondine said again, her voice sounding firm and satisfying to her ears. One little word, a world of strength behind it. "No."

The hazy skin of the magic bubble stretched and strained around them, but did not break.

"You think one simple word can stop me? Can stop this?" Mrs. Howser flicked her hand and the bubble wall grew thicker, stronger, the people on the other side blurred into vague shapes. New fears tugged at Ondine. She was no match for this kind of magic.

"No," the word came out as a whisper, more an expression of shock and surprise than intent.

"You've got to expand your vocabulary child. And your magic. I can teach you how to do this. You have so much potential. Let me help you shine."

Honeyed milk, that's how the words played over Ondine. All smooth and lovely and sweet and special. Like an extra treat after a long day of working so hard she could sleep forever. *Sleepity sleep sleep.* Now there's a thought. Sleep would be so good. If only there were some place nearby where she could lie down and sleep and . . . Outside the bubble, Hamish had stopped moving. His blurred face came into focus through the skin of magic between them.

Hamish. She felt all kinds of magic when he was around. They'd been doing something here, something she couldn't quite remember but . . . it had seemed important at the time.

A giggle formed. Ondine felt so light and carefree she could have sworn she was floating. Looking down to her feet, she saw a gap between her boots and the snowy ground. Yes, definitely floating.

Oh what a marvellous feeling. She could get used to this.

"I wonder if Hamish can see me floating?"

"Let's float away from here," a soothing voice said. Such a calming voice. Such a persuasive voice.

Belonging to Mrs. Howser.

Why did Ondine not like her? She seemed so nice. And yet the rest of her family had it in for her. Silly, really. Maybe it was her great aunt being jealous? That must be why they hated each other with such venom. How strange, now that she thought about it. It took so much energy to hate someone, when liking them was so easy.

So very easy.

Like Hamish. She'd fallen in like with him from the start and it hadn't taken long for it to turn into full-blown love.

A cold seed of doubt sprouted in her belly as she floated inside her bubble. Had she and Hamish fallen in love because they wanted to, or had they fallen under some kind of spell?

Turning her head, she saw Mrs. Howser smiling so sweetly.

"You made the spell," Ondine said.

"What spell, my dear?"

"The spell that made Hamish fall in love with me."

"You're welcome," Mrs. Howser tilted her head to accept the praise.

Only Ondine wasn't praising her. She was accusing her. Accusing her of exploiting her feelings and yearnings. Hamish was in love with her, but was it real or only magic?

"What if it's only the spell that's making him love me?" Ondine asked.

"You have nothing to worry about, child. He truly loves you. No spell is so great it can circumvent free will."

"Is that so?" Ondine asked in her dreamy state. The confirmation gave her a boost. She landed on the ground on steady feet. Then she looked Mrs. Howser straight in the eye and said, "Then I can stop you, and I can stop this."

Panic flickered across the witch's face before she composed herself. "What I meant to say was –"

"– No. You're going to shut up now." Ondine waved her hand towards the bubble's edge and poked it. The skin pressed outwards under the pressure, then shredded like a popped balloon. "You are going down," Ondine said.

Instantly Mrs. Howser waved her hands and a new bubble sealed around them. Ondine poked it again – same shredding effect.

"How are you doing that?" Mrs. Howser rapidly erected a third bubble.

This was getting tiresome. Ondine said, "Stop meddling in everyone's lives and leave us alone!"

"So you can be with your beautiful Hamish, I suppose?"

Oh, she had her there.

Time to be honest. That was pretty much the hardest thing to do, but it always achieved the best results. "That too. You'd love it if all I could think about was Hamish, but I've worked it out. Sure it took me a while, but even I can see truth. I'm not selfish all the time."

Mrs Howser creased her forehead. "There's nothing wrong with being selfish. It's how we get things done."

"You're right. I was so selfish I couldn't see past my own little bubble with Hamish. But I can see past that now," she said, glaring at Mrs. Howser.

Mrs Howser shot back, "Don't you look at me like that!"

The way out of this shone clear in Ondine's mind. "You don't have magic."

"Excuse me, I have more magic in my little finger than you'll ever have –"

"Magic's not in your hands. It's in here," Ondine said, pressing her hand slightly to the left of Mrs. Howser's bony sternum, where her heart would be. "And up here." With her free hand, she tapped the side of the old woman's head. Then Ondine turned and for the last time looked at the bubble surrounding them. She blew a puff towards the skin of the bubble, turning it into smoke. Another puff and the smoke wafted away like a snuffed candle.

"If you were really psychic, you should have seen this coming," Ondine said, pouring lemon juice on the old woman's wounds.

"Ondi, get back!" a girl behind her yelled. Suddenly Melody was grabbing at her, pulling her away.

"It's OK, I'm fine," Ondine said.

"Your hands!" Melody yelled.

"What about my –" Turning her palms over, she watched the tips of her fingers dissolve into smoke and drift off in the breeze. A scream filled her ears. Then more screams as the people around them saw what was happening.

Jupiter's moons. The smoke had dissolved down to the first knuckle already. Panic took over. All Ondine could do was stand there and scream and scream until she thought she'd black out.

CHAPTER 26

Like four fat incense sticks plus a stubby one on the side, Ondine's fingers and thumbs ended not in bitten-down nails but curlicues of smoke and ash.

"They're burning!" she cried out. Mrs. Howser would pay for this.

In a flash, Hamish scooped snow off the ground and sandwiched her hands between his. Drip, slurry, slop. The melty-ice dribbled to the ground. When Ondine looked at her hands again –

"They're still burning!"

"They look a bit red," Hamish said as he slapped another pack of slurry onto her skin.

Red? They were on *fire*!

"She's getting away!" Melody and Old Col called out at the same time.

So many things happened at once it was hard to put them in order. Ondine's fingers were trailing smoke and freaking her right out. Mrs. Howser dashed off towards Lord Vincent on the stage. Melody took off after her.

But the strangest thing – Hamish was not panicking anywhere near as much as he should.

"Mebbe yer too cold; ye need yer gloves on."

"They're burning!"

"Aye, my hands are so cold they feel hot at the ends too."

"No!" It wasn't nice to yell at her beloved, but he clearly wasn't listening to her. Shoving her hands directly in front of his face, she said. "They're smoking! Like Chimneys!" Any more exclamation marks and her head would explode.

Clasping her hands in his again, Hamish kissed the tips. The smouldering, ash-lined tips. "Ondi lass, they feel colder than a glare from ye Da, but they're nae on fire. I promise ye, they're only so cold they're hot, but they're nae on fire. Howser's messing with yer heid, so she is."

"But they're . . ." Confused and frightened, she pulled her hands out from Hamish's warm embrace to see they were perfectly normal. Incredibly cold and yes, the tips felt hot, possibly an early sign of frostbite because she wasn't wearing gloves. But they were normal, all the way to her completely normal fingertips. "Oh thank goodness, they're back to normal. Thank you Hamish."

"She touched ye, didn't she?"

Actually, Ondine had made the mistake of touching Birgit Howser.

"She *goat* ye in the head," Hamish said, his eyes filled with kindness as he turned her palm over and kissed the centre.

Oh lush.

Whoa, no time for that. "Jupiter's moons, she's going for Vincent!" But why would she do this, in such a public setting, would ruin everything for her. Had she completely lost her mind? They turned to see Mrs. Howser take a flying leap onto the stage. Lord Vincent flinched at her approach. Security guards leapt on her.

It looked like it was all over.

Melody and Old Col raced to the security pile-on. A puff of grey smoke swirled through the bodies and into the sky. The security crew untangled themselves and looked about, confused as all get-out.

Everyone looked like they were thinking the same thing. *Where did she go?*

"She's got Vincent," Melody yelled as she stood up on the stage.

The security guards leapt on Melody and Old Col instead and buried them under a hill of people.

"You've got the wrong witch!" Old Col shouted, pointing to Vincent and the smoky shape of Mrs Howser standing behind him, on the stage. "Get *her*."

The squeeing tone from the crowd changed to all-out screaming, and not in a good way.

Eerily calm, Vincent remained standing, confident the security would do its job. The guards were utterly useless against a whiff of smoke swirling around them. Invisible hands clonked the guards' heads together and they fell like rag dolls.

Another puff of smoke appeared behind Lord Vincent, swirling around his body, then his head, like a translucent scarf. He turned to see where it had gone. Then it zipped over to the other side of him, before slamming into his body.

He jolted forward as if he'd stuck a nine-volt battery on his tongue. [1]

Ondine was having such a hard time keeping up she didn't know how to properly describe it, but from the looks of things

---

1. Do not try this at home. The turning yourself into a shadow and leaping into someone else's body bit. The battery on the tongue? Go ahead, loads of fun. *Bzzt!* You're welcome.

Mrs. Howser had turned herself into a shadow and jumped inside Lord Vincent.

"Silence!" Lord Vincent yelled out.

No megaphone could carry his voice half so well. The audience of screaming fan-girls were stunned into quiet. Even the security guards looked gobsmacked.

The pastiness of Vincent's face reminded Ondine of the time at Coven Con. They'd had an audience with Duchess Anathea and Vincent had turned bonkers.

"She's got into him!" Ondine gasped. Because as sure as winter brings on blackouts across Brugel, Mrs Howser's smoky form was in Vincent, infiltrating his brain and body. She was going to overtake him completely and make him her puppet.

Beneath the hill of women and men in uniform, a crumpled and half-broken Melody tried to crawl out. They slammed her down again, convinced they were doing Vincent a favour. Meanwhile the man they should be protecting was already possessed.

On the other hand, if the security detail were busy flattening Melody, they wouldn't be able to stop Ondine. She leapt onto the stage, heading for Mrs. Howser-as-a-smoke-form-residing-in-Lord-Vincent.

Without a clue what to do when she got there.

In Brugel, there is a word for this kind of chaotic mayhem, but it doesn't translate very well into English. But the most chaotic type of chaos ever seen broke out as Ondine neared Lord Vincent.

Everybody screamed and shouted. Except Vincent, who stood there looking utterly lost.

Ondine stared at Vincent and yelled, "Get out of him!"

Security detail from goodness knows where launched at Ondine, knocking her sideways. Through a gap in the arms and legs restraining her, she saw Great Aunt Col had gotten away from her captors and was standing in front of Vincent.

"Time's up, Birgit, you've lost," she said to the woman inside him.

Vincent clamped his mouth shut. He wobbled and shuddered, his face paled some more until it turned the colour of curdled milk. Then he collapsed.

Was it over? Ondine hoped so.

"Man down!" Great Aunt Col cried out.

The audience by now were screaming, the noise of it piercing Ondine's eardrums. But her arms were pinned by security so she couldn't block the noise drilling in. Way off at the other end of the stage, she saw Duchess Anathea and the First Minister clamping their palms over their ears.

Anathea cried out, "Make it stop".

Suddenly Hamish was on the stage, peeling back the layers of people smothering Ondine.

The security in suits were about to pounce all over Ondine again when Old Col threw her hands out and cried, "Freeze!"

The men and women froze in place. Hamish held out his hand to help Ondine back to her feet. Then his warm hands held her face steady, her gaze captive to his. His green eyes sparkled with mischief. "Have ye forgotten what we came here for?"

A strand of candy-silk-loveliness spun inside her tummy. Oh yes. They were supposed to get loved up and make people's wishes come true. When her gaze locked with Hamish's, the commotion and chaos died away, leaving the two of them in a magical world of their own making.

"D'ye remember the first time I turned into me. We were gettin' ready for yer sister's engagement party and I pulled the table cloth down ontae meself . . . and ye were there."

Heat stole over her face at the memory. He'd transformed from his Shambles-ferretness into his gorgeous Hamish self, with only a tablecloth for modesty. A girl didn't forget a moment like that! The memories set more flurries free until the flurries were joining hands and dancing along her veins.

He made a lopsided smile and began to blush. "So ye do remember?" His eyes shone with mischief. If Ondine didn't know better, she'd swear he was using some kind of wonderful magic on her. He lowered his forehead onto hers; their temples warm despite the deep winter chill. "I love ye Ondi. Ours is a love for the ages. No magic can hold us back."

And then he kissed her. The sweetest brush against her lips. A tender buss of his nose against hers. Another kiss, frustratingly light again and yet so perfect an angel might have put it there. Needing more, her face tilted upwards, her lips at the ready.

"I love ye Ondi, yer my heart and soul. I want to grow old with ye. Will ye marry me?"

Oh!

Time stopped. Her heart as well. Then it kicked against her ribs and a husky, "yes" tripped from her. The rest of the world could have fallen into a snowdrift as Hamish's lips descended on hers. Warmth and love and the sweetest caress blocked out the cold winter's day. Her eyelids fluttered shut as sunshine filled her body.

"OK you two," Old Col said. "You'd better start k–. Oh, I see you're already at it. Carry on."

Buried under an avalanche of sensation, Ondine had no idea what was happening around her in Savo Plaza. All she wanted was for these magical kisses to continue. They sent her mind into a spin, her belly into a flip-flop and her heart into a canter.

Hamish wanted to marry her.

Old Col's bony hand pressed down on her shoulder and pulled her away. "That's enough."

Ondine's lips detached from Hamish's with a schmack of lost suction. Dizzy with love, she turned to see why her aunt had called a halt to it.

Savo Plaza had become a sea of flowers.

The ribbon over the entrance to the snow maze was still uncut as Anathea tossed bouquet after bouquet to the cheering crowd. Yes, cheering now, not screaming. Thank heavens for that.

"It worked?" Ondine could hardly believe it. Maybe they should kiss a bit more, just to make sure it wasn't a fluke.

Nearby, they heard a reporter make a speech to a camera, in which she described Anathea as the fairest of them all.

The clouds parted, filling the square with bright winter sun.

A light so bright it exposed a dark shadow behind Vincent. A shadow that looked suspiciously like Mrs. Howser holding strings that tied themselves in knots around Vincent.

The crowd gasped.

Mrs. Howser jumped back. Fully exposed, she had nowhere to go. The security guards flattened Mrs. Howser in the fastest ever game of Stacks-On.

They had her!

Oh dear. They only had her body. Her smoky shadow slipped away from them and headed straight for Anathea.

"No!" Ondine and Hamish yelled in unison as they leapt at the shadow.

Hamish threw himself on the dark shape, but it slipped out from beneath him. Ondine tried to grab at it – anywhere would do – but each time she clamped her fingers around a section, it morphed and squeezed away.

They were fighting a shadow. And losing.

The wind flurried snow around them, swirling the oleaginous shape into the air.

Jumping, Ondine tried to grab at it, but it was out of reach. The smoke shadow was zigging and zagging around the stage. Biscuit the dog barked like he'd been electrocuted as the smoke headed for the Duchess and First Minister. It wound around

Anathea's body, then rolled itself around her neck and head like a long smokey scarf with a mind of its own.

Behind them, doing her job as she should, was a janitor vacuuming the golden carpet.

"Anathea! Use the vacuum cleaner!" Ondine screamed and pointed at the same time.

Several miracles happened at once. Anathea heard her, she saw where Ondine was pointing and she took action, grabbing the vacuum hose out of the janitor's hands. The rest of the machine was strapped to the cleaner's back.

"Everyone get down!" Anathea shouted.

Everyone did just that.

Anathea held the nozzle into the air. Mrs Howser's elusive shadow that could withstand choking and flattening had no defences against the fabulous sucking motion. Floating in the air, it had nothing to cling to, and with a howl of wind it slurped into the hose.

Anathea handed the vacuum hose back to the puzzled cleaner. "The contents should be incarcerated. And in a separate facility to Mrs Howser's body."

"Yes, Your Lordship." The cleaner did a quick curtsey and scarpered off, looping the incredibly long extension cord over her shoulder as she went.

"Anathea is amazing!" Ondine said.

"Brilliant!" Hamish said.

The crowd roared with applause.

The two of them embraced Duchess Anathea like the saviour that she was. Busy rejoicing, they missed something, but the crowd was gasping. Ooops, had they overstepped the mark by touching the royal person? Embarrassed, Ondine pulled back, only to see that the crowd's reaction wasn't for them. It was for Vincent, who lay slumped on the ground like a dropped marionette.

"Darling!" Melody cried out as she sprang towards him.

"What's she up tae?" Hamish said.

Instead of tackling Melody, one of the guards guided her towards Vincent. There, she tenderly held the lord's hand and caressed a lock of hair from his face.

Old Col made her way to Ondine, Hamish and Anathea. "Well done, all of you. Your Lordship, that was some fast thinking."

Duchess Anathea beamed. "It was, rather, wasn't it? It couldn't have been done without Ondine."

Beaming at the compliment, Ondine looked again towards Melody and Vincent. Near them, the security detail dragged away a deflated and weak Birgit Howser, empty and soulless without her dark shadow.

"She is to be placed in the city asylum," Duchess Anathea called out. The hefty security people nodded and dragged her away.

Ondine pursed her lips in thought. "Does this mean Lord Vincent is free of Howser's influence?"

"That is to be hoped," Duchess Anathea said. "Perhaps he can be reasoned with now?"

"Er, he looks a bit busy," Hamish said.

Ondine, Old Col, Hamish and Duchess Anathea, in fact the entire crowd for that matter, watched as Melody helped Vincent to his feet, caressing and calming him all the time. His eyes were locked with hers. As he righted himself, he gave her a tender kiss of thanks on her cheek.

The crowd went insane with cheering.

"It would seem that in all things, everyone has an agenda," Old Col said. "That includes Melody."

Ondine could scarcely believe it. "Melody has a thing for Vincent?"

Hamish squeezed her hand. "Aye, every girl in the crowd has a *thing* for Vincent."

Ondine bristled. "Except me."

"Weil, yeas, but ye have excellent taste." He touched his nose to hers again, making her warm all over.

Vincent must have been wearing a microphone, because they could hear Melody's reassuring voice on the loudspeakers nearby. "You're free now. She can't ever harm you again."

Ondine couldn't work out if Melody put Vincent's arm across her shoulder or angled herself in such a way that he had to. Either way, they were leaning closely together.

"I did *noat* see that coming," Hamish said.

"She's a dark horse that one," Col said.

"Saturn's rings!" Ondine said. "We were so caught up in making Anathea's wish come true, we didn't pay attention to what Melody was wishing."

"Let's not get sidetracked," Col said. "The two of you did your job and did it well. Ondine, by giving Anathea a method of defeating Birgit, you made her the hero of the day in the public's eyes. Well done."

"Thank you, Ondine, I'd say you've more than earned Hamish's freedom," Anathea said, as her eyes wandered over towards Vincent.

Ondine beamed, "Do you have the papers?"

But the Duchess wasn't listening anymore as her attention found a new focus. "Now, if I may be excused, Vincent needs a good talking to."

They watched as she walked over to her nephew, the lad who wanted to kick her off the throne. Melody was smiling as the Duchess approached. So was Vincent.

"There has been so much enmity between us," they heard the Duchess say.

Yes, he definitely had a microphone on, and everyone could

hear their conversation. What a clever woman that Anathea was, Ondine thought, to make sure they had a crowd full of witnesses to this event.

Vincent nodded. "Your Lordship, thank you for your fast actions today. You have not only saved my life, but my soul."

"We are family. Family is the most important thing in the world," the Duchess said.

How uncharacteristic of her to speak in active voice all of a sudden, Ondine thought. Perhaps the old dear was changing for the better as well?

"Peace?" Vincent held out his hand.

The Duchess shook it. "Peace."

The crowd roared its approval.

When the crowd calmed down and the security team made sure they wouldn't be interrupted again, Anathea took hold of an over-sized pair of scissors to cut the ribbon at the entrance to the snow maze. The crowd roared with the kind of noise you'd hear at a football match after a winning goal. Anathea beamed. Even little Biscuit looked happy to be there.

In years past, Duke Pavla (may he rest in peace) would have been the first to explore the maze with a guide. The same was about to happen for Duchess Anathea. But instead of going straight in, she held her hand out towards Vincent, in front of thousands of witnesses, inviting him to explore the maze with her.

"I'd be honoured," he said.

Melody stayed by his side, ready to support him should he wobble.

The media turned their cameras on Anathea and Vincent as they held hands and walked together through the ice-bricked entrance.

Keeping two paces behind, Melody followed them into the

maze. Colours bloomed inside the icy walls, as if lit from within. The crowd cheered and applauded like crazy.

"Looks like our work here is done," Col said with satisfaction.

Ondine turned to her. "You never told me what you wished for."

Old Col rubbed her hands together against the cold. "I do believe I wished to knock some common sense into Vincent and Anathea."

A laugh escaped Ondine. "That was a really smart wish."

"It was rather!" Old Col giggled.

The crowd milled and chatted and became a bit noisy, as crowds do. The winter sun shone weakly, bands began to play and the smell of fried cheeseballs permeated the air.

After a short while Anathea and Lord Vincent emerged from the snow maze entrance into the open. [2]

Arms looped at the elbow, like old friends.

They were even . . . Ondine had to blink a few times to make sure . . . yes, they were laughing!

"When you wish, Auntie Col, you wish good!" Ondine said.

Everything was absolutely, wonderfully, perfectly perfect.

"Uh-oh," Hamish said when another development developed right before their eyes.

Saturn's rings. "Lord Vincent and Melody are kissing."

"Just when you think you've seen everything, eh lass?"

A wave of relief spread over Ondine. They had defeated Mrs. Howser and set Duchess Anathea on the road to becoming the most popular and loved ruler in Brugel's history. [3]

---

2. They hadn't made it all the way through the snow maze, because it was enormous and could take hours to get through. They'd simply waited around the corner, had a chat, explored a little, then used cheat codes to find their way out again.

3. She still had to behave herself and do the right thing by Brugel.

Everything had been put to rights.

And yet, as they walked home to the family pub, Ondine couldn't help feeling deflated, despite their success. Would Anathea come through with Hamish's work papers, allowing him to stay in Brugel? More importantly, would they ever break the mutating magic spell they were under?

CHAPTER 27

Such expensive clothes!

Even at her sister's wedding, Ondine hadn't worn the like. The tag itched the side of her ribs, but she was under desperate instructions not to remove it. Or leave any stain or smell on the fabric. Ma warned her, "You can't take clothes back for a refund with sweat stains on them, can you?"

If it was cold as the snow outside, perspiration wouldn't be a problem. But inside? Someone had turned the heating way up to keep everyone toasty warm, which meant Ondine couldn't help feeling hot under the armpits.

The air felt supercharged with electricity as Ondine, Hamish, Old Col and Ma sat in the balcony of the Dentate's public gallery to watch the vote officially recognising Anathea as Duchess of Brugel. The long bench seats were made from thickly padded leather, with pull-down timber desks for people to take notes, should they want to. Around the walls hung paintings from Brugel's history, from the early days of labour-intensive wheat production right through to the development of the plough.

Looking down on Brugel's elected representatives dressed in

their finery, Ondine couldn't help feeling as if she too were present during a great moment in Brugelish history. Every time a politician mentioned Duchess Anathea, a cheer went up in the gallery. The speaker of the house acknowledged their excitement but had to call order so they could actually take the vote before they broke for a celebratory lunch.

Provided they had something to celebrate.

"They should call the vote sharpish," Hamish said. "Me stomach's about tae eat itself."

That put a fresh smile on Ondine's face.

"Don't forget the reason you're here. Your work is not over yet." Old Col said.

Which wiped the smile straight off Ondine's face. It was ridiculous that she should fear the outcome of this vote. Their make-other-people's-wishes-come-true magic had helped Anathea become Brugel's most popular leader of all time, but the Dentate members still had to vote and make it a reality.

Hamish curled his fingers into Ondine's and caressed her palm with his thumb as the speaker called for the members to cast their votes. He nuzzled into her ear and kissed the tender spot just below her ear lobe.

Everything turned fuzzy and a wee bit lovely for a moment.

"You're in public, keep it nice," Ma said.

"It's for Brugel, Ma," Ondine said, surprised with how coherent she sounded as Hamish playfully nipped her ear and turned her brain to syrup.

They lost track of time and completely forgot there were people around them, as couples are wont to do when they are so deliciously loved-up.

"You can stop now, they've all voted," Ma said with an elbow to Ondine.

Heart almost stopping with anticipation, Ondine waited for the numbers to play out, with the counting of 'igens' to pass the law and the 'nincs' to shoot it down. [1] At the end of the tallying, the vote cleared with one hundred and eighteen in favour of the bill, eighty-three against.

"Ye did it!" Hamish nudged her shoulder and gave her his wickedest grin.

"We did it," she said with a massive sigh of relief.

Looking across the gallery, they saw Anathea in the royal box. She was on her feet, waving to the politicians below and blowing kisses to the public gallery. The new law secured Anathea's tenure as the Duchess for life. In time, it could even be possible for her daughters to inherit ahead of Vincent, but that would be another vote for another time.

"Vincent will be spitting cheeseballs," Hamish said.

"He promised he'd make peace. We all saw it," Ondine said. "Anyway, I'm sure he's distracted with Melody right now."

"Just as we shall soon be distracted with a free meal," Old Col said with a gleam in her eyes. "The Duchess invited us to a celebratory luncheon. Come along."

Ondine, Hamish and Ma followed Great-Auntie Col to the Dentate dining room. Ondine gave Hamish's hand a squeeze as a waiter showed them to their table. How lovely to be dining out somewhere other than her family's pub. Not that the food would be up to Henrik's standards, but she felt so much more relaxed knowing she didn't have to clean up afterwards.

She didn't even have to pay the bill!

Talk about posh! The tables were covered in cream-coloured linen with matching napkins. Each centrepiece had sprigs of budding willow surrounded by lush red tree peonies. As they sat down (the waiter held her seat back for her) Ondine couldn't resist turning over the cutlery. A surge of national pride came

---

1. The literal translation of "nincs" is "No way José". Someone who says "no" to everything is known as a "nincompoop".

over her as she saw the silver maker's hallmarks and the hexagonal stamp of Brugel.

Somebody else filled their glasses with chilled water and asked if they'd like anything from the wine list.

"I'm not sure I should," Ondine said, feeling heat roar up her face. What would her mother say?

She didn't have to think long about that. Sitting at the adjacent table, her mother leaned over and said, "I'll give you a taste of mine."

That seemed like a fair compromise, so she ordered a pineapple juice in the meantime.

A hush stole over the room and everyone stood to attention. Ondine looked to where everyone else was looking. The doorman announced the arrival of "The Honourable First Minister of Brugel, Natalya Cebotari." After the applause softened for her, he announced, "Her Lordship, the Duchess of Brugel."

Rousing applause greeted Anathea as she made her way to the centre of a long table, raised on a dais so everyone could see her.

Under their table, situated towards the back of the room, Hamish rubbed his foot against the side of Ondine's. "Look at us, eh lass."

"I know!" giggled Ondine. She could hardly believe they were here. Having lunch in the most exclusive, invitation-only restaurant in all of Brugel – The Dentate Dining Room.

"Ye deserve it, for all ye've done." Hamish held up his glass of water. Ondine responded by clinking her glass against his.

Mercury's Wings, this was the life.

The courses – and they were numerous – were each more delicious than the last. For a moment Ondine wondered if Henrik had a doppelganger working in the Dentate kitchens, the food was *that* good. After the waiters took the main meal plates away, Duchess Anathea rose from her seat.

Everyone in the restaurant stopped what they were doing and rose from their seats in respect.

"Thank you," Anathea said. "This luncheon has been beautifully prepared. The chef is to be congratulated."

The guests applauded in agreement. Ondine nearly called out "hear-hear" but held back in case it was a breach of protocol.

As Anathea looked out across her audience, her eyes rested on Hamish and Ondine. She smiled and made the slightest nod in recognition. That's when Ondine noticed Biscuit the dog was not around. Wow, that had to mean this was a seriously formal occasion if she didn't have the dog with her.

"Ladies and Gentlemen, thank you from the bottom of my heart for taking time out of your busy schedules to attend today's historic vote in the Dentate and dine with me."

Polite applause. For Ondine, her busy schedule included washing dishes. Hmmm, menial housework or go to lunch? What a no-brainer.

Anathea smiled as much as her barely-moving face could smile. "In these changing times, we seek certainty in all things. Brugel has experienced times of uncertainty, but the late Duke Pavla's legacy will be carried on now that the tenure of the Duchy is secure."

Despite the goodwill in the room, Ondine felt she couldn't relax. Not until Hamish had his papers so he could stay in Brugel instead of facing deportation.

"We'll all be jogging home to work this off," Ma said as she patted her stomach.

"Enjoy it," Old Col said as a waiter came and refilled their wine glasses. "Oh, no more for me please, I'll fall off my broomstick."

"Yes ma-am," the waiter said without a blink. "May I suggest a stroll through the gardens after your meals? Don't worry about being cold, the conservatory is virtually tropical this time of year."

"Thank you," Ma said. "That's a lovely idea."

After their lunch was over, they took the waiter's advice and visited the orangery, where the outdoors came indoors. Trees and shrubs grew in proper dirt and flowers bloomed in well-tended beds, all under the protection of huge sheets of glass overhead.

"Ru-ru-ru-ru," they heard a dog yap.

Hamish turned to Ondine. "That sounds like . . ."

"Biscuit?" Ondine said. They turned to see a familiar white fluffy dog barrelling towards them.

"Not the clothes!" Ma held up her foot to ward the dog away.

"Biscuit, heel!" Duchess Anathea said as she came into view. She'd changed into a cream-coloured suit that swished with each step she took. "Ondine, Hamish, thank you once again for all your help. I would never have thought about using the vacuum cleaner without your prompting."

"You're welcome," Ondine and Hamish said together.

"And now, there is a debt to be repaid." She turned to Hamish and reached into the inside of her jacket for a sheaf of folded paper. "Thank you again, for everything you've done for Brugel. This document, signed by myself and First Minister Cebotari, grants you Brugelish citizenship and gives you the freedom of the city."

Tears of happiness blurred Ondine's vision as Hamish took the papers from Anathea and made a low bow. When he finished, he said, "Och, come here," and gave the Duchess a massive squeeze.

"Steady!" Anathea said. "This suit can't be returned if it's wrinkled!"

"Aye." Hamish un-squeezed himself from Anathea. Then he unfolded the document so he and Ondine could gaze upon it. She couldn't read it through her happy tears.

"Thank you," Ondine said, as she wiped her cheeks. No crying onto the paper, it would leave splotches. And she dare not cry onto her clothes either because tear stains left salt-rings.

"Now, we need to talk about Birgit," the Duchess said.

"Must we?" Hamish and Ondine said together.

"Is she still . . . ?" Old Col asked.

"In a secure facility? Yes," Anathea said. "In two of them, in fact. Her person is in the asylum and her soul is in the vacuum cleaner bag, in a safe. As long as we keep the two pieces apart, she can do no further damage."

Old Col made a sniffing sound. "That's the best we could hope for I suppose."

Tucking the certificate inside his coat pocket, Hamish turned to Ondine and reached for her hand. "I think we did good, lass."

Ondine beamed and nestled into him, feeling that at last, all was right with the world.

"Don't crease your clothes," Ma said. "Or we won't get the refunds.

"Yes, Ma," Ondine said with a giggle.

"Come on kids, let's go home." Old Col said.

EPILOGUE

Weak afternoon sunshine greeted them as they walked to the railway station. The banks of snow on the streets were melting into brown slurry. It sloshed down the steps to the platform, spraying Ondine's boots. She raised her hem to avoid staining her skirt, but the act only exposed her legs to cold splashes of mud.

"Allow me," Hamish scooped her up and carried her in his arms.

Ondine snuggled into him, feeling warm and protected. She heard Old Col tisk behind them.

They caught the train home, but dared not sit on the wet wooden bench seats in case they left stains on their fabric. Throughout the day other passengers had brought slurry on the train with their boots and bags, coating every flat surface with slop. Possibly because passengers had been standing on the bench seats to avoid the river of slush sliding and slopping up and down the aisle.

At last they reached their station. The late afternoon sun tried desperately to wring out the last little bit of shine on the neighbourhood. The streetlights were already on and the neon dragon out the front of *On The Fang* flickered into life.

"Oh how sweet!" Ondine squeezed Hamish's hand as she saw an early sign of spring. The raised garden beds near the station still had plenty of snow, but a clutch of bright yellow crocus flowers had broken through.

"Aye, I'll be glad to see the back of winter."

"On that, I agree," Old Col said.

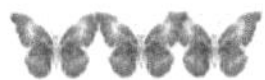

LATER, after they'd swept the last of the customers out into the cold, slushy February night, Ondine banked the open fire and locked the screen in place. Her back ached from leaning over the sink all evening washing dishes and she was about ready to collapse into bed.

"Yer mother works ye too hard, lass."

She turned to find Hamish grinning at her, holding something behind his back. With a self-conscious flourish, he produced a bouquet of golden crocus.

"They're beautiful," she held them to her chest, "thank you."

"Ye've been on yer feet all night; ye need to sit down fer a while."

Good idea. Ondine plonked her crocuses into one of the table vases, then reached for a dining chair and pulled it out to face the fire. Hamish did the same and sat beside her. It felt so natural to rest her head on his shoulder and, oh how lovely, he put his arm around her and held her close.

In the background, the radio news invaded their idyll with stories of strange magic spreading to the United States, Japan and even as far away as Australia.

With a heavy sigh, Ondine said, "I can't help wondering if that's all my fault."

"Dinnae fash yerself," [1] Hamish said as he played with her hair.

"I can't help it," she said with an even louder sigh. "I mean, we've won this battle and helped Anathea, but I can't help thinking there's a bigger war that's only just beginning."

The last coals of the fire glowed dimly, giving out scant heat. Ondine shivered as the cold air and even colder thoughts took place.

Hamish produced a blanket and tucked it over her, keeping her warm. She snuggled in further, sharing the warmth. He'd thought of everything, hadn't he?

"This is going to sound strange," she said, "but I think I like being magic. I like making other people's wishes come true. And if there is more of this weirdness going around, I'd much rather have some magic in me to tackle it, than no magic at all."

"Aye, that's because ye've got a heart as big as Brugel," he said, touching the tip of his nose to hers.

She luxuriated in his attention, then pulled back for a moment. "You have put your papers somewhere safe, haven't you?"

"In the strong box under the floor in the kitchen." He pressed his forehead lightly against hers. "Now dry yer eyes, all is right with the world."

"No Hamish, don't say that out loud. The minute you do, the universe conspires to make something awful happen."

Hamish chuckled and held her closer. "OK, I'll nae say it again. I'll just think it."

"Don't even think it." She gave him a poke in the ribs.

He tickled her in retaliation and they became silly and giddy

---

1. Stop fussing, lassie, there's not much you can do about it now anyway.

for a moment. When they eventually stopped, and Ondine caught her breath back, she said, "I don't think I've ever been as happy in my life as I am right now."

"Och, lass, it's just the beginning."

He kissed her so sweetly she thought she'd float away. There was no heat left in the fire, yet her body radiated warmth.

"I love you, Hamish."

"And I love you, Ondi."

They shared more sweet kisses and snuggled under the blanket, feeling yummy and lush. They stayed there, wrapped in each other, until the sun peeked over the hills heralding the beginning of a new day.

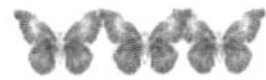

I HOPE you had a wonderful time in with Ondine and Hamish as winter set in.

Their romance concludes magnificently in the fourth and final novel, The Spring Revolution. Read on for the first chapter.

THE SPRING REVOLUTION

CHAPTER 1

Astral projection. Some people are great at it; others are famous for sleeping right through it.

Take the almost-sixteen-year-old Ondine, for example. By all accounts she's a healthy teen, eats well, has her regular share of bad and good hair days. (Long, wispy and brown. What can you do?) Being our brave and clever heroine, Ondine is blessed with 'resting curious face', which means she often looks like she knows what's going on. Even if she doesn't.

At the end of a long day of working for her family in their pub, *The Duke and Ferret* in downtown Venzelemma, the capital city of Brugel, Ondine is also blessed with the ability to fall asleep three minutes and twenty-two seconds after climbing into bed. She has neither the energy nor the inclination to develop her astral projection abilities. It would involve meditating, then separating her spiritual body from the physical to then journey – along what is known in psychic circles as the astral plane – from her mind and project herself into the mind of another.

Or travel to various psychic destinations.

On the other hand, witch-in-training Melody, who is getting the colour back into her cheeks after the strain of working with the 'bad witch' Mrs Howser, is an absolute natural at astral projection. Melody and Ondine first met at Psychic Summer-camp, three seasons (and three books) ago. Melody proved to be so good at astral projection, she can now travel by day or night and visit people who are either asleep or awake – sometimes without the recipient even knowing. Plus, Melody can take people with her on these journeys, visiting places or people anywhere in the city, or indeed any part of Brugel (a country in eastern Europe that has still not won the Eurovision Song Contest).

So it came as no surprise to Ondine, as she was asleep in her bedroom above the family pub, to see and hear Melody appear at the end of her bed one rainy spring evening, sitting as comfortably as you like. Even though it was the middle of the night, and, as previously stated, it was raining. Pouring down, it was. Hitting the windowpanes at a fierce angle and diluting the last of the winter snow into slurry. Exactly the kind of weather you don't want to be out in, even if you do have seriously important news you simply can't wait until morning to tell your friend. Which is again why astral is so useful, as travel along the psychic plane is not weather-dependant.

Melody looked dry and warm as she folded her travelling witch cloak over her knees and smiled her brightest smile for Ondine.

"You're totally owning astral," Ondine said.

Melody beamed with confidence. "Yeah, I am. You're still asleep, by the way."

"Am I?" Ondine made to rub her eyes, like she normally did upon waking, but found that her arm had turned rubbery and she only mooshed her head into the pillow instead. The pillow felt as soft and squishy as pizza dough. So doughy. So drowsy.

"I have something you need to see," Melody said, holding out her hand. "Come with me."

"Do I have to wake up?" Ondine nibbled at the corner of her pizza dough pillow. Mmmm, yeasty.

"No, it's best if you stay asleep for this," Melody took her limp palm. "This is really important, so hold my hand the whole time and don't fall asleep on me, OK?"

"I thought you said I *was* asleep?"

"You know what I mean."

As Ondine's hand slipped into Melody's, she saw a third person appear in the room.

"Hey there sleepy head," Hamish said, giving her a cheeky wink.

Suddenly Ondine hoped she wasn't having one of *those* dreams where she turned up to school naked. She checked herself and noted, with a relieved sigh, she was completely decent. If you could count her nattiest flannel pyjamas with holes in the armpits decent.

For his part, Hamish was dressed in a dinner suit straight out of a classic 1920s movie. High white collar, black bow tie, tight-fitting dark grey suit and black lapels. Not to mention the creased pants and shiny black shoes. Despite his fancy appearance, Hamish's black hair refused to sit right, with a disarming lock blocking the vision from his cheeky green eyes. ('Cheeky' is so a colour.) He tugged at his neck and complained in his endearing Scottish accent, "I couldnae dream about being at a toga party, could I? That would be far too comfortable."

Curiosity ate her up as Ondine took in the lush sight of him. "What were you dreaming about?"

"My worst nightmare. Ballroom dancing."

For many, ballroom dancing would be the subject of an

exciting dream, but considering Hamish's back story, where he was first cursed by Ondine's great-aunt Col to be a ferret when attending her debutante ball, that kind of setting was a source of constant upset.

"Was I in it?" Ondine asked.

Melody made an exaggerated harrumph. "Can you two stop gushing and pay attention? This is serious."

"Yes ma'am," Hamish said.

Ondine nodded.

"Good," Melody said. "Now, prepare yourselves this won't be pretty. Lord Vincent is visiting his mother at the asylum, and we need to make sure he doesn't do anything stupid." [1]

"What sort of stupid?" Ondine wondered.

"Seriously stupid," Melody said. "You know Mrs Howser is being kept at the same facility, don't you?"

"No," Ondine and Hamish said together at the mention of their nemesis and Ondine's former Psychic Summercamp teacher.

"And you know that the vacuum bag with Mrs Howser's soul in it has gone missing, don't you?" [2]

Did they have to be talking about Birgit Howser? The woman had gone from being a batty old pest to becoming Ondine's mortal enemy. Sickened by the revelation that the bag was missing, Ondine looked first to Hamish then to Melody. "I didn't know that."

Melody's eyebrows shot up. "It's been all over the news! What have you two been doing?"

---

1. Did you think I'd forgotten about the footnotes? Not a chance! Vincent's mother was previously known as Duchess Kerala. However, now that Kerala's husband Duke Pavla is no more, mostly because Kerala fed him pastries made from poisonous rhubarb leaves, she is known as The Dowager Duchess Kerala.
2. If none of this is making any sense, it's most likely because you've accidentally picked up the fourth book in the series instead of the first.

Something on the floor became incredibly interesting as Ondine studied the carpet at her feet.

"Fine!" Melody tisked loudly and tightened her grip on Ondine's hand. "I'll catch you up to speed on the way there."

"Eh lass? I can't go out like this."

Ondine looked up to see Hamish's spiffy suit had vanished, replaced by the more comfortable toga he'd requested. He even had a laurel wreath on his head, his dark locks brushed forward to fan his temples.

"It doesn't matter what you're wearing, they won't see us anyway, we're astraling," Melody said. "Now stop yammering and pay attention. The future of Brugel is at stake!"

"It sounds so dramatic when she says it like that," Hamish said as he gave Ondine a wink.

The bedroom melted away and they floated out into the dark sky above. It rained all around them, yet they didn't get wet. It wasn't even cold, for which Ondine was incredibly grateful.

"Are we spying on Mrs Howser?" Ondine asked.

"Only a little," Melody said, then quickly added, "I know last time didn't end well, but this will be different."

The 'last time' of which Melody referred, had ended very badly. Mrs Howser had seen straight through Melody's magic and had screamed at them for invading her memories. It was the kind of unpleasant encounter that put Ondine right off wanting any repeats. Now Melody was dragging her straight back to the old witch.

"Is it too late to go back home instead?" Ondine asked.

Melody wore a determined look. "That would be a 'yes'. We're here already."

Looking around, Ondine took in what Melody meant by 'here'. They were in a hallway with fake wood panelling to mid-height; the rest of the walls were painted in custard-yellow, while the ceiling was half a tone lighter. Prints of cottages in impossibly pretty country settings were set along the walls. Beige linoleum covered the floors and curved the first few centimetres up the walls.

The acrid smell of cold chicken soup hung in the air.

Hamish wrinkled his face. "Are we in hell?"

"No, we're in the Duchess Yelena Memorial Asylum," [3] Melody said, "If I've done this right . . ." she leaned sharply towards a door, nearly clonking her head on the knocker. Instead of being hurt, the top half of the young witch's body vanished right though the wood, like a ghost. Just as Ondine was about to yelp with the shock of it all and loosen her grip, Melody pulled herself back into the hallway. She gave a smile of triumph and finished the sentence she'd started so much earlier, "... Vincent and his mother are behind that door."

"And they didnae see you, lass?"

A wary look came over Melody. "Course not."

Ondine murmured, "You said that last time."

Ignoring their scepticism, Melody said, "We're going to be very quiet and float in like dust motes. Then we're going to listen in. No talking, OK?"

The instructions had Ondine wrinkling her forehead. "I thought you said they couldn't hear us?"

"They can't, but if you're nattering on I won't be able to hear *them*, got it?" Melody said.

"How about I wait out here?" Ondine asked.

Hamish gave her a lopsided smile and said, "You're not worried it's going to all end badly are ye?"

Zhoop, before Ondine could answer, they dissolved through

---

3. "It's fun to stay at the DYMA," is a popular Brugelish refrain when someone starts acting loopy.

the door and into the room. Here was Vincent sitting beside his mother, the Dowager Duchess Kerala.

At first Ondine didn't recognise the frail woman in the room, her hair thin and balding under a cotton cap. She was missing her shiny dark helmet of hair and ubiquitous glass of wine (which had turned out to be apple juice, just to throw people off the scent of her nefarious activities). The room was a far cry from the splendour of the Autumn Palace at Bellreeve. The linoleum from the hallway continued in here, as did the enforced cheer of the yellow colour scheme.

"If ye weren't crazy already, you soon would be, eh?" Hamish whispered.

Ondine nodded and murmured back, "It's giving me a headache."

Melody glared at Ondine. "Be quiet."

"How come you told me off and not him?"

"Because he's charming and you're not, now hush."

Moving closer, yet also keeping their distance (Ondine still wasn't convinced they'd be unnoticed), the trio floated towards Kerala's bed, where they found the former duchess sitting up, dressed in a mauve, velour tracksuit.

As they were floating above their targets, Hamish tilted his head to indicate a small patch on the top of Vincent's golden head with less hair than the rest. What with Vincent's glossy dark shoes, neat suit, perfect gold tie and golden cufflinks, he looked like a young man with the world at his feet. If only people didn't look too close to the scalp. Ondine snorted at the sight of the lord's future bald patch, which earned her another glare from Melody. With a waft of her hand, Melody sent a trail of glimmering dust through the air towards Vincent, repairing his tresses to their youthful lustre. Ondine threw up in her mouth a little at the sight of Melody's blatant adoration of Vincent. Honestly, the girl really needed to get out more.

When Ondine turned back to Hamish, her breath hitched. Amongst his lustrous dark locks were three glaringly silver strands of hair. Silver! Alas, they weren't here to worry about Hamish's hair – or Vincent's – they were here to eavesdrop on a conversation. Ondine stopped her noisy internal thoughts and listened in.

"You're doing so well, I knew you would," Kerala said, softly touching Vincent's cheek in a loving gesture.

The former duchess and husband-knocker-offer had certainly changed in strength and tone from the last time Ondine had seen her. Much calmer now. Not ranting and weeping like she had over Duke Pavla's frail body, pretending to care even though she'd been the one slowly poisoning him all that time.

Vincent's voice was calm and low as he spoke. "You're being good here, aren't you? Taking your medicine?"

"I'm a good girl." Kerala became infantile and needy as she spoke. "I've always been good."

Is this it? Is this what they'd come to hear? In that case Melody could have come on her own. "Is this relevant?" Ondine asked.

With a tilt of her head, Melody indicated Vincent's satchel, which he'd left slumped on the floor. Something moved inside it, like a rolling lump of . . . something lumpy.

"I brought you a present," Vincent said, reaching into that very satchel. He withdrew a bulky present, wrapped badly with too much paper and sticky tape. He must have done it himself, in a hurry.

"Is it my birthday?" Kerala asked, her face wobbling in fright. "Did I forget it was my birthday?"

"No, course not," he said. Kerala's smile returned as Vincent pressed the gift into her hands and said, "Can't I give you a present just because?"

"Of course you can. I love presents." Her fingers dug into the paper and battled with the tape to reveal an over-stuffed teddy bear. "Oh I love it!" She squeezed it to her chest, making dust blow out.

Looking to Hamish, Ondine mouthed, "Dust?"

"I have to go now, dear Mother," Vincent said, giving her a dutiful kiss on the forehead. "Be good now and keep taking your medicine."

Kerala hugged the teddy, sending more dust into the room. The teddy's stomach bulged under the pressure.

Vincent turned, lifted his now-empty satchel from the floor and tucked it over his shoulder as he walked out. Melody began to waft after him, tugging Ondine's hand towards the door. "Was that an heirloom or something?" Ondine asked.

"Aye, I was wondering that meself, although it looked new," Hamish added.

"It is new. You haven't worked out what's inside it, have you?" Melody said as she drew them after Vincent.

"A bag of dust . . ." Ondine thought out loud. She would have slapped her forehead in realisation had she not been gripping Hamish and Melody's hands so tightly. "It's the dust bag from the vacuum cleaner. The one with Mrs Howser's soul in it."

"That's why we're such good friends, because you're so smart," Melody said, giving Ondine a wink of encouragement.

"But why would Vincent give Howser's soul to his mother? Are they going to merge or something so Kerala can use Howser's magic to escape the asylum?"

"I doubt it," Melody brought them through another closed door, where they found Vincent crouching down to speak to a woman who was kneeling in the corner of the room. She was curled up, her arms tucked tightly over her knees, rocking slowly back and forth. Her hands were covered in mittens, which were securely fastened to a solid jacket she wore.

Vincent touched the woman's shoulder, but she didn't react to him. With a tug of her hand, Melody pulled Ondine and Hamish around to get a better view, which resulted in them emerging through a connecting wall.

The woman was Mrs Howser. Her face was gaunt and grey, the lines deeper after rapid weight loss and perhaps a nervous breakdown. The shocks kept coming when Mrs Howser opened her eyes to reveal opaque irises and pupils; like dirty window-panes in need of a good clean.

Cold fear prickled Ondine's spine. They thought they'd been safe from Mrs Howser, after her body and soul separation last month in Savo Plaza. But now only a child-woman and her teddy bear separated the most powerful witch's body from her evil essence.

Thank goodness for the mittens, so she couldn't touch anyone and transfer magic, Ondine thought.

"Now you see why I brought you here," Melody said, pulling them upwards, away from Vincent.

"He won't stop till he's Duke, will he?" Ondine asked, although she already knew the answer, so it was more like a statement.

"Exactly." Melody said. "Which is why I already have a plan. I'm going to work with Vincent and keep an eye on him. Meanwhile, you have to help Anathea any way you can. We'll meet up and share what we know, to make sure Brugel stays on the straight and narrow."

Of course Melody would volunteer to work with Vincent.

"Ma's going to kill me," Ondine said. "She doesn't want any of us having anything more to do with the royal family ever again."

"Then don't tell her," Melody said. "What she doesn't know won't hurt her."

"Aye. It'll be like old times eh lass?" Hamish gave her a wink.

Ondine's lips twisted in thought. Could she really do this? "I thought we'd have a little more time for normal things before everything turned bonkers again."

"Come on." Melody gave her hand an encouraging squeeze. "As if you could ever stay away from the crazy."

ABOUT THE AUTHOR

Ebony McKenna is the author of the well-loved four-part Ondine series, about a girl whose pet ferret starts talking with a Scottish accent. (The ferret is really a man who offended a witch, and Ondine will do whatever she can to break the spell.)

She has lived all over Victoria, including Lorne, Maldon, Narre Warren and Ballarat. But not in that order.

At one point her mother *almost* bought The Clarkfield Hotel to turn it into a restaurant, not knowing it was one of the most haunted buildings in the state. But that's another story.

These days she lives in suburban Melbourne and is busy dreaming up more adventures under the pen-name Ebony Oaten, as she writes sweet and saucy regency romances with that name. (Using a different name is her way of differentiating between audiences.)

She loves train sets, trivia nights and the Eurovosion Song Contest.

You can find Ebony at her website:

www.ebonyoaten.com

Would you like to know when I have new books available? I have a newsletter to let readers know what's happening. Click here to grab a free, sweet Regency romance novella when you join in.

ALSO BY EBONY MCKENNA

THE ONDINE SERIES (IN READING ORDER)

The Summer of Shambles

The Autumn Palace

The Winter of Magic

The Spring Revolution

A Brugel Fairytale Treasury

OTHER NOVELS

The Girl and The Ghost (RWAus Ruby - Romantic Book of the Year - winner.)

Robyn and the Hoodettes

NON FICTION

Edit Your Own Romance Novel

Marketing Books to Australian Libraries, second edition.

Find the rest of my titles here: ebonyoaten.com